MW00587715

SMOKE,
IN
CRIMSON

SMOKE, IN CRIMSON

a novel by
GREG F. GIFUNE

CEMETERY DANCE PUBLICATIONS

Baltimore
2023

Smoke, In Crimson
Copyright © 2023 by Greg F. Gifune

Cover Artwork and Design © 2023 by Kealan Patrick Burke
Interior Design © 2023 by Desert Isle Design, LLC

All rights reserved. No part of this book may be reproduced
in any form or by any electronic or mechanical means,
including information storage and retrieval systems,
without permission in writing from the publisher, except
by a reviewer who may quote brief passages in a review.

Trade Paperback Edition

ISBN:
978-1-58767-929-2

This book is a work of fiction. Names, characters, places and
incidents either are products of the author's imagination or are
used fictitiously. Any resemblance to actual events or locales
or persons, living or dead, is entirely coincidental.

Cemetery Dance Publications
132B Industry Lane, Unit #7
Forest Hill, MD 21050
www.cemeterydance.com

For Jane

Our madness, vice and crazed binges were a lifetime ago. We were so lost, and maybe in some ways I still am, who can say? What I do know is you deserved better than you got in life, and your time in this world shouldn't have ended the way it did. I'll always remember laughing until we cried, and crying until we laughed. This one's for you.

PART
ONE

"I want you at the end of your rope, lashed to
the mast of my dreams."
–Steve Erickson, *The Sea Came in at Midnight*

CHAPTER **ONE**

MEMORIES OF HER BLOOD haunted him. More powerful than any ghost or nightmare, they clung to him, burrowing deep into his flesh like the rancid parasites they were.

So much of life was gone now. He hadn't seen Fay in a few years, but he always thought of her in one of two very distinctive ways. Either dancing and flailing about, free and full of laughter and mischief, so high and drunk and horny—exploding with life—or frozen, staring at him with hopeless, bloodshot eyes, hair wild and her face a grimace of confusion, shock and horror. Her wounds oozing, slowly dripping…

She was gone now, or so Deacon had been told, and though he hadn't quite come to grips with that yet, the potential finality of it all was so devastating and sad, it was as if he'd vanished along with her. In the time since he'd last seen her, she'd been relegated to his dreams. Strange, he thought, how rapidly that transition occurred, Fay so god damn effortlessly slipping from one realm to another, like sand between his fingers.

A chilly autumn breeze blew in off the ocean and whispered through the dunes, causing the tall stalks of grass to sway and rousing the smell of seawater, secrets and magic. In a fiery blur, the sun appeared, breaking slowly over the horizon. Like a dream from some other place and time, it rose, shining not for the blessed, but the damned.

As the light of a brisk new day assumed its reign, Deacon, who until then had been hidden in the tall grass of the dunes, slowly sat up. Sidestepping nightmares, he took a few moments to convince himself he was safe, or as safe as could be expected. His body remained tense, unconvinced, so he lay back in the sand a moment and watched the morning sky. A bevy of seabirds circled overhead.

He reached into his pocket, pulled out a small green stone he'd carried with him for years and rubbed it between his fingers a moment. There would be no end to this pain, no escape from it. Deacon knew that. All that remained was the struggle to prevent it from overtaking him. Maybe that's why he'd really come back here after these last few years, to find meaning amidst the darkness and loss. If such things still existed, that is.

Suddenly, Deacon sensed movement. Bolting upright, he returned the stone to his pocket and ran his hands

SMOKE, in CRIMSON

through his hair, pushing it back and away from his forehead before looking around and realizing no one was there. In the last months his hair had grown to his shoulders, the longest since he was a teenager. He grabbed his knapsack and quickly rummaged through it until he found a red bandana. Folding it first, he tied it around his head. Hair secured, he stretched a bit, loosening muscles and working his sore joints. There was rain coming, no doubt about it. Though still a relatively young man, the older he got the more his body became a barometer of aches and pains.

With a sigh, he lit a cigarette. As Deacon's nerves settled, sorrow replaced fear.

One ghost exchanged for another.

Exhaling the first drag, he coughed, rubbed his eyes and looked out at the Atlantic beneath the strengthening morning light. Such beauty, and yet, in the distance, dark clouds had gathered.

A storm was coming.

But so was something else, and with greater urgency. It rushed up over the dunes and headed right for him. He could hear it, *feel* it.

Flicking the cigarette away, Deacon rolled onto all-fours, ready to pounce at whatever was on its way to him. But he was too late.

A heavy burst of hot breath slammed his face, followed by something wet and cold pressed against him. And then, hair, soft and thick and cradling a frame rugged and powerful but low to the ground.

Christ, he thought, *it's just a dog.*

Relaxing, Deacon let the pup knock him back, and together they rolled across the sand, finally coming to rest a few feet away. What he'd initially feared as an attack turned playful as the dog smothered him with big sloppy licks and kisses, wagging his tail so enthusiastically that the entire lower half of the animal wiggled in time with the motion. Grunting playfully, the dog looked into his eyes the way only a creature of such innocence could, then sat back on his haunches as if to say, *Okay, now what?*

"That's quite an entrance you got there, pal," Deacon said breathlessly.

A midsized dog, he was a mutt but predominantly yellow Labrador retriever. His tail continued to wag, furiously sweeping back and forth across the sand and grass.

"Are you all alone out here, boy?" Deacon noticed a collar, but the tags hanging from it were so old and worn he couldn't make out any information. Giving the dog a pat on the head, he stood up, brushed his jeans off and looked out across the dunes to the road beyond.

A young boy of perhaps nine or ten was approaching on a bicycle.

Deacon waved, but the boy hadn't yet seen him.

SMOKE, IN CRIMSON

"Larry!" the boy called. "Where are you? Come on, Larry! Larry!"

"Somebody's looking for you," Deacon said, squatting next to the dog.

Larry offered his paw.

Unable to prevent a smile, Deacon took hold of it and they shook. He couldn't remember the last time he'd felt such warmth and connection to another living thing. "Nice to meet you, Larry, I'm Deacon."

Letting the paw go, he stood back up and saw that the kid had gotten a bit closer. "Over here!" Deacon called out. "He's here!"

The boy stood up, balancing his bike between his legs. Thin and gangly, with a mussed shock of dark hair in need of a trim, the boy sported inexpensive mismatched clothes and a pair of badly worn sneakers. He didn't look dirty, just disheveled.

He also looked leery.

Deacon grabbed his knapsack, slung it over his shoulder and gave his leg a pat to let Larry know he should follow him, which he did. Crossing the top of the dune, he moved to within a few feet of the boy, but stopped when he noticed him tense up, ready for flight if need be. "It's okay," Deacon said softly, motioning to Larry. "He's here."

Larry gave him a quick look then bounded over to the boy, tail wagging furiously.

"Nice dog," Deacon said.

"Yeah, he's cool," the boy answered, turning his bike in the opposite direction but keeping his body turned so he could still see Deacon. "Thanks. Come on, Larry."

Deacon gave a quick nod as the kid peddled away without another word, Larry gleefully running alongside him. It bothered him that the boy reacted to him that way. He didn't like being the kind of person children didn't feel comfortable around, but maybe the kid was dealing with more than Deacon knew or understood. Regardless, it was good for children to be careful. Not everyone was harmless.

Sometimes strangers needed to be feared.

Deacon walked out across the dunes and onto the paved road. Everything was quiet and shut down, the tourist season over until next summer.

Up ahead, he saw the boy gliding away on his bike, weaving back and forth across the empty street. Larry ran next to him, hopping out of the way and juking about, barking now and then as if to encourage him.

Years ago Deacon might've been that boy.

Something whispered to him from the very edges of his consciousness, stealing those possibilities and the memories they fostered. It could've been the wind, but Deacon didn't hear, see or feel any evidence of that. Yet he knew he heard something.

It was there. Just like Fay's bloody wounds, it was there.

SMOKE, IN CRIMSON

Deacon listened for more, but all he heard now was the gentle lap of waves against shore. *It's only the past,* he told himself.

He looked back at the road from which he'd come the night before, stretched out behind him like a serpent of dust and lies, dangerous as any of the gods it served. Much as he wished he was wrong, Deacon knew the truth.

There was no such thing as a road to nowhere.

CHAPTER **TWO**

WALKING WITH PURPOSE, DEACON stayed close to the dunes and ocean on his left as he continued along the lonely street. The world was still awakening around him, but the storm was alive and well and making its move. Any pleasantness the early morning light had brought was fading. The sun was already losing its battle with an invading army of dark clouds rolling in across the ocean, and the light was turning now, shifting, as the gentle morning breeze became a wind.

A few moments later the rain began to fall. Hard and sudden, it hit like bullets. Pulling his jacket in tight around him, Deacon pushed on through the storm, moving away from the road and slogging back across the sand.

Out over the ocean, lightning strikes slashed the sky, crackling and spearing the water in brilliant blue bolts that looked almost too spectacular to be real. Alone in the chaos,

Deacon hurried through the downpour until he was able to see the small cottage in the distance.

Set atop a broad and rounded bluff and nestled among the dunes, it overlooked the ocean. Even with the change in light, at this distance it was impossible to tell if anyone was there, so Deacon pressed on.

Once he reached the base of the bluff, he followed a narrow but worn path up through the tall grass until he reached the property. Stepping onto the small back porch, he took refuge as best he could beneath the slight overhang of roof.

At closer range, Deacon could see that there was light coming from inside, and to his right, he was able to make out a portion of the short gravel driveway around the side of the cottage, and the two vehicles parked there. One was a Mercedes Benz SUV.

The other was a police cruiser.

Soaked to the bone and shivering, Deacon tried to focus as the storm thundered around him. The rain kept coming, falling in heavy sheets now, the overhang providing only minimal shelter. He glanced at the small wood bench, the chipped and weathered clay pots along the edge of the porch—the flowers long dead and rotted—and a small slate plaque next to the back door that read WELCOME and featured a pair of smiling cartoon cats waving hello. He remembered them all, particularly the plaque, because

SMOKE, IN CRIMSON

he'd bought it for her. Deacon touched the cool slate, his hand shaking. Flashes of Fay erupted across his mind's eye, how happy she was when she opened the giftwrapped box it came in, and how she insisted it be hung up right away, in that very spot.

Deacon tried to bury the memories, something he'd become quite adept at of late, but now that he was actually here, his emotions ran roughshod over him. Like the rain, tears came to him abruptly, violently, and refused to stop.

As he wiped his eyes, unsure of where the rain ended and his tears began, Deacon imagined Fay here over the last few years, alone in this town at the literal ends of the earth, skulking through the streets, watching the sand, perched atop dunes and gazing out at the ocean like some mad, darkly bewitched sentinel.

In his mind he stood watching the old cottage from down below on the beach, alone in the rain and waiting for her, unaware that he hadn't made it in time. Or maybe he knew better than anyone that she'd be gone before he could reach her. Maybe he'd known all along.

Maybe they both did.

Deacon remained where he was, making no attempt to knock on the door just yet. Instead, he waited, focusing on his visions, memories, nightmares—whatever the fuck they were—and hoped the door might open and he'd be discovered standing there in the rain like the fool he was.

If I'm quiet, he thought, *they'll never know I'm here.*

With his mind reeling and rain crashing down in a steady and constant downpour, surging along the gutters and gushing through downspouts, causing more of a racket than he'd first realized, Deacon slid his knapsack off his shoulder and dropped it to the porch. Fay was nowhere in sight, yet she was all around him. He could feel her moving on his skin, taste her on his tongue, smell traces of her in the rain, and even faintly hear her voice as it rode the wind.

Fay always believed the only way to quiet the madness and fear, to truly stop the pain, was to strip oneself of all identity and purpose then wander off into oblivion.

She was right. There was no turning back now.

From deep within the shadows she grinned at him, that decadent smile he'd grown to love slowly curling her lips. With smoky brown eyes wide and looking not at but *into* him in a way only she could, Fay whispered promises they both knew she couldn't keep. Not then, not now. But it didn't matter, never had. He believed her anyway.

IT WAS STRANGE STEPPING into the cottage again after such a long time. Familiar, in the sense that nothing had changed much since he'd last been there, but none of it seemed exactly, *precisely* real. Close, just slightly askew, in

SMOKE, IN CRIMSON

the way dreams often were, as if the entire place had been frozen in time then secreted away when no one was looking and replaced with an exact replica. Yet the same old ghosts rattling the same old chains remained. They didn't know any better, probably couldn't tell the difference. Maybe they just didn't give a shit. But they were all around him.

Deacon hung his jacket on a hook inside the back door, watching as it dripped rainwater onto a small throw rug. The kitchen was warm and cramped. Heat rose from an old wrought iron woodstove against the opposite wall, logs crackling and throwing off a stifling, heavy heat unique to indoor wood-burning. The modest table in the center of the room still sported a silver bowl Fay always kept there, a couple envelopes and a ring of keys sitting in it as if she'd just tossed them there moments ago.

Still wet from the storm, Deacon pawed what remained of the rain and tears from his eyes then forced himself to look beyond the table into the living room. Despite the silence, they all knew at some point they'd have to speak to each other and at least try to sort some of this out. That didn't make it any less awkward. In fact, he already felt more out of place within these walls than he ever had in the past. Any sense of belonging had apparently left with Fay. He was the intruder now, the outsider, the visitor, and why shouldn't he be? It wasn't his place, not really, never had been. Technically it wasn't even Fay's. The cottage belonged to her father.

Stevie, his back to Deacon, stood before the long windows facing the ocean. Decked out in full cop regalia, he held a Styrofoam cup of steaming coffee. A small radio unit on his shoulder spewed distorted, clipped voices. With his free hand, he reached up, lowered the volume. "When'd you get to town?" he asked.

"Last night."

Lance, who had been sitting on the couch, slowly rose to his feet and stepped around a squat coffee table. Appearing somewhere between pained and inconvenienced, he offered his hand while still a few feet away. "Deacon," he said with a nuanced smile. "It's so good to see you again. I'm sorry it has to be like this."

Ever the business executive, Fay's father, a blue-eyed, square-jawed WASP with the vapid look of a catalogue model, wore a turtleneck beneath a cream-colored cable knit sweater, expensive wool slacks and a pair of loafers. Despite having crossed into his 60s, his tanning-bed-bronzed skin, brilliantly white capped teeth and full, perfectly combed, dyed-to-perfection sandy brown hair conspired to convince anyone that didn't look closely that he was aging slowly and gracefully. But Deacon knew better. Look long enough into those dead, soulless eyes pretending to be warm, and it became apparent there was nothing good staring back. It was all smoke and mirrors, a dance, a sleight-of-hand parlor trick he'd perfected through years of practice. Demons

SMOKE, IN **CRIMSON**

swam in those eyes, and just like their host, they'd been neither young nor innocent in a very long time.

Unable to come up with anything worth saying, he just shook Lance's hand. It was warm and soft, his grip firm but unaggressive, and like everything else about the sonofabitch, calculated. As if being in his presence wasn't enough, making physical contact with him, even after all this time, turned Deacon's stomach.

Stevie finally came away from the windows. Unlike Lance, in just a few years he'd aged significantly. His hair had thinned a bit on top and had begun to slightly gray at the temples. Although he was just forty, the lines around his eyes and mouth had grown deeper and more pronounced. His small, deep-seated eyes were dark to the point of appearing black, and although he was clean-shaven, his beard was so heavy he had a perpetual five o'clock shadow. A big man at six-foot-three and well over two hundred pounds, he'd maintained his powerful build, but since Deacon had last seen him he'd added a few pounds around his middle. With a guarded expression, Stevie extended his free hand.

Deacon pretended not to notice it, and instead drifted toward a comfortable chair in the corner. "Has there been any news?"

"No." Stevie dropped his hand, slapping it against his thigh as he did so. "Look, I know you and I have had our differences, but—"

"I'm here for Fay, Stevie. I can't be any clearer than that."

Stevie's expression shifted to a typical *how-dare-you-disre-spect-me* cop stare. He'd been playing the part of a policeman for so long he'd likely lost the ability to differentiate it from his former self, the stripped down original version sans gun, badge, perfectly pressed uniform and high-shine black mirror boots. "We're *all* here for Fay," he said in his best traffic-stop tone.

"I asked Stevie to track you down," Lance offered. "I felt you needed to know what was going on. I also hoped you might know something more."

Deacon shook his head no.

"I understand Stevie located you in upstate New York."

"Utica," Deacon said.

Lance arched an eyebrow. "Tough town from what I've heard."

"It can be."

"What are you up to there?"

Lightning flashed through the windows, but all he could see was Fay. She was everywhere here, even when she wasn't. "Just where I wound up," Deacon said.

"Working as a short-order cook in a dump of a break-fast and lunch joint," Stevie said with an air of superiority. "Flipping burgers and making omelets, right?"

"Yeah, we can't all be Dirty Harry."

"Real original," Stevie said with a huff. "You're the same bum and drifter you always were, and if it was up to me—"

SMOKE, IN CRIMSON

"Yeah, well it isn't."

Stopping a step shy of putting himself directly between the two men, Lance raised his hands. "I understand you two don't care for each other—and that's fine, not everyone has to be friends—but I'm going to go ahead and ask that you try to put that sort of thing aside for now and focus on Fay, all right? I didn't ask you two here to argue and make matters worse. That's the last thing I want."

"I'm sorry, Mr. Dillon." Stevie reached out and gave him a pat on the shoulder. "You're right, and I apologize. What's important right now is Fay, not us. You've got enough on your mind with your daughter missing, you don't need this arguing."

"Stevie, we've all been adults for a long while now. Call me Lance. You too, Deacon, we're all grown men here. How about we all bear that in mind and do our best to act like it? Is that acceptable to all parties?"

Rain splashed the tall windows and sluiced along the panes, blurring the world outside. In the distance, thunder rumbled and lightning flashed over the ocean.

"Yes sir," Stevie said, looking to Deacon for confirmation.

Rather than give it, he just stood by the chair waiting for more information.

"Okay, well." Lance sighed dramatically and sank back onto the couch. "Given the circumstances, I was hoping you two might be able to get along. If not for my sake, then Fay's, but apparently that's too much to ask."

GREG F. GIFUNE

"Not on my part," Stevie said, hands on his hips.

Deacon rolled his eyes and turned to Lance. "So what do we know?"

After several seconds of silence and staring at the floor, Lance finally answered. "Fay's been missing for two weeks. I hadn't heard from her in a while, so I called to check in on her, as I often do. She didn't call back, so I tried texting, even emailed her, but never got a response. That's not like her, so when a few days went by and I still hadn't heard anything, I became concerned and decided to come up here to see if she was all right. I found the place empty and looking just as it does now, like she'd only left moments before. No clues, nothing missing. I waited here another day but still heard nothing, and by the following day, when she still hadn't come home, I started to panic."

"She took her car? I didn't see it in the driveway."

"Actually no, it was in the garage getting an oil change and a new inspection sticker," Stevie explained. "Apparently Fay dropped her vehicle off the Friday afternoon before last and walked back here. It's only about a mile or so to Dempsey's, where she was having the work done. She was supposed to pick up the vehicle Saturday morning but never showed. Dempsey's Garage called her on the following Monday, and again on Tuesday. According to Jeff, the head mechanic there, he left messages both times, but Fay never returned his calls."

26

SMOKE, IN CRIMSON

"What about her phone, or her computer?" Deacon asked.

"Stevie and I looked everywhere," Lance said. "They're not here, so she must've taken her phone and laptop with her when she left."

"And before you ask, yes we've tried calling her phone." Stevie looked at him defiantly. "It goes straight to voicemail."

"It seems she took nothing else with her, no clothes, nothing," Lance offered. "So either she hadn't planned to be gone long or this was a spur of the moment type thing, I just don't know."

"Can't you track her through her phone?" Deacon asked.

Stevie gave a curt nod. "Yes, but it has to be on in order to do that. The last ping we got was that Friday, when she made a call from this location to Ricardo's Restaurant. I checked with them and a pizza was delivered here at 12:47 that afternoon. According to the delivery kid, Fay answered the door, signed the credit card receipt and tipped him. He said she seemed fine."

"It's the last time anyone saw her," Lance added, glancing up at Deacon sadly.

"Since then her phone has not only been off, but the battery has likely been removed," Stevie explained. "That's why we haven't gotten anything more."

"Why would she do that?"

"Obviously, if she's gone to all that trouble, she doesn't want to be located. Fay's only got one VISA and a debit card, and neither has been used since the pizza delivery. She also has a checking account, but there's been no activity."

"And you don't find that suspect?"

"Of course I do, but that doesn't mean—"

"How's she living if she's not using her cards, did she have lots of cash on hand?"

"Not that we know of. But she could be with someone else, and that's how—"

"Did you have a chat with the pizza delivery kid?"

"Yeah, Deacon, I did." Stevie shook his head, offended at being questioned by a civilian. "He was back at the restaurant in minutes. Numerous witnesses, including his boss, say he worked the rest of his shift behind the counter."

"What about after his shift?" Deacon asked.

Stevie smiled condescendingly. "My investigation accounted for that."

"Okay, and?"

"He takes MMA at a local dojo, went straight there from work and then home, where his parents told me he stayed for the entire evening. He's a good kid, never been in trouble and he's worked at Ricardo's for the last two years without a single complaint or incident. There's no reason to suspect this young man has anything to do with this."

Lance rose from the couch again, wringing his manicured hands. "I also see no reason to assume anything nefarious has happened. We all know Fay can be—well—eccentric and troubled at times, but there's no evidence to suggest foul play."

Visions of Fay danced through Deacon's mind then burned away like film in a hot projector. Her whole god damn life was foul play.

"That's correct," Stevie said. "It appears more likely that Fay just up and left."

Deacon stared at him. "Just up and left, huh?"

"That's what I said."

"*On foot*, Stevie, with her laptop and phone and credit cards, none of which she's used since?"

"Yes, unless someone else came and got her."

"Like who? Did she make some new friends these last few years?"

"We don't think so," Lance answered for him. "But you know how Fay is."

"Yeah," Deacon said through a heavy sigh. "I know how Fay is."

As if to confirm that, with a seductive smile and eyes of fire, she crawled through the shadows of his mind, a smear of blood in her wake.

"Sometimes when people decide to disappear—and they do all the time by the way—they do things that don't initially make much sense," Stevie continued.

"You mean like dropping her car off to be serviced?" Deacon forced Fay back into the darkness from which she'd come. "Why would she do that if she planned to leave? That only makes sense if she went back and got the car and then took off."

Stevie shrugged. "Who knows what was going through her head?"

Hell. Hell was going through her head.

"We thought maybe you might've heard from her," Lance said.

"I told Stevie on the phone I haven't spoken to Fay since I left town."

"Yes, but…" Lance hesitantly moved closer to him. "Deacon, you know Fay a lot better than anyone, and—"

"Not anymore. It's been a long time."

"My point is that you know her differently," Lance said softly, as if fearful someone else might hear. "You know her *intimately.*"

Deacon glared at him, hard enough for Stevie to take notice.

"Do you have *any* idea at all where she might've gone?" Lance asked.

He pictured Fay walking into the sea. He knew they'd all considered it, and Stevie probably even investigated the possibility, but Deacon left it alone. "No."

Lance masked his annoyance with another deliberate expression of pain. "Just no, that's it?"

"That's it."

SMOKE, IN CRIMSON

Brow knit, he frowned. "I need to ask you something else, and I want you to be brutally honest with me. Do you think Fay may have harmed herself?"

Rain spattered the windows again, drummed the roof. Deacon listened to it a while before answering. "It's always a possibility."

"Is it?" Lance asked, his eyes moistening.

"You tell me."

"I'm her father."

"True enough, you are that."

"I don't want to think about my only child hurting herself, but—"

"Truth is we don't have any evidence of that either," Stevie interjected. "And it's not like Fay had a history of suicide attempts or suicidal thoughts, so—"

"How the fuck would you know?" Deacon snapped.

Stevie blanched. "What's that supposed to mean?"

"Hold on," Lance said grimly. "Let's not get into all that."

Fay talked about death a lot, and thought about it even more. Much as it terrified her, she was also fascinated by it, and there had been an incident once years before Lance had kept quiet. Deacon let it go. "Most people have those thoughts now and then."

"That's not the same thing," Stevie said.

"Like I said, it's been a long time. A lot can happen to a person over the years. Deacon made eye contact with

Lance. "Then again, a lot had already happened to her over the years, hadn't it?"

"It wasn't easy after Fay's mother passed. I made my share of mistakes, sure, but you both know Fay and I have always been close."

"You don't have to explain yourself to anyone, least of all this clown," Stevie said. "Fay loves you, Lance. She told me that many times. She loves you very much."

To whatever degree that might have been true, Deacon knew she also despised him. "Okay, so why am I here?"

"Because you care," Lance answered, wiping his eyes. "And because I thought you'd be able to help. Why else would I ask you to come all the way from New York?"

Ignoring the ghosts circling him like the hungry wolves they were, Deacon focused on the steady rhythm of the rain, but offered nothing more.

"I need to get back to my Boston office," Lance said, clearing his throat and seeming to remember his corporate warrior shtick. "There's a lot going on I have to attend to, it's a very busy time. I can't stay here indefinitely and dedicate all my time to this, much as I wish I could. And Stevie, you've been an enormous help, but you have other duties and responsibilities that require your time and attention. At this point, you and the local department can't really do anything more than you've already done."

"And you think I can?" Deacon asked.

SMOKE, IN CRIMSON

"Tell me, when are you expected back at work?"

"I'm not. I walked."

"I didn't mean for you to lose your job, Deacon."

"I quit. It was time to move on anyway."

Stevie shook his head, disgusted.

"I'd like to offer you the chance to stay here a while," Lance said. "Rent free, of course, to see if anything breaks."

"I don't understand," Deacon said. "Breaks how?"

"What Lance is trying to say is he thinks Fay just walked away," Stevie said, his officious voice temporarily drowning out the sounds of rain. "And that she did so of her own volition."

"Wow, somebody's been reading his thesaurus."

"He's right," Lance answered before Stevie could. "That's what my gut tells me. To put it bluntly, I think this is one of her, well, for lack of a better word, *stunts*."

"Stunts," Deacon muttered, wanting to choke the smug fuck into unconsciousness right then and there. "I see."

"Let's be honest here. We all know what I'm talking about. The drugs and the drinking, the running around, the endless drama, I'd hoped she'd outgrown that nonsense but apparently she hasn't. You of all people know what I mean, Deacon. That said, I truly believe you're also the only man my daughter has ever been in love with, and I know you care for her very deeply as well."

Stung, Stevie turned away and lumbered back to the windows.

"You spent an awful lot of time together in this cottage," Lance continued. "You practically lived here at one point. Maybe you two weren't always best for each other…"

You have no idea, Lance old boy. You have no idea at all.

"But I always stayed out of Fay's personal life. It's all relative, of course, but ultimately I believe she was happiest when she was with you. Here, in this place."

He wasn't wrong necessarily, but it had never been about being happy. Not really. Something similar perhaps, but like all good hauntings, it was a hell of a lot more complicated than that. "How will my staying here help anything?"

"For one, I'd prefer the place not remain unoccupied," Lance said sullenly. "And I know I can trust you with the property. Whatever's happened, whatever *is* happening that made Fay take off like this, if you reach out to her maybe she'll answer. Her cell number is the same it's always been. I assume you still have it. Have you tried to contact her?"

"Not yet."

"What the hell were you waiting for?" Stevie snapped, turning back toward them. "Why didn't you try the minute you hung up with me?"

"Go back to counting raindrops, dipshit."

Lance held a hand up to silence Stevie. "If at some point she comes back or even calls—there's still a landline here— if it's you she sees when she walks through the door, or you she hears on the other end of that phone, well then I—I think maybe..."

Deacon let silence take hold a while.

"She was always so fond of you, Deacon. God knows Fay never felt that way about many people, but she always did with you. Maybe you can convince her that whatever the problem is it isn't insurmountable and we're all here to help. If she needs rehab again, I'll pay for everything just like the other times. If there's some other issue, we can work it out. This doesn't have to be the end of the world."

Why did everyone always assume the end of the world hadn't happened yet?

"So do me this favor, please," Lance pressed. "Stay. Even if just for a little while, and see if she makes contact."

Deacon wanted to tell him he wouldn't do him a favor if he had a gun to his head, but he knew Lance was already well aware of that fact. At best Fay's old man was a pretentious and narcissistic degenerate, at worst, an evil sociopath. Either way, he was far from stupid, though after all these years, it hardly mattered. Anything Deacon had done to this point or would do moving forward was for Fay, or possibly himself, but certainly not for Lance. "What if you're wrong?"

"About what?" Lance asked.

"What if Fay didn't take off? What if something happened to her?"

"I just got through telling you I conducted a thorough investigation," Stevie said, then sipped his coffee. "There's no evidence to suggest that."

"So keep looking for her, isn't that your job?"

"Frankly, no, it's not. When adults go missing, unless there's some sign of foul play or reason to believe they're in immediate danger, we don't spend a lot of time on these things. We don't have the resources or manpower to track people down. Anybody can walk away from their life if they want to. It's not against the law necessarily."

"Maybe it's time to hire a private detective then," Deacon suggested.

"That remains an option," Lance said. "But I think it's premature at this point."

"Why's that?"

"Given Fay's drug problems in the past, I think they could very well be behind this. She could be off somewhere on a binge with a bunch of other druggies."

Druggies, Deacon thought. *Funny how people use that word as if they're referring to something rather than some*one. "Even if that's the case, a private investigator can likely track her down."

"Fay told me she was clean," Lance said as if he hadn't heard him. "Now I wonder if it was just more of her lies."

"Sad to say, but it wouldn't be the first time she lied about that," Stevie added.

SMOKE, IN CRIMSON

Deacon sighed. Part of him wished he was back in the tall grass of the dunes, lying beneath the stars and listening to the wind off the ocean as waves gently rolled to shore. It was all so close, just outside the door, and yet the cottage felt like an alien craft drifting through the dark and empty expanse of space, lightyears from Earth and existing solely on the periphery of his dreams, the outskirts of his bleak nightmares.

To his right, between the kitchen and the living room, a short hallway led to the only bedroom and bathroom in the cottage. It was dark now, but Deacon could still see her there, watching him from the shadows. Wearing only panties, her otherwise nude body glistening with sweat, she smiled helplessly, hopelessly, then raised her hands and showed him her palms. He could see her wounds just as he remembered them, the blood slowly leaking, running down along her wrists and curling around her forearms, staining them with crimson vines of barbed wire.

Fay dropped her hands, allowing the blood to drip, then bowed her head and watched as it collected in little puddles around her bare feet.

Deacon closed his eyes, but that only made things worse.

When he opened them again, the hallway was empty.

Fay wasn't gone. Not by a longshot. She just wasn't there anymore.

CHAPTER **THREE**

THE STORM CONTINUED TO rage. In the relative quiet of the cottage, Deacon made a pot of coffee, poured himself a mug then sat at the small kitchen table to drink it and smoke a cigarette. Despite his history here, he couldn't help feeling like some crazed thief that had broken in while no one was home. But time was the only thief here, his dark dreams and memories of loss the only forfeitures of sanity.

He hadn't searched the entire cottage yet, but he had gone looking for things he knew he'd find. Bottles of booze—vodka, tequila and whiskey—in various stages of depletion, lined one of the kitchen cupboards, and Fay's stash of mushrooms, a few tabs of LSD, a baggie of cocaine, and weed—flower, joints, edibles and vapes—packed one of the drawers. In the bathroom cabinet he discovered a bottle with a few Oxys in it, and another with prescription muscle relaxants. So much for rehab, but then, Fay never really wanted to be clean and sober. That was theater, a performance for her father and others, because she knew most saw her as a drunk and drug addict. But for Fay, drugs and alcohol were more than dulling agents or an escape from everyday life. They served as a conduit, not only to higher levels of consciousness, but to other planes of existence. Like sex, they were her religion, her church, and she believed, a pathway to the gods.

"What the hell am I even doing here?" Deacon muttered, though he already knew the answer. Fay was *his* religion, and despite his best efforts, he was still a true believer, a hapless addict in need of a fix and willing to do whatever was necessary to get it.

Memories of lying next to Fay in the dark came to him, her nude body slick with sweat, her eyes stabbing into his like knives and her harried breath panting hot against his throat. "There's more," she whispered from the past. "We just have to find it. We just have to get there."

Deacon sipped his coffee as a sense of unrest swept through him. Instinctual and dark, it was all around him here, and while that was nothing new, there was no denying it had grown stronger, more malevolent somehow. He could feel evil within these walls, in the rain lashing the cottage and running off the roof, in the grass along the sand dunes, on the beach below and in the ocean beyond. With Fay, and this place, there was always a degree of

SMOKE, in CRIMSON

that—it was the bad that came with her good, and he'd always written it off as such—but this was different. The horror had become more aggressive again in his absence. Everything dripped with it now.

There were no framed photographs on display, nothing to link Fay to anyone or anything, past or present. The cottage possessed the same transient feel it always had, yet Fay's presence lingered. Lance had purchased the cottage decades before, not long after Fay's mother died from cancer. The plan was to make it a summer place and a weekend getaway spot from the city, which it was, until Fay was in her mid-twenties. When she lost her job as an RN, along with her license, for drug offenses, her nursing career abruptly came to an end. After a stint in rehab, her second, she moved into the cottage permanently with the alleged hope of straightening out her life and starting anew.

Years later she was still unemployed, still living in Lance's cottage rent-free, and supported herself with a hefty allowance her father provided each month. As much as she hated Lance in many ways, Deacon never once saw her refuse his generosity—if that's what it was—or his money. And she had no remorse or shame about it whatsoever.

"He's not paying me, he's paying me *back*," she once told Deacon in her typically cryptic way, even after such semantics were no longer necessary. "He owes me."

Deacon pushed away from the table and stood up. He needed to move, to shake off the past like the funereal shroud it was. He needed to run, to grab his jacket and knapsack and get as far away from the cottage as possible. He needed to get out of this town and never come back. But that wasn't going to happen. Deacon had been on the run his entire life, bouncing from place to place like the vagabond he was, and although exhausted, he harbored no illusions that this would be the end of his road. Not if he survived, and he planned to do just that. Of course there were no guarantees. All that dwelled within the darkness would never let him go, not without a fight.

And this time that fight would be to the death.

As he left the kitchen and drifted into the living room, watching the rain-blurred windows, he thought about Stevie Avado. Like everyone attached to Fay, he was her puppet. It was just a matter of degrees, though in Stevie's case it was particularly pathetic. Despite being long-married with three children, Stevie was madly in love with her and had been pining for her for years. A few grades ahead of her, he'd known her since their high school days, and while he'd regularly injected himself into her life ever since, often uninvited, and made certain he was constantly at her beckon call, he was never anything more to Fay than a casual friend. Anyone who *was* more, Stevie reviled, and Deacon topped that list.

SMOKE, IN CRIMSON

Earlier, he'd made it a point to linger while Lance was leaving, so he'd have a moment alone with Deacon. When that moment arrived, he waited near the back door. He didn't move, didn't say anything. He just stood there.

"Is there something else?" Deacon asked.

"Yes," Stevie said softly, almost guiltily. "I didn't want to bring it up in front of Mr. Dillon. He has enough to worry about, and I know you do too, but what I've got to tell you is unpleasant, so I thought it'd be best if I waited until it was just the two of us. It's a personal family matter."

"My family's dead."

"When you made town, did you come straight here?"

"I got in late last night, slept on the beach. Why, want to ticket me for vagrancy?"

"You haven't been to the cemetery yet then."

Stevie phrased it more as statement than question, but Deacon answered anyway. "No, I haven't. Why, what's the problem?"

"There's no easy way to say this so I'm just going to give it to you straight." Stevie's face flushed. "Somebody vandalized your sister's grave."

Deacon's gut twisted. "*What?*"

"Happened about a week or so ago, and due to the amount of damage we suspect it was more than one person. They tipped over the stone and tore up the ground pretty bad, looked like wild animals had been digging at it. Gina's headstone was damaged, but the caretaker—you remember Pete Briggs—he straightened things up as best he could."

"What kind of damage to her stone are we talking about?"

"Bastards managed to split it in two, must've used a sledgehammer. We would have notified you sooner, but nobody knew where you were or how to get hold of you."

Heart and mind racing, Deacon searched for a response. It eluded him.

"I know you and I aren't exactly friends, but I truly am sorry to have to tell you this, Deacon. It's an awful thing. An *evil* thing, you ask me."

Fay was back. Deacon couldn't see her, but she was there. So was Gina. The two of them with bleary eyes, arms wrapped tightly around each other like frightened children huddled together in a storm.

"Who did it?"

Stevie shrugged. "We don't know. I'm thinking probably teenagers."

Why did cops always blame everything short of genocide on teenagers?

"You don't know anybody that might've done something like this, do you?"

Deacon gave him a stern look that answered the question for him.

"Didn't think so, but had to ask. You understand. Anyway, I want you to know we'll keep looking into this until we find the perps, whoever they are, and I don't care how long that takes. I give you my word on that."

Deacon was so close to the woodstove the waves of heat wafting from it made drawing a full breath difficult. "Was Gina's grave the only one they bothered?"

"It was, and we have no idea why they singled hers out in particular."

Deacon watched him a while. Stevie didn't look dangerous enough to be a cop just then, more like a nervous little kid who'd been cornered into telling the truth about something he would've rather lied about. "Is that what you think happened?"

"Either that or they chose it at random. Where her stone's at the end of a row not far from the entrance, it's possible—likely even—they picked it out due to its proximity to the road. We just don't know for sure."

Wind rocked the cottage as whispers drifted from the bedroom, down the hallway and into the living room behind him. "Thanks for letting me know, I appreciate it."

"Sure." Stevie opened the back door, letting in the sounds of the rain, then hesitated and looked back at Deacon like he had something more to say. After a moment, he gave an awkward wave then stepped out into the storm, closing the door behind him.

Deacon sipped his coffee as Stevie's troubled face faded from memory.

The last thing he wanted to think about was his sister's grave disturbed and damaged—attacked—but he was powerless to prevent the torrent of pictures rifling across his mind's eye. Deacon hadn't thought of his sister Gina in a long time, not in anything more than a fleeting sense. He rarely allowed himself to. It was too painful on too many levels. With Fay missing he was already staggered. This latest news felt more like a knockout blow.

His sister glared at him from the past, her dark eyes, tears and black streaks of makeup staining her cheeks in long swaths like war paint.

Maybe betrayal was the worst desecration of all.

Deacon closed his eyes.

Fay's face, sullen now, breached the darkness. "All our demons have come out to play," she whispered, slinking closer. "Every last fucking god damned one of them."

Rain sprayed the windows, snapping him back from the brink. But the respite would be short-lived. Drowning remained his fate. No one could tread water forever.

DESPITE ORIGINALLY HAVING BEEN Gina's college girlfriend, Deacon assigned Fay legendary status the moment he first laid eyes on her. Naively, and because they'd deliberately concealed it, he'd mistaken her relationship with

SMOKE, IN CRIMSON

his sister as platonic. So when he first saw her laying on her stomach, stretched out on a towel under summer sky while sunbathing with Gina, his nineteen-year-old body was incapable of resisting her. Watching them in the backyard, he'd never felt more detached and alone, and never more alive. But as much as he longed for her, at the time he had no idea what Fay was really all about. It wasn't until a few years later that she took him by the hand and led him across the bridge separating her soul from his. It was then that he grew mature enough to see Fay as a whole, three-dimensional entity. Until then, she'd been sandy-blonde hair, big brown eyes, a certain scent, a sexy laugh, tits, ass, a coy glance. *Smoke…*

Unlike her brother, Gina was a pack animal rather than a loner, so predictably, when she and Fay broke up after being together for two years in college and three years after graduation, it was messy and ugly. Given the circumstances, it couldn't have been any other way, and by the time it came about, Fay had already turned her attention to Deacon. Initially he remained unaware of her true relationship with Gina, so when that gap closed it did so rapidly, and it didn't take long for him to understand that Fay was anything but typical. She was no high school girl with stars in her eyes. Fay was something different. She was undiscovered country, as dangerous as she was mysterious.

In a constant state of flux, Fay attacked life—assaulted it—while others seemed mere spectators, if not outright victims of it. Deacon not only related to the eccentric and rebellious behavior she fed on, he also discovered a freedom and form of expression he'd been unaware of prior, and soon found himself as hungry to be between her ears as he was her legs.

One night, right before they fucked, Fay finally told Deacon that she and Gina had been lovers. Lying in bed together afterwards, they shared a cigarette and stayed quiet for several minutes. Sated in a way he never believed possible, drenched in sweat and still trying to get his mind around what he'd learned, Deacon watched the ceiling fan rotate in the darkness above them. "Don't you feel guilty?" he asked softly.

With light laughter, Fay blew a stream of smoke into the air. "Should I?"

"How can you not?"

"Do you know who Rita Mae Brown is? She's an author and playwright." Fay's soft, faintly raspy voice was barely audible above the hum of the ceiling fan. "She said that one of the keys to happiness is a bad memory. And she was right."

Dread clung to him like a second skin. "You have an excellent memory."

"I'm not talking about me," Fay said. "And you didn't ask if I felt happy. You asked if I felt guilty."

"I don't understand."

SMOKE, IN CRIMSON

With a devilish grin, she handed him the cigarette. "You will."

THE BEDROOM WAS EXACTLY as he remembered it. Nothing had changed. Even the bedspread was the same. A small room, it consisted of a single window which faced the beach, a bed, two matching nightstands, a bureau and a modest closet.

Deacon stood in the doorway, unsure if he wanted to step inside. He could still feel Fay here, and from the inside. Yet it looked like no one had set foot in the room for ages. The bed was neatly made, everything was dusted and almost too clean, and nothing was out of place. The top of the old bureau was empty, and a small wood framed mirror above it, which at one time had been lined on either side with photographs from over the years, was now barren.

Odd, Deacon thought. *Her photographs meant so much to her.*

Drawing a deep breath, he stepped into the room and slid open the top bureau drawer to find numerous pairs of socks, panties and bras. He slid it closed, opened the second drawer and found neatly folded jeans and khakis. The third drawer housed various t-shirts, tank tops and blouses, but there was still no sign of the photographs.

Behind him, the closet, which had no door, revealed a few skirts, dresses, belts and some formal tops, all on hangers. Along the floor were a couple pairs of heels, some flats, sandals, flip-flops and sneakers, all in uniform little rows. Stacked along the single shelf in the closet were clear plastic bins filled with sweaters and winter clothing, including scarves, gloves, mittens and knit hats.

The cottage had never been this organized in the past. Although always relatively neat and clean, this version looked like someone had come here before he'd arrived and meticulously straightened everything out. Lance, no doubt. The question was why.

Deacon turned back to the bureau and caught a glimpse of himself in the mirror.

Behind him, on the bed, Fay crawled toward him on all-fours, and while the memory was disturbing, he was thankful for the distraction. She smiled coyly, as if reading his mind, then licked her lips, her eyes consuming him. Despite her lusty, feral qualities, there remained something unmistakably poetic and ethereal about Fay as well. Those aspects were so profound they radiated from her as much as fear and hate and love did. She existed in multiple worlds simultaneously, one a reality of pure impulse—raw, animalistic and instinctual—the other furtive, spiritual and transcendent. Ravenous wolf and phantom waif, Fay was somehow both, and decidedly so.

SMOKE, IN CRIMSON

Bracing himself against the bureau, Deacon bowed his head and waited for the memories to pass. Once they'd left him, he made his way around the foot of the bed to the first nightstand, careful not to land on his reflection again.

A squat lamp sat atop it, but there was enough dull light from the window, so he checked the single drawer and found a mishmash tangle of USB, HDMI, charging and earphone cords. The other nightstand was sans lamp, and in its drawer were a few pens and highlighters, a blank pad of white lined paper, dog-eared copies of the Jerzy Kosiński novel *The Painted Bird*, Kate Braverman's poetry collection *Lullaby for Sinners*, and worn copies of both *The Anunnaki Bible* and *The Book of Enoch*.

Against his better judgement, Deacon reached down and touched the bedspread. It was cool and soft, with a silky feel he remembered well. He'd slept in that bed beneath these covers countless times, with Fay wrapped around him like a snake slowly squeezing the life from grateful prey. The first time they ever fucked was in this room, in this bed, and he could still feel her on top of him, taking over once he'd cum twice and lay there out of breath and exhausted. He remembered her uncanny ability to bring him back, to get him erect again and again, even when he was sure he couldn't and no longer wanted to, her fingers caressing his scrotum and shaft as she whispered in his ear how badly she wanted it, how desperately she *needed* it. How sore he'd been for days after, his penis swollen, the head and base chafed and raw. He remembered begging her to stop, as she climbed onto him again and again, somehow getting him hard and slipping him inside her then smashing down into him with such force the entire room shook. And how finally, thankfully, Fay fell away from him for the final time that night, drenched, dripping and panting wildly, finally sated.

"Where are you?" Deacon asked. His voice sounded hollow in the otherwise empty room, like that of a mourner, someone who'd already buried her long ago.

But he knew better. Fay was alive.

The only one dead and buried was Gina, and even she hadn't been allowed to rest. Much as Deacon searched his mind, he couldn't come up with any connection between Fay and the desecration of his sister's grave. Fay was crazy, but she wouldn't do such a thing, and it seemed farfetched at best to suggest her disappearance had something to do with it. Deacon wanted to believe they were unrelated events, but again, he knew better. There were no such things as coincidences.

How were they connected then, and why?

His sister's sad face emerged from the shadows of the past. *Come and see, brother. Come and see what they've done to me.* A single tear slid the length of her face, clung to her jawline a moment then fell away to darkness. *Come and see.*

Deacon nodded, and then slowly made his way back to the kitchen for his jacket.

CHAPTER **FOUR**

THE WORST OF THE storm had gone, and though the rain had letup somewhat, it continued to fall. His hair still secured with a bandana, Deacon walked back along the beach to the main road, then followed it to the downtown area, which was only about seven or eight minutes away on foot. He was soaked and chilled to the bone by the time he got there, but his focus was on how much the town had changed in just three years. There were more boarded up buildings, more empty lots neglected and overgrown with weeds, and more dark corners, both commercial and residential. Several business properties were empty year-round now, relics of prosperity from days past, and one area, which had once been a thriving shopping plaza filled with numerous name brand discount outlets, was reduced to a seedy-looking flea market which was closed for the offseason. The town itself had always been a tourist trap—bustling in the summer months and dead, bleak and desolate through the fall and winter—but it had somehow managed to become even more soulless and drearier in Deacon's absence.

Of course the version of town he'd known growing up was almost completely gone, and had been for a very long time. With the exception of a few seasonal stores specifically designed to sell crappy trinkets to tourists, the mom-and-pop shops of Deacon's youth were nonexistent, even in what outsiders viewed as a quaint, albeit typical, little seaside vacation spot. It was all corporate now. The little A&P his mother shopped at on Main Street was long gone, and a giant Stop & Shop had popped up across town near the state highway exit, along with a CVS and an Olive Garden. A Blockbuster Video and another independent video store had shut their doors years before, yet both buildings were still vacant and left to rot. Dell's, a small hamburger joint operated by a cranky old guy named Arthur Dell since the 1950s, had become a Wendy's. The office supply place a local couple owned for decades was a law office now, the general store had been torn down and replaced with an insurance office, and the independent pizza parlors had become a Papa Gino's and a Domino's franchise. The only family-owned properties that had survived along the three blocks that constituted the commercial district were a modest hardware store, a couple seafood joints and a saltwater taffy stand.

SMOKE, IN CRIMSON

With a head full of memories good and bad, Deacon crossed to a side street and followed it another couple blocks until he reached Holder Road, a quiet tree lined street populated by modest but well-kept houses, all with neatly squared little front lawns and paved driveways. He stopped before a gated picket fence in front of one house in particular. There was a fence when he lived there too, but it was the rusty chain-link variety. The old shingles, removed and replaced with vinyl siding years ago, the yard, most of which had been dirt back in the day, the intricate stone walkway to the front door, and the expertly-pruned shrubbery beneath the two windows facing the street left the house of his youth barely recognizable. In the driveway sat an SUV, rather than his father's beat up old pickup truck and his mother's Ford Escort. Even the mailbox was different, the dented metal job replaced with a fancy-looking wood number that looked like a replica of the house. Ironically, though still a working-class neighborhood, Holder Road was one of the few areas that actually looked better than it had in the past. But looks, as the old saying went, could be deceiving. Then and now.

Wind whipped up the narrow street. The gutters on either side of Holder Road were packed with leaves wet and matted down from the storm. Deacon could remember the scraping sound the dead leaves made when they were dry, as they swept across the street. The way they danced and swirled, suddenly brought back to life for as long as the autumn winds saw fit. As a little boy, he'd lay in bed at night, listening to those leaves on windy nights, wondering if it was really leaves he was hearing, or something more sinister.

Deacon looked out at the street. He could almost see himself the day he learned to ride his bike, and how his father screamed at him, frustrated with Deacon's inability to pick it up quickly.

"Is that yelling really necessary?" his mother had asked, coming outside due to the noise. "The whole neighborhood can hear you."

"I don't give a good god damn what they can hear!" his father growled. "This kid's gonna learn how to ride that thing if it's the last thing he does!"

And Deacon did. By the end of that afternoon, knees and palms scraped from multiple falls, exhausted, trauma-tized and crying uncontrollably, seven-year-old Deacon was damn near an expert rider.

He looked back at the house. The little boy and teen-ager that grew up there was as dead and gone now as his parents were, his father to a heart attack at just fifty-one, his mother from liver disease three years later at forty-nine.

By the time Deacon was twenty-one and Gina just twenty-three, their parents were gone. Their father worked as a custodian in a local plant, their mother was a CNA at a nursing home two towns away, and despite having lived in that house and paid on it for years, when they died they still

SMOKE, IN **CRIMSON**

owed a great deal because they'd taken a second mortgage out to pay for Gina's college. Once the house sold and the debts were paid, all that was left was about ten thousand dollars, which Deacon and Gina split. His end had run out long ago. He never knew what Gina did with hers.

Not that it mattered now. It never really had.

All these years later, Deacon wanted to feel something more, but couldn't seem to get there. His childhood home didn't conjure memories particularly good or bad. In reality, he felt almost nothing at all, and somehow, that was worse.

Other memories did exist here, however, and he knew it was only a matter of time before they slipped free of their hiding places deep within those walls and came for him. So Deacon hurried off through the rain to the end of the street, turned at the corner then followed another to the cemetery next to the highway where his family was buried.

Standing next to the open gates, Deacon could see his parents' grave from there, and Gina's next to it. The cold wind gusted across the empty highway, slashing through him before continuing on across the graveyard and into the wall of trees at the rear of the property. Like sentries guarding the dead, their branches swayed and bounced in the rain, spraying the already drenched ground below.

He thought he could outrun the dark memories slowly escaping that old house, but he was wrong. There was nothing to outrun. They were here, waiting for him all along.

GINA'S APARTMENT WAS A small place located over a garage in town, just blocks from the house she and Deacon grew up in. Her job as a nurse at the local hospital afforded her rent and utilities, groceries, a monthly payment and insurance on a decent compact car, and enough extra cash for pizza delivery once a week and a movie out or dancing and bar-hopping on Saturday nights. Before the breakup, she and Fay spent their time there or at the cottage, but they were rarely apart, which is why it was still odd to find Gina sitting on a couch, alone in her tiny space. In jeans and a light sweater that looked as if she'd slept in them, she sat staring at the wall, her eyes red and saddled with dark bags, her skin pale and drawn. Even a year and a half later, Gina had yet to recover from the breakup. In fact, she'd gotten worse. Though never much of a drinker, she'd made herself a rum and coke, and from the look of her and what was left in the bottle, it wasn't her first.

Standing in the doorway between the kitchenette and the living room, Deacon cautiously uttered her name.

"Yeah, by all means, just come right in," Gina said without looking at him, a cigarette smoldering in one hand and her drink in the other. "Mi casa es tu casa."

"I knocked a couple times," Deacon told her. "Your car's out there so I knew you were home, just wanted to make sure you were all right."

SMOKE, IN CRIMSON

"Oh, how sweet," Gina said with a quick side-glance. She took a long pull on the cigarette and rolled her eyes. "What do you want?"

Deacon wished he could take it all back, but it was too late for that, and they both knew it. "I wasn't sure if you heard about Fay."

"Her father was nice enough to call and let me know, said maybe it'd be nice if I went to see her since we'd been such good *friends*, you know? Told me he's sure she *misses* me and seeing me might cheer her up, if you can believe that one. Those are the words he used. *Cheer her up.* What an asshole."

"Yeah, he's a piece of work."

"You have *no* idea, kid." Gina laughed lightly, bitterly, and puffed on her cigarette. "Then again, maybe you do. You're the one she tells her secrets to now."

"Gina—"

"Get out." She crushed her cigarette in an ashtray on an end table next to the couch. "Seriously, just get the fuck out of my house. Go see your girlfriend. Tell her I said I'd be by to *cheer her up* but I'm a little busy trying not to end up in the same place her dear old dad has her tucked away in. Boston, he said. Have to keep up appearances, right? His daughter's enough of an embarrassment, can't have *this* getting out and risk having it make him look bad. Shit, if they only knew, right, champ?"

"You have to stop with all this," he told her. "You have to get your life back."

Gina finally looked at him. "I'm sorry. Didn't I just tell you to get the fuck out of my house? And yet, you're still here, standing there like some emotionally wounded puppy that can't figure out why he's in trouble."

"I didn't take her from you, Gina, and she didn't leave you for me. We haven't even been together for months."

"On-again off-again is Fay's modus operandi. You'll get used to it."

"I don't..." Deacon searched desperately for the words he needed. "I don't want you to be mad at me anymore. I don't want us to be like this."

Gina smiled, but it was tortured. "It's terrible to want something you can't have, isn't it?"

"Why are you punishing me?"

"Because I can," she said.

"What do you want me to do? Tell me. What can I do?"

She pointed to the door with her drink. "You can leave."

With a sorrowful nod, Deacon did just that.

Later, as those memories dissipated, he watched a train glide along tracks overhead before vanishing into curtains of fog and dust.

The neighborhood was not what he expected, nothing at all like his nightmares.

SMOKE, IN CRIMSON

Two skinheads stared at him from across the street. Clad in bomber jackets, fatigues and combat boots, they leaned against the base of the overpass listening to a boom box spewing hate-metal.

Deacon paused at the corner to light a cigarette, reminded of bullies in high school. This duo looked decidedly more dangerous than the worst teenagers, but it was more or less the same principle, it seemed to him. They were all sad, weak, angry and frightened boys raging nonsensically against people and things that had absolutely nothing to do with their own problems and shortcomings. Self-hatred turned mindless weapon of hatred for others, that's all it was. And that was more than enough.

Even then, despite being out of high school only a few years, it seemed far off, a memory so distant his experiences could have easily been assigned to someone else.

One of the skinheads was gobbling up a chili dog with revolting devotion. It smelled rancid, and as Deacon passed by, he was certain that despite his love of them, he'd never be able to eat a hot dog again.

The other one said something under his breath in a snide tone, but Deacon ignored him and continued toward the massive building at the end of the street, perched there like some jaded monolith.

Once inside, a long row of fixtures on the narrow ceiling cast a tan-yellow tint that was somehow soothing and disquieting all at once. Through another set of doors Deacon found an enormous desk. To his right was a waiting area that consisted of several nondescript chairs and a small coffee table covered in tattered, dated magazines. He noticed a vending machine and another hallway to his left. Somewhere within these unremarkable walls they'd tucked Fay away.

A passing nurse eyed him suspiciously. "Can I help you with something?"

Deacon wondered how he'd avoided coming to live here himself. It wasn't so difficult, really.

"Are you here to visit someone?" the nurse persisted.

"Yes," he answered in a tone better suited to an admission of guilt than the most basic reply. "Fay Dillon."

As the nurse escorted him along the corridor, patients babbled in distant rooms. Others screamed as if being tortured—perhaps they were—and it was clear to Deacon that if one were not mad before walking these halls, the onset of mental illness could not be far behind once one had.

The nurse stopped and motioned to a room to her right. "You can go right in."

There was no door, and he hesitated to look in at Fay, aware that she had not yet seen him. In an iron bed, tucked beneath top sheet and a thin brown blanket, she gazed out the wire-encased window on the far wall like a child who had just had her tonsils removed and was now awaiting the

SMOKE, IN CRIMSON

promised bowl of ice cream. Her hair was chopped shorter than usual, and her face bore no makeup. Her lips were dry and cracked, her right wrist wrapped in bandages and heavy gauze.

In all the time Deacon had known her, he'd never before seen Fay look so utterly, darkly, hopelessly, commonly *human.*

As if she'd heard his thoughts, Fay turned, focused on him, and summed up all there was to know about them with a single uninhibited smile. "Deacon," she said softly.

He remembered her smiling the same way through the darkness, her hands gliding over his body, her breath hot against his chest. Deacon wanted to answer, but his throat constricted.

"*Deacon,*" she said again. "How did I know you'd come?"

"Your father called me," he answered, clearing his throat. "And Gina."

Fay arched an eyebrow. "Really?"

"I was surprised too."

"By his phone call or my theatrics?"

"What do *you* think?"

"I think I'd sell my soul for a pack of Marlboros."

"Can't sell what you don't have."

She nodded, eyes still fixed on his. "True enough, baby."

"You look beautiful."

"Christ, you actually believe that, don't you?"

63

Eyeing her bandaged wrist, Deacon couldn't help but imagine the slashed flesh beneath. Amazed either of them were still alive after everything they'd been through, if that's what this could be called, he stood there stupidly, realizing he should have brought flowers or candy, answers, prayers, fresh razors—something.

An orderly appeared at the top of the hall pushing a metal cart.

Deacon stepped into the room and approached Fay cautiously; the way as a child he'd approached tigers at the zoo. "I should've brought you something."

Fay shook her head. "Nothing grows here."

"How much longer do you have to stay?"

"Thirty days they tell me."

"That's not such a long time."

"My father called me too, but of course he hasn't visited, can't be seen in a place like this. He chewed me out pretty good, said it's time to grow up. He even threatened to cut off the money if I don't get my shit together. I swear it sounded like the fool actually meant it this time. He's so full of compassion, my father. But then, he has no idea how it is to be us, does he?"

"Maybe that's for the best."

"I should tell him to go fuck himself. I'm not incapable of earning a living."

"I know, but—"

SMOKE, IN CRIMSON

"Sometimes I wish I could go back to nursing."

"Only nursing you can ever hope getting close to again is breastfeeding."

Fay laughed, and Deacon felt valuable.

"At least he had the sense to get a hold of you."

"Are you sure that's a positive?"

"How did he find you?"

"Probably Gina, but I'm not sure."

She nodded. "Guess I'm the one who lost track."

"That was your decision."

Her eyes pierced his. "Still getting high?"

It never made me high is what he thought. "Now and then," is what he said.

Fay let it go, and he was grateful.

"What have you been doing with yourself these days?" she asked.

"I work underground, below street level."

She seemed fascinated with this concept. "You mean in the sewers?"

"A shoe store in Providence," he explained. "I've been living not far from there the last few months, got my own place. Just a room, but I can walk to work. Anyway, you know those clunky white security things they put on shoes these days?"

She stared at him, oblivious.

"I stand at a table all day in a basement attaching those to the shoes with this little handheld thing, kind of like a hole-punch, before they go upstairs to the sales floor."

"Sounds enchanting," she said, clearly disappointed.

"It keeps the lights on."

"Why would you want the lights on?"

"Can't live your whole life in the dark."

"Who says?"

Deacon shrugged.

Her expression grew sad. "What do you remember most?"

"Laughing until we cried, and being unapologetically alive, indestructible."

She glanced at him as if she'd swallowed her tongue. "That's odd. I remember your face the first time you saw my scars, your innocent little-boy eyes and how often I dreamt of plucking them out. I remember you as a ghost, moving between people and things without ever becoming clearly defined yourself, and I remember feeling isolated and alone even when you loved me."

"Then I'm sorry."

"I guess that makes everything all right then." She laughed, but there was little humor in it, because there was nowhere for them to hide from what they both knew to be true, from what they both realized were genuine memories and not the flights of fantasy they so desperately wanted them to be. "It was never your fault."

"What wasn't?"

SMOKE, IN CRIMSON

Fay's eyes became moist, and Deacon noticed her hands were shaking, hands dainty and soft yet still tarnished with the blood and bodily fluids of all those ghosts only the two of them were able to see. "Me."

"I should go, Fay."

"Can't you sit with me just a while longer?"

"Love or hate, you never could decide."

"Both, god damn it," Fay said, taking his hand. "*Both*."

As warmth passed from her palm to his, Deacon knew exactly what she meant.

WITH AN UNSETTLING SENSE of being watched, and a light rain misting all around him, Deacon crossed through the cemetery gates. As he followed a narrow paved path to the first row of headstones, he purposely averted his eyes from them and instead gazed out at the massive trees along the back of the property. Branches sagging and heavy with rain effectively concealed what lurked behind and between them, things dark and unseen waiting for their chance to pierce the thin film separating the world of the living, and that which belonged to the dead.

Deacon turned away, and looked down at the stones. Gina's was first, followed by the plot where both his parents were buried. The entire family was here, with one exception, of course. No plot had ever been purchased for him here. He didn't have the financial means to buy one himself, and likely never would, but that didn't bother him. In fact, it seemed appropriate. Although there were times in his life Deacon was close to Gina, he'd always felt like an add-on to the family, the one member slightly out-of-step and apart from the rest. He couldn't remember it ever being any other way, even as a little boy. The others had always been more of a family unit, a dysfunctional one to be sure, but a unit nonetheless. For Deacon, there was a feeling of a separation, even when he was in their presence. And now, since their deaths, that had literally become the case. Whether that was a blessing, a curse, or something in between, he couldn't be sure.

The sudden feeling of something bursting through the trees behind him, flying over the sea of stones and closing on him like a predator was so strong, Deacon actually braced himself for impact as he spun around.

But there was nothing out there, nothing rushing up behind him.

He watched the trees a while anyway, listened to the wind and the occasional sound of a car passing on the nearby highway. Maybe the dead were watching him, or maybe it was someone else. Deacon couldn't be certain.

No one was ever truly alone in a graveyard.

Sometimes knowing things was a horrible burden.

SMOKE, IN CRIMSON

Holding back the fear, Deacon returned his attention to the family plots. Both stones were high-gloss and dark gray in color. His parents' was pristine and glistening in the rain, their names chiseled into the stone along with their dates of birth and death. Flashes of their decomposing bodies lying six feet beneath his feet came to him, their sightless eyes open as if aware of him, and their mouths sewn shut into thin grim lines.

As those hideous sights dissipated, Deacon focused on Gina's grave.

The stone had been split in two just as Stevie had described. One piece that had obviously fallen away when it was damaged was now leaned against the base. The other was still attached to the base but had been hit with such force it had become misaligned. The jagged sides of both slabs caught Deacon's eye, along with the patch of ground in front of the stone, which had been considerably disturbed and later, obviously raked by cemetery staff to look somewhat more presentable. Her name was broken in two, Gina on one slab, her last on the other, and a cross that lay on its side etched into the granite was now split between them as well.

Unlike his parents, Deacon had no visions of his sister beneath the earth. He had no sense of her here at all, really, but standing before such desecration did nothing to deter the anger burning through him.

"I'll find out who did this, and why," he said, his voice strange and alien in this ghostly place of whispers and tears.

Something compelled Deacon to reach out and touch the stone still attached to the base. When he did so he felt something odd beneath his fingers, and realized there was something atop the stone he hadn't noticed.

Very old and made of either iron or severely tarnished brass, Deacon picked it up and held it out before him in the rain.

Someone had left a skeleton key on Gina's headstone.

CHAPTER **FIVE**

DEACON WASN'T FAR FROM the cottage when he heard the barking.

A short distance from where he'd seen them that morning, the boy and his dog Larry were in the middle of the road that ran alongside the dunes. The rain had stopped but it was still overcast and cloudy, darker than it should've been that time of day. An ancient-looking tow truck was parked diagonally across the road, like it had stopped abruptly, the driver's side door open and the engine still running. The boy was straddling his bike, and a man, presumably the driver of the truck, was blocking his path, leaned against the front wheel with his hands gripping the handlebars. A plastic bag and a few spilled groceries lay at the boy's feet. The dog continued to bark with a nervous edge.

"What's going on?" Deacon asked.

The man, who was filthy, at least six-feet tall, well over two hundred pounds and looked to be somewhere in his

71

mid-to-late fifties, released the bike and turned toward Deacon. With stringy, greasy, badly thinning dark hair, pockmarked skin and hands black with grime, he was dressed in jeans, a faded blue shirt advertising a gas station, and a pair of work boots. Rather than answer, he sized Deacon up without subtlety, and then laughed under his breath as if amused by the sight of him.

Larry recognized Deacon and dashed over to him playfully. As he squatted down to pet and calm the dog, Deacon kept his attention focused on the man. There was a deeply depraved look in his eyes, the kind Deacon had seen before. "Maybe you didn't hear me," he said, petting the dog. "I asked what was going on."

"Nothin'," the man grunted, standing there like a slump-shouldered ogre.

"You okay?" Deacon asked the boy.

He gave a hesitant nod but said nothing.

"How old are you, son?"

"Eleven," the boy said. "And a half, almost."

"We was just talkin'," the man said, wiping his mouth with the back of his hand.

"Is that right?" Deacon gave Larry another pat on the head then walked over and stood next to the boy. "What are you talking about, anything interesting?"

"It's none of your business," the man said, stepping closer.

He smelled even worse than he looked, but Deacon was busy working various scenarios in his mind. He hoped to

SMOKE, IN CRIMSON

avoid it, but if things turned physical he'd be three or four moves ahead of this oaf and put him on the ground before the guy knew what hit him. "A grown man bothering a little kid ought to be everybody's business."

"Who says I'm botherin' him?"

"I do."

"Yeah, and who the hell are *you*?"

"The guy that's asking what business you have with an eleven-year-old child."

The man narrowed his sickly eyes. "That's between me and him."

"Do you know this guy?" Deacon asked the boy without breaking eye contact.

"Sure he does," the man answered for him. "Me and Henry is old friends."

Deacon noticed the sewn-on name patch on the man's shirt. "You friends with lots of little boys, *Albert*?"

"Fuck's that mean?"

"You tell me."

"Huh?" The man seemed genuinely confused.

You can hear his blood pulsing through his veins, can't you, Deacon?

"Leave the kid alone, okay?"

You can see his bones snapping.

"Told you we just talkin'."

You can taste his tears.

"Conversation's over."

You can feel the warmth of everything that's alive inside of him all over you.

Albert smiled, revealing big square brown teeth. Again, he seemed to find Deacon amusing. "I'll catch you later, Henry," he said, heading for his truck. "Don't forget to tell Mom I said hi."

A gust of wind blew in off the Atlantic, cold and raw. Deacon didn't look. That's what the ghosts wanted. Whatever else they had to say or show him could wait.

With his ignorant, condescending smile still in place, Albert watched Deacon the entire time he strode to his tow truck, struggled up into the cab then slowly pulled away.

"What was that all about?" Deacon asked once he'd gone.

"He's just a jerk."

"No doubt, you sure you're all right?"

"Yeah, thanks." Henry climbed off his bike long enough to put a half-gallon of milk, a loaf of bread, a small container of butter and a tube of toothpaste back into the plastic bag.

"So you're Henry?"

The boy stood his bike up and hopped on. "Yup."

"I'm Deacon. Saw you and Larry this morning down on the dunes."

"Yeah, I remember."

Deacon looked over his shoulder. The tow truck had

pulled to the side of the road quite a distance away. "So how do you know Albert?"

"I just sorta know who he is. He works at the gas station downtown."

"You need to let your parents know he's been bothering you, okay?"

Henry nodded but seemed unconvinced. "I got to get home now," he said. "I was supposed to go to the store and come right back. Come on, Larry."

Deacon looked again. The truck was still there. "You guys live nearby?"

The boy pointed to a cottage perhaps half a mile down the beach from Fay's.

"See the other cottage on the bluff?" Deacon asked. "That's where I'm staying for a while, so I've got to go right by your place anyway. Mind if I walk with you guys?"

Henry shrugged. "Free country."

Deacon couldn't prevent a brief smile. "Well, more or less." He took another look back, this time continuing to stare until the tow truck lurched from the side of the road and sped off, finally vanishing into the distance.

With Larry galloping along behind him, Henry slowly peddled for home.

Deacon followed.

The cottage, which was nearly identical to Fay's, had been there for decades, but Deacon never knew who lived there. There were a total of four cottages along the stretch of shoreline, which covered more than five miles, but most were summer getaways and empty this time of year. At the end of the beach were the ruins of an abandoned hotel.

As they reached a gravel driveway of bright white stones, Larry ran ahead of them, bounding up the back steps to the backdoor. It opened and a woman in a sweater and jeans stepped out, bending down quickly to ruffle the dog's fur with a quick pat.

"What took you so long? I was getting worried and I…" As she straightened up she realized Henry and Larry were not alone. Nervously, she brushed a wisp of auburn hair from her eyes and hooked it behind her ear. "Oh. Hello."

Before Deacon could respond Henry held the bag up as if in evidence and said, "I got everything. There's two dollars and something left." He hopped off his bike, leaned it against the wall, climbed the stairs to the back porch then jerked a thumb behind him. "That's Deacon."

"Go put everything on the counter for me, okay, sweetie?" she said, stepping further onto the porch and folding her arms across her chest.

There was something familiar about the woman, but Deacon couldn't place her. "Hi, I'm staying a ways up the beach," he explained as Henry and Larry disappeared inside. "I just wanted to make sure they got home safely, happened to be passing by when this guy in a tow truck was giving your son a hard time."

76

SMOKE, IN CRIMSON

The woman rolled her pale blue eyes. "That would be Albert."

"He was blocking Henry's way and holding onto his bike."

She sighed. "Albert's asked me out a few times and I said no, so—"

"Gee, can't imagine why."

"I know, quite the catch, right? But now he stops Henry whenever he sees him around town by himself and apparently asks about me. Far as I know he's relatively harmless. He scares Henry something awful, though. I was hoping to avoid having to call the police about it."

"Never been a big fan of cops, but in this case I think that might be a good idea."

"Thanks for helping him. That was nice of you to do."

"Sure," he said.

Her expression turned a bit coy. "You don't remember me, do you?"

"Should I?" Deacon asked. "Do we know each other?"

"Little bit, a long time ago." The wind caught her hair again. She moved it from her face. "We went to high school together. You were a year ahead of me. I'm Lauren. Lauren DiCicco. It was Petty back then."

As he studied her face the memories returned. She'd aged, of course, but gracefully, and her hair, which she wore shorter as a teenager, now hung just below her shoulders. "Lauren Petty. You did gymnastics, right?"

"I did, yes! I can't believe you remember me. I was a little mouse back then."

Slowly, more memories came to him. A quiet girl with a mouth full of braces, Lauren was petite and pretty, but shy. Not hugely popular, though never the outsider Deacon was, he was aware of her only vaguely, as a girl he passed in the halls, sat a distance from in the cafeteria, or saw in yearbook photos highlighting the gymnastics team. Until just then, he was certain they'd never actually spoken to each other.

"I *do* remember," Deacon told her. "So what are you up to these days?"

"I work for a medical billing company in Plymouth. What about you?"

"I'm between jobs right now."

Lauren considered this a moment. "And you're staying at the Dillon cottage?"

"Yeah," he said carefully. "You remember Fay?"

"I remember Fay, yes," she said in a tone not quite malicious, but close.

"She's gone missing."

"I heard. Is there any news?"

"Not yet." Deacon arched an eyebrow. "Word travels fast, huh?"

"It's still a small town."

"It's been a few years but it seems even smaller than the last time I was here, if you know what I mean."

SMOKE, IN CRIMSON

"I do, actually, and I've been back for quite a while." Lauren looked away, out at the sea. "Right after college I moved to Florida. Met a guy, got married, had Henry. My husband was in the military. He was killed in Afghanistan when Henry was four."

Deacon could feel her pain; see it etched across her face. "Jesus, I'm sorry."

"Thanks." She smiled sadly. "So I came home a widow and single mom—God, seven years ago now—with what little we had in our savings. I bought this place with the insurance money. I always used to think it'd be so nice to live in one of these cottages out here, you know? I'd walk the beach as a kid and wonder who lived in them and what they were doing, and since this one just happened to be for sale and I had the money, I went for it. Unfortunately turns out it's nowhere near as romantic as I imagined."

Nothing ever is, Deacon thought.

"I'm sorry," she said. "Listen to me babbling on and on, I—"

"Not at all, you're fine."

Lauren moved to the steps and sat on the first one. "So you're staying at Fay's place again?"

"For now," Deacon said.

"You two aren't together anymore I take it?"

"Not for a while."

"I remember seeing Fay around without you so I assumed you'd left town."

"Her father contacted me, asked if I'd come back and stay at the cottage a while, see if I could help figure out what's going on."

"Are you staying there by yourself?"

"Yes," he said.

"I remember when you lived there before. I'd see you two now and then, coming in or out or walking the beach, but I never saw you around otherwise."

Deacon chased away the images falling through his head. "We didn't leave the cottage much."

"What do you think happened to her?" Lauren asked.

"I'm not sure."

"What about the police? Do they think Fay just up and left or—"

"I really don't know, but they say there's no sign of foul play."

Lauren nodded, hugging herself as an awkward silence followed.

"Listen, it was good seeing you," Deacon finally said. "But I should get going."

"Good seeing you too." Lauren stood up. "If you get bored over there all by yourself, maybe you could come over for dinner one night. Believe me, I love my son and that goofy dog more than life itself, but I do miss adult conversation now and then."

SMOKE, IN CRIMSON

Lauren's shyness had apparently gone the way of her braces, but Deacon found that endearing. "Sounds nice," he said. "I might just take you up on that."

"Do you have a phone?"

He held it out for her.

Lauren took it from him, tapped the screen a few times then handed it back. "Now you've got my number," she said with an impish grin. "You know, in case you want to give me a call."

"Thanks," Deacon said, waving as he moved down the driveway. "Talk soon."

"Take care, and thanks again for helping Henry."

By the time Deacon reached the road, Lauren had already gone inside. Watching the place a moment, he tried to remember the last time he felt as alive as he had just then.

For an instant, the darkness had receded and taken Fay along with it.

But even as Deacon acknowledged that, she and all that came with her were back. As real as the ground beneath his feet and the wind in his hair, those same old demons returned too, folding their leathery wings around him, encasing him in a black cocoon and dragging him down into that pit of bottomless darkness he knew all too well.

There's no escape, baby, not from Hell.

Fay was right. There was no escape. Salvation was the only way out, but Deacon could no longer be sure where damnation ended and deliverance began.

GREG F. GIFUNE

As he made his way across the sand and back to the cottage, to his past and all that awaited him there, he couldn't help but wonder if he ever had.

CHAPTER **SIX**

IN THE DIM LIGHT of the bathroom, Deacon stood before the small mirror over the sink, hands clutching the counter and his head bowed. In a sudden outburst of rage, he'd punched the mirror and shattered it. Several shards lay scattered about, so he carefully collected them and dropped them in the wastebasket. He didn't want to see his reflection anyway. The stories it told, the perpetual sorrow in his ever-fading eyes, the light within them that once burned so brightly gradually skulking closer to extinguishment, all of it conspired to drive him deeper into madness. He looked at his hand, it was sore but fine.

"If we live long enough we forget who we were," Fay once told him as they sat together in the sand on a cold winter day, watching the ocean. "When we get older, we become cheap imitations of ourselves. Replicas, that's all we are, and not even very good ones. Wild horses reduced to lap dogs."

"What's wrong with a good and noble lap dog?" Deacon asked.

"Nothing, if that's what you're born to be, but slowly altering ourselves over the years until we *become* that lap dog is something else. One is a dream, an honorable destiny fulfilled. The other's a slow-death nightmare, a prison of what-ifs. Deep down, we recognize it. We know what's happening, and we still can't stop it."

"Maybe we're not meant to. Everything ages, Fay, even wild horses."

"They age, yes, but they're still wild."

"You mean free."

She looked at him, eyes moist with tears. "Until the day they die."

These few years later, standing in that bathroom, Deacon now understood what Fay meant. Infuriating as it was, she'd been right once again. Running into Lauren made him realize it. The reaction had at first made him happy, almost carefree in a way he hadn't felt in years, but that joy was short-lived. Soon, it morphed into something far more accurate and sobering. Maybe Lauren liked what she saw, but she didn't know any better. In the years since high school, she didn't know who or what Deacon had become.

I'm half the man I used to be. Why poison them with my demons?

SMOKE, IN CRIMSON

Fay watched from the darkness of his mind with reptilian-like sluggishness.

Because it's what we do, it's our nature. We can't help ourselves.

Deacon ran the water, splashed some on his face then dried off with a hand towel. Rather than folding and putting it back on the rod where he'd found it, he tossed the towel on the counter and ventured out into the hallway.

In the kitchen, he poured himself a glass of vodka and studied the key he'd found on his sister's gravestone. Although he had no reason to believe it was tied to Fay or the cottage, he tried it in every lock anyway, even on the door to the small storage shed next to the driveway. It fit none of the locks, inside or out. Not that he'd expected it to. The key was obviously an antique. At first he thought it might've been tarnished brass, but closer inspection revealed it to be iron, and while Deacon was far from an expert on the matter, he was reasonably sure keys hadn't been made from iron since the 1800s.

He picked it up a moment, hoping it might tell him its secrets. As if trying to figure out where the hell Fay had gone wasn't enough, now he had to deal with Gina's grave being desecrated and the bizarre key left behind too.

Deacon dropped it on the table, grabbed his vodka and took a long drink. As a thought occurred to him, he grabbed his phone and did a search for the town's cemetery department. Once he located it, he dialed the main number.

"Department of Cemetery Services," a gruff male voice answered.

"Is Pete Briggs in?"

"Yeah, this is him."

"It's Deacon, I'm calling about the vandalism done to my sister Gina's grave. Stevie told me about what happened."

"Terrible thing," he said. "Hell of a thing."

"I'm in town, I just came from there."

"Never seen nothing like that before, not in all my years working the cemetery. There's no respect for nothing no more. Things are changing, and not for the better, I can tell you that. Ain't like it used to be, that's for sure. The world's gone nuts."

Deacon pictured Pete Briggs sitting alone in his musty little office in a small hut of a building at the edge of the cemetery. He remembered him as a stout and often abrasive, hardworking guy about fifteen years or so his senior. Usually in overalls and work boots, he was bald on top, with wild sprigs of unruly chalk-white hair jutting out comically from the sides of his head. His face was round and pasty, his nose bulbous, and he had a few missing teeth, which left him with a jack-o'-lantern smile. He was one of those townies whose families had been in the area going back to the Pilgrims, a strange and solitary man that never left town, lived alone and seemed to exist solely within the confines of his job and the town in which he performed it.

SMOKE, IN CRIMSON

"I straightened it up best I could, but I'm by myself out here these days, the only full-time employee left," Pete continued. "Damn fool selectmen have been making cuts to this department left and right the last few years. They expect me to do everything by myself, and when I do get help now and then it ain't nothing but short-time part-timers that don't care about nothing and do a half-assed job. Anyways, I would've got hold of you when this happened but I didn't know how. I never knew you that good and the info I had wasn't—"

"I understand, don't worry about it. But listen, Pete, I want to ask you something. Do you remember seeing anything on Gina's stone?"

"Not sure I follow."

"Anything left on top of it, like a coin or a key maybe?"

"No, don't remember nothin' like that. Doubt I would've missed it, I know every inch of these grounds, but if there was anything on her stone, with the mess them bastards made, it's probably long gone. Why, are you something missing?"

"No, just wondering is all."

"Uh-huh," Pete said, sounding unconvinced. "There was a bunch of flowers somebody left on her grave, but they was all torn up and tossed around. Only one I ever seen at the grave was Fay Dillon, so I figured they was from one of her visits."

"Was Fay there a lot?"

"Not much. Few times a year, maybe. Heard they been looking for Fay, she wander off or something?"

"Looks like it. I'm trying to figure that out too."

"Never knew her good, but she had a reputation as trouble, no offense." Pete sighed heavily. "Between this and her, sounds like you got your hands full."

"Like you said, the world's gone nuts."

"Damn straight. Anyway, about the stone, you got to get it fixed or taken down. It's against department policy to leave it as is."

"I'll take care of it soon as I can," Deacon assured him, though he had no ability to pay for such things.

"I can put you in touch with a local monuments and memorials place. They can take the old stone away and install a new one if that's what you want, up to you, but—"

"I'm going to be in town a while. I'll be by to see you before I leave and you can give me their contact info then, okay?"

"Just make sure you do," he said, then blew his nose with a honking sound.

"One more question. When's the last time you were at Gina's grave?"

"Passed by yesterday doing my usual rounds, but I ain't actually stopped to inspect that section in a few days. Before all these cuts, I used to be able to—"

SMOKE, IN CRIMSON

"It's cool, I was just curious. Thanks for your time, Pete. Talk to you soon."

"Yup," he grunted then hung up.

Deacon sat at the table and poured himself another drink. Now he knew the key hadn't been left there when the grave was desecrated. It was left after the fact. Pete checked on the site a few days before and hadn't seen it, which meant he either hadn't noticed it, or it wasn't there. Given Pete's work ethic and attention to detail, the latter was more likely.

Whoever left the key had done so in the last two or three days, which meant they timed it in the hopes that Deacon would be the one to find it.

It also meant they knew he was coming.

IN THE HEAVY RAIN, on the outskirts of Boston's Back Bay, as he climbed the rusted metal steps to Dana's back alley apartment, he sensed that Fay was there, and not alone.

In those days, Fay was seldom a solitary creature.

Dana—shaved head, inverted crosses dangling from both ears, angry tattoos, multiple piercings and Salvation Army wardrobe—sat straddling a worn beanbag chair in the center of the room, her black foggy eyes glaring at Deacon with the ravenous instincts of a predator interrupted mid-feed. "Look what the wind blew in."

Deacon moved past her and into the bedroom like she wasn't there.

Just weeks out of the hospital, and Fay was back in bed, naked, lying on her side and propped up on an elbow, a cigarette dangling from her crimson lips, her creamy skin a striking contrast to the dirty bare mattress decorated with an array of stains and spills, like a Jackson Pollock painting begun but never finished. The walls around her were unclean, the wallpaper ripped and torn, peeled away in some spots, faded and covered in drug-fueled graffiti disguised as blackout poetry in others. Food wrappers, empty beer cans and spent liquor bottles, ratty pornographic magazines and a recent edition of *The Boston Phoenix* littered the floor. Next to the bed sat a small and rickety table serving as a nightstand that looked as if it had come directly from a garage sale. Painted red and blue and yellow and green—hastily from the looks of the feverish brush marks left behind—it resembled something conjured in the mind of a toddler.

And then, of course, there came the smell. A combination of perspiration, urine, cum, pussy, cock, weed, booze and cigarettes, it hung in the air, unseen yet hiding in plain sight like the sniper it was.

A curly-haired man somewhere in his early to middle twenties sat huddled in the corner, right hand clamped down over the bend in his left arm, his jeans and underwear

SMOKE, IN CRIMSON

in a tangle at his ankles, his pasty glistening flesh a testament to his lack of judgement. A small silver ankh lay at his sandaled feet as if casually tossed there, the tip blackened and smeared with congealed blood. Trembling, he stared at Deacon, bug-eyed behind oval wireframe eyeglasses, the lenses badly smudged and scratched. "Hey, man," he said in a small voice. "Can you help me out? I think I should go, I—I want to go. Is it okay if I do that, if I just go? I think you—you cats got me all wrong. I want to go home now."

Deacon turned to Fay. "Are you all right?"

She nodded dreamily and reached for him with the arm she'd used, the scars visible along her wrist now that the bandages were gone. "Of course," she whispered.

As he sat on the edge of the bed, Deacon glanced at the network of scars across her otherwise beautiful breasts, and despite the tightening deep in his gut, assured himself the sight no longer wielded the power over him it once had. He cocked his head at the guy on the floor, who continued to stare at him through his dirty glasses as if expecting answers, resolution, perhaps rescue. He'd discovered a different kind of pain, they'd made sure of it, and the poor soul still didn't realize he should've been careful what he wished for. In that dingy, horrible little room, sometimes wishes did come true.

"Where'd he come from?" Deacon asked. "Did Dana get him for you?"

Fay smiled, feigning vulnerability. "You mean the slut in the other room?"

"Yeah, you know, as opposed to the one in here."

"Is that supposed to shame me? Am I supposed to defend it as if it's a sin?"

"I'm trying to understand."

"You understood the first time we fucked. You're just jealous and afraid, that's all. Like a little schoolboy." She giggled, groping him. "Women are like chocolate. Great from time to time but nothing I'd ever make an exclusive diet of."

Deacon stroked her hair, her shoulders, and her scars. "You sound like a man sometimes, you know that?"

"Fuck the gender police!" Fay threw her head back and laughed. "And the blue and pink horses they rode in on!"

"Did Dana get him for you, Fay?"

"Deacon, baby, you ask the *strangest* questions." She spread her legs, pushed Deacon's fingers inside her. "Don't you know by now that *I* get them for *her*?"

Dana was suddenly in the doorway.

"Speak of the Devil," Deacon muttered.

"And she appears." Dana grinned at him as blood sloshed about in a small plastic bag hanging from her moist, plump fingers.

"Get dressed, Fay." Deacon rubbed her lower back and the supple curve of her buttocks. "I'm taking you out of here."

SMOKE, IN CRIMSON

"Look out, everybody," Dana said. "It's a *hero.*"

"Fuck off," Deacon said without looking at her.

"You think you can tell me that in my own fucking place?"

"I just did."

Dana hissed at him like an angry cat. By then she was so far gone there was no coming back. She no longer seemed capable of typical, or even appropriate human emotions. Once upon a time she'd been someone else, someone more common, Deacon supposed, but he hadn't known that earlier version of her, so for him there were no memories of *that* Dana, only assumptions.

Stepping into the room, Dana closed the door behind her then leaned back against it. Her chest rose and fell, her breathing excited as she took everything in.

"He thinks he's clean now," Fay told Dana.

"Come on," Deacon said. "We're leaving."

"You're so predictable," Fay scolded playfully. "Baby, we're not going anywhere. Tell him, Dana."

"We're not going anywhere." Like a shark just before it bites, Dana's eyes rolled to white, her body swaying and pulsing to a venomous melody Deacon and Fay could not yet hear. "And neither are you."

GREG F. GIFUNE

DEACON STOOD BEFORE THE windows, watching the ocean and the slowly setting sun. He'd given up on the glass a while ago and was now swigging directly out of the bottle. Vaguely aware that he was drunk, and had been for a while, it occurred to him that he was standing in the exact spot Stevie had been standing in earlier when he first entered the cottage that morning. But he knew all too well that he and that sad, aging, small town cop saw very different things out there among the waves. Stevie saw all that might have been. Deacon saw what never should've happened.

He lit a cigarette, drew the smoke deep into his lungs and exhaled, remembering how Fay would often slink in behind him when he stood before these same windows, her arms snaking around him as she lapped at the back of his neck.

Where have you gone, Fay?

Deacon took another pull of vodka from the bottle.

What the hell have you done?

The past was never far, time was a miserable liar, and now night was coming, creeping up over the dunes like clouds of mustard gas slowly drifting across a battlefield. And for Deacon, that darkness could be just as deadly.

Night was a weapon.

CHAPTER **SEVEN**

DARKNESS HAD FALLEN. ALTHOUGH the storm outside finally came to an end, those raging inside Deacon had only grown worse. He wandered about the cottage drunkenly, his angry rants shattering the silence as he stumbled after the ghosts hiding there, chasing them from room to room in search of answers he knew they'd never give him. Drink after drink, cigarette after cigarette, memory after memory, they all led him back to her.

But Fay had slipped through his fingers and returned to shadow, to smoke.

When they first came together, it was just the two of them, though Gina was never far. The last remnants of an echo, a screech of agony from the end of a dark hallway, his sister's presence lingered like a bloodstain that wouldn't come clean. And it was only the beginning. What Deacon didn't know then was that Gina was condemned. She'd be that mark, along with those of the Devil, on their souls forever.

Deacon and Fay spent their days having amazing conversations, snorting cocaine, popping whatever pills fit the bill at any particular moment—speed, Quaaludes and codeine—and drinking and smoking pot and cigarettes until all hours, laughing until it hurt, telling each other their darkest secrets, even the ones they didn't like to admit to themselves. Deacon had never had such honest conversations with anyone. They struck him as a kind of magic, a cleansing ritual of sorts, and in the early days of their relationship, he learned to easily dismiss things like judgement and guilt. Fay had an uncanny ability to put things in perspective, to explain things that made everything all right, even when it wasn't. And slowly, like a dance, despite making little sense, they'd sit together like awkward teenagers hoping the other would make the first move. Deacon knew now it was his own hesitation and fear of not measuring up to this goddess he'd constructed, one that possessed all the answers and experience he didn't. And for Fay, it was her version of early seduction. Patient, sweet and sexily hesitant—she was an empress awaiting defilement from her timid slave boy—until she wasn't. The sex would come moments later, usually very late at night, and last into the early morning hours. Fay fucked angry, like she was seeking revenge, and despite having lost his

SMOKE, IN CRIMSON

virginity a few years before, Deacon had never experienced anything like her.

In those days and nights they spent together, Fay lived in the cottage, but she also spent a lot of time in Boston. Wherever they were, it was as if nothing else—no one else—mattered or even existed, but as with all things, that eventually changed. Not slowly—suddenly—it became something more. Like any addiction, Fay could be as dangerous and exciting as she was alluring and exhausting. She drew him toward her gradually, until their positions shifted, and by the time Deacon realized it, he was too far gone to care. He was hooked, and happily. Even when the power fell mostly to Fay, he followed her around like the perfectly content junkie he'd become. It was then that Deacon saw beyond the animalistic lust he and Fay shared. She read novels and stories by authors like Jerzy Kosiński and Anna Kavan, Jean-Paul Sartre, Thomas Mann and Franz Kafka, Christopher Isherwood, Herman Hesse, Fyodor Dostoevsky and Albert Camus, studied the works of Friedrich Nietzsche, René Descartes, Angela Davis and Carl Jung, devoured the poetry of Sylvia Plath, E.E. Cummings and Kate Braverman, and urged him to read them too. She introduced him to Lou Reed, David Bowie, Patti Smith and Miles Davis, Iggy Pop, Dusty Springfield, The Sherbs and Joan Armatrading, and when they were in Boston they'd sneak off to foreign films like Benjamin Christensen's *Haxan*, Jean-Luc Godard's

GREG F. GIFUNE

Breathless and *Alphaville*, along with others they saw huddled together in the darkness of near-empty little arthouse theaters in obscure parts of the city. But Fay was more than a narcotic. She was a high priestess mingling Heaven and Hell into a single doctrine of madness and wonder. It couldn't last forever, not uninterrupted, but respites were not cures. Deacon was an addict and always would be, whether he partook of Fay or not. As with any curse, the addiction remained.

Deacon found himself in the bedroom. Part of him wanted to collapse onto the bed and let sleep—or something similar—take him, but he couldn't let go. He had to bleed himself, here in this old cottage, and allow the demons to do their work. It was the only means of escaping them, even if just for a little while, and his chance at communion with Fay and all the blood trails she'd left behind that might lead him to her.

He closed his eyes, remembered one particularly humid summer night they'd been in bed together, talking quietly in the darkness of the cottage.

Fay always claimed the Rapture was real, and if it wasn't, it should've been. She said she knew Jesus had and did exist, even though she wasn't a Christian herself, and claimed there were greater powers at work in the universe few understood or were even aware of. Not only was there an afterlife, she insisted, it was closely aligned with life on Earth.

SMOKE, IN CRIMSON

"It's all one vast ocean," she told him. "We're born into it and either swim or drown. What they don't tell us is that it doesn't matter either way. Not until the end."

The Rapture specifically, was how it would actually come about, she believed. Would people truly rise up into the heavens? And go where, outer space? No. There were creatures that would come to collect those still here by then, beings assigned that task. Neither angels nor demons, instead, these were entities that existed outside those confines and beyond our understanding.

"Are they good or evil?" Deacon asked.

"They're indifferent." She took a finger and dabbed at a trickle of sweat between her breasts. "Good and evil are human constructs."

"So?"

"So they're not human." A flame cut the darkness around them as she lit a cigarette. "Don't you believe in the Rapture?"

"Not really, no. I've always found it a little silly."

"But you believe in God."

"Yes."

"And you believe in an afterlife."

"I do."

Serpents of smoke leaked from her nostrils. "You believe in Jesus, don't you?"   "Yes."

"You're a Christian then?"

"I'm a type of Christian, sure."

"Are you the type of Christian that doesn't believe in the Bible?"

"I don't believe in it literally, no."

"How else is there to believe in something but literally?"

"Figuratively," he said. "As metaphor or parable, lots of ways."

Fay left the cigarette to dangle between her lips and propped herself up on an elbow. "So you pick and choose what to believe and what not to believe then?"

"That's what intelligent people do, they discern. They choose things that make sense and put aside what doesn't. Why do *you* believe in something like the Rapture? It's a Christian belief, and you've said many times that you're not a Christian."

"It makes sense to me," she said, gently stroking the dark hair on his chest. "There's something horrific and wildly erotic about it."

"Why erotic?"

Her eyes widened comically. "Maybe it's the whole being taken thing."

"I'm serious, Fay."

"So am I. I think."

Deacon weighed the validity of that a moment. "Do you think you'll be taken?"

Fay shifted her position, deeper into the shadows. "No."

"Why would you be left behind?"

SMOKE, IN CRIMSON

"You know why," she said quietly. "Maybe even better than I do."

"Do you think I'll be taken?"

With a sad face, she shook her head no.

"Why won't they take me?"

"Because, baby," she said, leaning in close enough to brush her lips against his. "I already have."

As those memories crumbled to dust and returned him to the cottage, Deacon staggered out of the bedroom, bouncing against the walls of the hallway and taking another swig from the bottle as he made his way back to the kitchen. He knew how ridiculous he was, stumbling around drunk, but it was working. The walls were slowly dissolving, the curtains coming down. Fay was no longer confined to his head, she was scuttling across his skin now, an insect in the dark, felt but not yet seen.

And Gina, god damn Gina, she'd come to the party too, as he knew of course she would. Standing there with her torn clothes, battered face and shattered skull on the outskirts of Deacon's mind, her intestines a tangle of diseased eels, slick, bloody and quivering with the last vestiges of life as they dangled from a blown-out cavity in her abdomen. *I died alone*, she said, spitting teeth from her mouth while bile as black as tar drooled out over her bottom lip and onto her chin. *And so will you.* Spreading her arms, she turned her scraped and bloody palms upward and gave herself to whatever gods had claimed her. *You just don't realize it yet, little brother, but death is nothing but cold and lonely.* His sister's blood-red eyes slid closed, her raw lips moving silently now as she was absorbed back into the thick fog of memory from which she'd come.

DEACON REMAINED JUST BEYOND her reach on the bare mattress.

"A bottle," Fay said, running her fingertips across the scars on her wrist.

He looked away from the blood-spattered fool in the eyeglasses slumped on the floor, and focused his attention on her instead. "What?"

"You never asked me what I used when you came to visit me in that awful place."

"That couldn't possibly be because it doesn't matter, right?"

"Bullshit, I know you've been wondering."

"What, no impalement?"

"How very theatrical of you," she said, sighing with disappointment. "No, Deacon, it was a broken bottle."

"I don't want to fucking hear about it."

"You never even asked me why. I knew you wouldn't."

"I already know why."

SMOKE, IN CRIMSON

Immortality is a lie, a coin never tossed for fear of what the outcome might reveal.

"You're so smart," she said. "It makes me wet, but it pisses me the fuck off too."

"I know the feeling."

Suddenly Fay was beaming. "I meant to tell you, Dana's mother has a little place out in the middle of nowhere in New Mexico. She's sick, needs to go into a nursing home. Dana's going to crash there a while. She's tired of Boston, said I'm welcome to come stay with her as long as I want."

"I bet. Are you going?"

"I suppose I'd like to see the desert before I die." Fay combed some hair behind her ear with a finger. "Want to come?"

From the corner of his eye he saw Dana, as nude as he was, standing with her back to them in the adjacent bathroom, washing blood from things in the already filthy sink. "I'll pass."

"That's my Deacon, pariah by choice, even from your own brood."

"Dana's part of *your* brood," he told her. "My only brood is you."

"Why do you always have to be so infuriatingly aloof? You could easily be far more powerful than I've ever dreamed of being, but you toss it aside like roadkill."

Outside those battered old walls, the city distracted him as day morphed into night. Some ran from the darkness that would soon take hold, others ran toward it.

Rats, all, Deacon thought.

He could feel them scurrying around out there.

Sodom and Gomorrah the whole thing to the ground, and me right along with it.

He could *smell* them.

Pillars of salt for the rest, mercy disguised as annihilation.

"That's the biggest difference between us, isn't it?" Fay asked. "You refuse to accept what you are, while I embrace it."

"Keep talking," Deacon said. "Maybe next time you try to kill yourself it'll take."

"*You're* the one that knocked on the Devil's door, baby boy."

"I remember."

"Then don't be angry with me because he answered it."

Fay leaned forward, and a silk robe she'd put on a minute before parted to reveal a swell of cleavage. Deacon refused to look away, recalling how earlier he'd squatted over her belly like a giant bird of prey and imagined it had been his cock, crushed and gliding between her wet breasts that had left those scars in its wake.

Tell me, Deacon…what else do you remember?

IN A DRUNKEN HAZE Deacon prowled the cottage like a thief frantically searching for anything of value. He

SMOKE, IN CRIMSON

touched whatever he could lay his hands on, running them across windows, doors and furniture, handling items in the kitchen, bathroom and bedroom, sliding them along the walls. He dropped to his knees, pressed palms and face to the floors, and looked under things he might've missed. He wanted to touch everything Fay had, drawing whatever traces of her he could find into himself.

"There are eaters of souls," Fay had once told him. "And there are those like us that eat what the soul leaves behind, a trail like the moist wake of a slug. Taste it, and it tells us all we need to know."

Exhausted, Deacon stumbled into the kitchen and flopped into one of the chairs at the table. Struggling to keep awake, his eyes slowly scanned his surroundings again. Squinting, he landed on the woodstove. It was almost out. He hadn't fed it in hours.

On wobbly legs he made his way over to the stove, plucked a wrought iron tool hanging from the side of it that fit into a slot on the main, largest burner, and pulled free the iron cover. Once he set it aside on the next burner, he staggered over to a wooden bin just inside and to the left of the back door that was filled with precut wood, and plucked a few pieces out. Just as he was about to return to the kitchen, he noticed a small basket on the floor tucked behind the bin. Squinting in an attempt to better focus his drunken vision, he saw it contained an open package of mesh adhesive wall patches, some sandpaper, a small plastic tub of joint compound, a can of paint, a putty knife and a paintbrush, neither of which had been cleaned very well.

That's a kit to repair a hole in drywall, Deacon thought.

The cottage had aged wood plank walls, not sheetrock. There was only one room that had drywall, and that was the kitchen, which Lance had gutted, rebuilt and renovated when he first purchased the place. The only thing they'd saved from the original kitchen was the woodstove.

Deacon returned to the kitchen and slid the pieces of wood through the circular opening into the fire. The flames claimed them, sending a small spray of sparks and a puff of black smoke into the air. Using the same tool, he shifted the small logs into better position. A burst of heat rushed up into his face just as he dropped the cover back over the burner. Wiping his eyes with one hand and fanning the air with the other, he stepped back and began searching the walls in the kitchen again, this time more carefully.

A thorough examination of the wall turned up nothing.

With a sigh, Deacon returned to the table, grabbed his cigarettes, shook one free of the pack and stabbed it between his lips. If a repair had been made using the materials in the basket, it had to be that wall. But it looked completely intact and seamless.

Deacon lit the cigarette, tossed his lighter on the table

and took a hard drag. As he exhaled, he ran his free hand across his face and studied the wall some more.

A foot or so from the refrigerator was an old wall phone, a rectangular unit with a built-in speaker. Leaving the cigarette between his lips, he grabbed the phone and lifted it from the metal mount beneath, which was screwed into the wall. Once he disconnected the wire, the unit came free and he placed the phone on the counter.

On the wall behind it, just to the right of the mount and previously hidden by the phone, an area about the size of a baseball stood out. Although the same color as the rest of the wall, it had obviously been recently painted.

Deacon ran his hand over the area. Fay, or whoever had patched the wall, had done a fine job, but made no attempt to conceal the fresh brushstrokes. The question was how could there be damage to an area *behind* a wall phone he remembered being there for years? Anywhere else on the wall made sense, accidents sometimes happened, but not where it was protected by a clunky old speaker phone. He smoked his cigarette a while, staring at the patch. It was an exterior wall, which meant there was more space between the sheetrock and the literal outside of the cottage behind it. Could Fay have damaged it on purpose and then patched it without telling anyone? Had she left those items behind so someone—maybe even Deacon—would find them?

He checked his watch. It was just after midnight, he wasn't about to call Lance at that hour and ask if he was aware of any damage that had been done to the kitchen wall.

Besides, he thought, *maybe I was supposed to find this, not Lance or anyone else. Maybe that's why it was hidden.*

After a final drag, he tossed the cigarette butt into the sink then quickly ran the water to extinguish it.

Or maybe you're a drunken asshole looking for crazy shit where there isn't any.

"Only one way to find out," he mumbled.

Grabbing the putty knife from the basket, he returned to the kitchen and began scraping at the patch. Within a minute or two he'd reached the edges of the mesh, and knew where the center of the patch was.

Deacon went back to the table, took another pull from the bottle of vodka then strode over to the wall and smashed the heel of his hand into the patch, imploding it. His hand stung a bit but with a quick shake it dissipated, and he took to pulling the mesh free.

Digging around the edges with the putty knife, he managed to loosen and dislodge the entire thing, so he ripped it free without giving any thought to the mess he was making, and threw it aside onto the counter.

The patch now gone, a hole was revealed.

And sitting inside it, in the wall, was a small, very old looking box.

CHAPTER **EIGHT**

THE FIRST TRACES OF daylight broke over the horizon. It was a peaceful, quiet world now, the ocean relatively placid and the storms of the day and night before gone, at least for the time being. But for Deacon, the new day brought only more chaos.

He hadn't slept all night.

With his heart racing he'd brought the box to the kitchen table, brushed it off then set it down and stared at it while he finished the bottle of vodka. He recognized it as Fay's. The same box sat on her bureau in the bedroom for years. Constructed of worn cherry-colored wood, with a lid that once unlocked became detachable, the box was rectangular in shape and roughly the size of a carton of cigarettes. He remembered it as a gift Dana had given Fay back in their Boston days. She claimed it was very old—ancient even—and had been passed between those who understood its power for generations.

A mirror box, she called it. Despite its ominous supposed origins, Deacon was never sure of its purpose, and far as he knew, Fay used it as a jewelry box, nothing more.

Also before Deacon on the table was the skeleton key he'd found on Gina's grave. It would fit the lock, and inside the box would be at least some answers, he had no doubt. He just wasn't sure he was prepared for what they might be, so it sat untouched.

You left that key for me to find, he thought. *It had to be you.*

Fay knew Deacon would likely be summoned to town, and that he'd come. She also knew he'd go to the cemetery to check the damaged stone. Could she have *caused* that damage though? *Would* she? He still didn't believe that. But if he was right about the key, according to the timelines as he understood them, Fay had left it on Gina's stone more than a week after she allegedly disappeared.

Where was she in the interim? Where had she been since?

Bleary, exhausted, and with the night nearly behind him, Deacon forced himself to pick up the key. Turning it over again and again between his fingers, it felt abnormally cold against his warm skin. He didn't remember it being so cold to the touch prior, but ignored the sensation and slid the key into the lock.

It fit, as he knew it would, and with a slow turn, unlocked the box.

SMOKE, IN **CRIMSON**

Carefully, he took hold of the lid and wrested it free.

A strange odor wafted loose, like something decayed or rotten, but dissipated quickly. His hand shaking, Deacon placed the lid on the table.

The interior of the box was lined with badly pitted red velvet. Inside was a single decomposed long stem rose, a black candle with Fay's name scratched into the wax along its base, a few pieces of cracked glass that appeared to have come from a mirror, and a good deal of dirt. Beneath it all, he found Fay's phone. Attached to the dark screen was a small yellow Post-it note with a single word written across it in Fay's hand.

-VIDEO-

THE PARK BENCH WAS a small alley club nestled between Boylston Street and St. James. With its black ceilings, walls and floors, it resembled a giant coffin. The dim lighting, provided by candles encased in small red globes on the tables and mounted along the walls, only added to the funereal feel. Except for the industrial-style, battered gunmetal bar, and a projection screen that took up nearly the entire back wall that showed obscure and mostly foreign black-and-white silent horror movies on an endless loop, it was decorated with what appeared to be a deliberate lack of detail and flair.

Despite Boston's stringently compartmentalized and segregated design at the time, no specific rule governed there, which resulted in a broad range of straight and gay clientele that included musicians, groupies, drag queens, goth college students, writers, artists, punks, poets, philosophers, filmmakers and even the occasional, self-professed intellectual coffee-sipper. Each time someone came or went through the black steel front door fumes from the nearby Greyhound station wafted in and lingered like a bad meal.

The woman was college age, with blonde hair, an expensive but casual wardrobe and clearly privileged beginnings. Deacon imagined she hailed from somewhere like Wellesley, Brookline or maybe Weston. Wholly out of place, she seemed nervous and self-conscious. She was also quite clearly turned on.

She is slumming, after all, Deacon thought with contempt. *How fun for her.*

The girl and Fay were so deeply entrenched in conversation neither had noticed his arrival, so from his table deep in the shadows, Deacon sipped his beer, lit a cigarette and watched them a while. The woman wasn't the typical catch. Sure, she had a WASP kind of beauty Fay sometimes felt drawn to, but this one was dangerous. This girl had family, people who loved her and cared about what happened to her. She was someone a lot of people would come looking for, people with power and influence. If she reported

SMOKE, IN CRIMSON

something—and those types always did—the authorities would pay attention and take it seriously, regardless of how crazy it might sound.

The door opened, spilling a temporary flash of light into the bar.

Fumes filled the air as a short blond guy with a bowl cut, large gold hoop earrings and matching glitter eye shadow made his way directly to a jukebox in the corner. Clad in black leather pants, a black mesh shirt and white go-go boots, he dropped a couple coins in and Iggy Pop's "The Passenger" began to play. Grabbing either side of the jukebox like a pinball machine, he bounced his hips in time with the music.

Deacon returned his attention to Fay.

She leaned in close and said something to her latest find. The girl, her pretty blue eyes wide and bright, laughed then shook her head as her snow-white face flushed deep red. As if mistakenly, their feet touched and tangled beneath the table.

Unseen from his dark table, a mishmash of stories he'd never tell shook out across his mind like a giant quilt unfurled. It seemed his sister came to him at the strangest times, but now that she had, acknowledging Fay or her mark in any meaningful way was no longer possible. Not with the incessant sounds of Gina's weeping echoing in his head.

So Deacon focused on Fay, in her worn Levi's, tits straining against a skintight low-cut sleeveless top, wooden Dr. Scholl's sandals kicked off beneath the table, her bare feet rubbing against each other, tan bra straps showing and a hint of belly revealed each time she laughed or sat back and the top rode up, separating from her jeans. Hair hacked short and purposely mussed, and her face sans makeup, Fay had her mojo working on the college girl like the evil spell it was, staring at her with doe-eyes and making her think she—and she alone—was the only thing worth noticing in the universe.

Run, little lamb, run.

Fay suddenly gave Deacon a quick sideways glance. She'd seen him, and he knew then he'd fooled no one. She was aware of his presence all along. As if to solidify it, her eyes widened and a subtle smile curled her lips. Seductive and terrifying, it looked as if the Devil had crossed her face. It happened so quickly he almost missed it, but he'd seen it. There, then gone.

He'd *felt* it.

Responding to her cue with a quick nod, Deacon crushed his cigarette in an ashtray, sat back, powered down the remainder of his beer and readied himself to join them at their table. The beer wasn't enough, but would have to do for the time being.

He couldn't absolve himself, much as he wished he could, though in that moment he still believed one day he might be able to. The only one he really cared about in those terms was his sister, but no matter what he did moving forward, she would never forgive him. And while in his darkest, most private moments, Deacon wanted desperately to forgive her as well, for things she had never admitted to him and likely never would, he didn't know it then, but it was too late for all that.

They'd never get the chance to cleanse each other of their iniquities.

Gina was already dead.

DEACON TURNED THE PHONE on. It came to life, revealing a nearly blank home screen. The entire thing had been wiped clean, everything deleted but for the base apps, one of which was the camera. Exhausted, nervous and unsure of what he might find, he tapped the icon.

The camera activated. In the lower left corner was a small box. He tapped it but there were no photos or videos, nothing. With a sigh, he closed the camera and next tapped the PHOTOS app. A list appeared, but again, everything had been deleted, so he scrolled down to UTILITIES.

RECENTLY DELETED PHOTOS & VIDEOS: 1

Deacon tapped it and another screen appeared with a single box of a video the phone had taken that had been deleted. At the bottom of the box it read: *5 days* which meant it would permanently delete after that amount of time if the file wasn't restored. Fay had taken quite a chance. There had to be a reason she'd given him a finite amount of time to find the phone, particularly after going to such lengths to conceal it. Despite the odds against it, Fay gambled the only person who would put it together was Deacon, and that he'd find it in time. Despite the odds to the contrary, she'd been right, and once again, like so many times in the past, somehow, Fay got away with it.

"So far," Deacon muttered. He knew all too well there could be damn near anything on the video. His finger hovered over the box, his mind still blurred with vodka and lack of sleep.

Come with me, Fay whispered to him across time. *Come...*

He remembered verses of compliance he'd recited long ago, the words swirling about in a frenzy of love, lust, fear, pain and disgust.

His finger dropped, tapping the box, and a video suddenly filled the screen.

Darkness and the sound of heavy breathing mixed with static-like bursts of wind hitting the microphone came to life before him. The phone tilted, blurred then righted itself, showing a flash of ocean, the waves rolling with whitecaps that stood out in the otherwise pitch-black night.

SMOKE, IN CRIMSON

"I know it's you, baby," Fay said breathlessly. "It's all for you."

Her face came into frame, those carnal eyes wide but bloodshot, her face pale, lips chapped. She was running along the beach, the phone held up in front of her as she made her way through the night.

"It's happening," she said, staring at the camera as if looking directly into his soul. "It's *happening*."

Unsettled by the sound of her voice, he tapped the screen, freezing the video a moment. Deacon looked to the bottom of the frame. The length of the video was listed as 1:42. He wasn't even twenty seconds in.

There's more. We just have to find it. We just have to get there.

With memories of Fay's wounds dripping blood across her nude body playing out before him, Deacon defiantly tapped the screen again.

Fay came to life, her face pushed close to the lens.

She looked completely and hopelessly insane.

The camera bounced and her breathing grew heavier as she continued running. "I don't know for sure how or when, but that doesn't matter now. None of that matters. It didn't have to be this way, baby. I know you don't understand yet. But you will. They're coming."

The camera turned away from her, showing flashes of beach as her bare feet slapped wet sand. And then she came to an abrupt stop and dropped to her knees. Deacon couldn't tell if she was crying or laughing, but she remained where she was for a few seconds, the camera still recording but the picture black.

A series of sounds he couldn't identify followed, and then her laptop was in her free hand, held out before her in front of the camera.

"It's a lie," she said. "All of it."

Suddenly she was splashing into the ocean, and when she'd gotten about thigh deep, she stopped and hurled the laptop into the waves, laughing maniacally as she did so. It vanished, swallowed by the waves, and then she was spinning like a top, the picture blurred and whirling round and round with dizzying speed.

Everything went dark and the recording stopped. But there was still about twenty seconds left on the file.

After a moment, it resumed, this time with a close-up of Fay's face.

It took Deacon a moment to realize what he was looking at. She was lying on the beach, her face and hair caked with wet sand, the phone propped up right next to her face, so close that each time she exhaled her breath temporarily fogged the lens.

"It's okay to be afraid," she gasped, still out of breath. "You just don't know it yet. I'm on the other side of that veil, baby, and when you're here, that's when you'll understand.

SMOKE, IN CRIMSON

Nothing can undo what's been done, what *we've* done, but we can make it beautiful again, Deacon, so motherfucking *beautiful*."

Just beyond her, shadows shifted, barely noticeable.

"They're coming. But I'm ready."

Snot and spittle bubbled from Fay's nose and mouth as she stared at the camera with eyes that may as well have been dead now. "I'm going back," she whispered, her voice barely audible over the sounds of wind and ocean. "But only so I can leave this for you. Don't let the others see. I'll find you, but if you have to come to me then come. You know what to do. Go back. Go back so you can go forward. Suffering is joy."

As she snatched the phone from the sand, there was a brief moment where Deacon was able to see a long stone jetty jutting out into the ocean. He knew that spot on the beach, realized exactly where she'd been when she'd recorded.

Behind her, in the distance and obscured by night, what looked like dark figures stood gathered in the shadows along the sand, unmoving and silently watching her.

Deacon backed it up then played that part again, but he couldn't be sure. They could've just been shadows along the beach.

Suffering is joy.

But it was more complicated than that. It always had been.

Leaving it all there at the kitchen table, he pushed himself to his feet, staggered drunkenly over to the couch and collapsed onto it.

Even with the ghosts surrounding him and picking at his bones, vultures all, Deacon fell away into something very deep and very much like sleep. As nightmares blanketed him, Fay was there too, as he knew she would be. Nude, covered in blood, panting, the whites of her eyes startling amidst a sea of red, she bit her bottom lip and rode him, her pussy tight on his cock, tits slick with crimson and bouncing, dripping the fruit of their shared sins across his waiting flesh.

Just like the rain, Fay whispered in his mind. *Just like the rain in Hell...*

CHAPTER **NINE**

THE RAIN HAD STOPPED, but it was an overcast and chilly morning, the wind off the ocean steady but not terribly strong. Walking purposefully along the sand, Deacon made his way toward the stone jetty in the distance. He'd come awake about an hour earlier, feeling nauseous as he slowly drifted toward consciousness, a headache jackhammering the back of his skull. He went to the bathroom, stripped off his clothes, leaving them where they fell, and then ran the shower until the water was steaming hot. After urinating and brushing his teeth, he opened the stall shower door and stepped beneath the water, but he was far from alone. Fay's floral body wash, pink razors, various moisturizers and creams, a luffa and washcloth hanging from a small caddie draped over the shower nozzle all conspired to keep her close. The luffa smelled like her—all of her— and as he ran it across his body, he slowly became erect remembering the times they'd showered together. Visions of her slowly dropping to her knees came to him, her nude body slick and wet, partially concealed in steam. Deacon closed his eyes, let the hot water soothe his tight, sore muscles. Pushing his head beneath the stream, the water pulsed against the back of his neck, relaxing him and lessening the pain of his headache. Moments later, standing before the remains of the mirror, his reflection a blurred shadow, Deacon ran his hands through his hair, pushing it back, away from his face, and into a ponytail. Nude, he strode into the kitchen, giving the hole in the wall a glance. He'd had a lot to drink the night before and needed to be sure of what he'd seen on Fay's phone.

A second viewing left no doubt.

After finding fresh clothes from his knapsack, he dressed and headed out.

Now, on the beach, he could still sense Fay was with him. Not like in the cottage, but she was there. Her residue, perhaps, he couldn't be sure, but it felt like she was aware of his presence and what he was doing, almost as if she was watching him somehow.

When Deacon finally reached the stone jetty, he stepped up onto the first large rock and took a quick look around. Fay's cottage was perhaps half of a mile away down the beach. Lauren's cottage was a bit closer. There were lights in the windows but no sign of movement. In the other direction, not

SMOKE, IN CRIMSON

far on the other side of the jetty, the beach turned to rocky shoreline, and the ruins of a once successful hotel. Behind him was the road that ran parallel to the beach. Between it and him, near the edge of the sand, an old snack bar that had been there for decades stood boarded up for the winter.

As he turned and walked along the jetty, the footing difficult and uneven, Deacon gazed out at the vastness of the sea before him. The waves were a bit rough but not as bad as the day and night before, and though they steadily splashed against the jetty, the tops of the large rocks remained relatively dry.

It wasn't until he reached the end that he saw it.

On the last rock, painted in tan paint—the same color the walls in Fay's kitchen were painted—was a crude rendition of an ankh. Heart dropping, Deacon considered the symbol a moment, hands stuffed into his jacket pockets as the wind blew his hair about.

The bottom of the ankh, rather than being straight and flat, instead came to a point. Long as he'd known her, Fay had worn a sliver ankh around her neck with the same pointed end. Flashes of her licking it clean of blood while it was still on her flashed in his mind, her eyes wild as a devilish grin creased her lips.

Deacon imagined her there, painting this symbol in the dark like some crazed witch marking her territory in the dead of night, knowing he'd eventually find it.

He knew what it meant, but there had to be a greater purpose for having left this for him, so he continued studying the ankh until he got his answer.

Fay had drawn it with the bottom tip facing back toward the beach from which he'd come. Slowly, Deacon looked over his shoulder.

His eyes settled on the snack bar near the far edge of the sand. It had been there since he was a kid, and was book-ended by two crudely designed cinderblock open-air showers.

The ankh was pointed right at it.

Typical Fay, he thought. *Send me on a wild goose chase with her cryptic bullshit rather than just tell me what the fuck is going on.*

With a sigh, he started back across the jetty.

When Deacon reached the sand, he stabbed a cigarette between his lips then hunched over and cupped the flame against the wind as he attempted to light it. After a couple tries he got the cigarette going.

"Hey there!" a cheerful voice said to his left. "Good morning!"

Startled, Deacon turned in the direction of the voice, exhaling a stream of smoke from his nostrils that was quickly carried away on the wind.

Lauren stood a few feet away smiling at him. "Sorry, didn't mean to sneak up on you like that."

"It's okay," Deacon said. "Hi."

SMOKE, IN CRIMSON

"I walk the beach every morning." She strolled closer. "Well, not *every* morning, but as often as I can. Didn't expect to find anyone out here this early, especially this time of year, it's usually just me. I bring Larry with me sometimes but he decided to sleep in with Henry this morning."

Deacon forced a smile. "I thought I'd get some fresh air, clear my head a bit."

"I didn't mean to bother you. I just saw you and thought I'd—"

"You're not bothering me." This time his smile was genuine.

"You're looking a little hungover," Lauren said with a chuckle. "And by a little, I mean a lot."

Deacon took another pull on his cigarette. "It's that obvious, huh?"

"That came off rude, didn't it? It's just my sense of humor, I didn't—"

"No, you're right, I had a tough night."

Lauren continued smiling, but her eyes were gauging him, assessing him. "You do know the best cure for a hangover is a big plate of greasy food, right?"

"So I've heard."

"It's true," she said, playing along, and then cocked her head toward the road. "The diner right up the street's open, want to grab some breakfast? My treat."

"I can't right now," he told her. "But—"

"It's okay," Lauren held her hands up in front of her. "I don't mean to keep…"

"Hitting on me?"

She raised an eyebrow. "Is that what I'm doing?"

"Isn't it?"

"I just thought maybe you could use a friend," she said.

"What about you?"

"What about me?"

"Could you use a friend?"

She watched him a moment, cautious now. "I can't figure out if you're teasing me, flirting with me, or if I'm annoying you and you're making fun of me."

"You're not annoying me." Deacon flicked his cigarette away. "And I would never make fun of you. I just can't go to breakfast right now, much as I'd like to."

"I'd try for lunch," she said, nibbling her bottom lip. "But my afternoon's booked with grocery shopping, cleaning the house and doing laundry. We're talking a nonstop funfest of epic proportions here, let me tell you."

Leave her alone.

"Wouldn't want you to miss out on that," Deacon said.

Don't drag her into this.

"But the dinner invitation stands," she said.

Don't drag her into you.

When he hesitated, Lauren gave an awkward nod, her embarrassment evident. "I get it," she said softly. "I'll stop bugging you. I've obviously made a fool of myself not once but twice now, and I'm mortified. So, if you don't mind, excuse me. I'm going to walk into the ocean and drown myself."

"Lauren, it's not like that, I—"

"It's okay," she said. "Really, it is. Take care of yourself. I hope the whole thing with Fay works out."

He nodded, giving in as he knew he had to. "You take care too."

Lauren turned and continued on her way, back down the beach toward her cottage. Deacon watched her go. He felt her loneliness, understood it on a deeper level than she could ever comprehend. Part of him wanted to stop her, to tell her that he was hurting too, that he wanted to forget all this madness with Fay, desecrated graves, bad dreams and horrible memories, and run to her instead. He'd fought so hard these last few years, convincing himself he was finally clean—cured—far enough away in both space and time to begin to believe there was a real difference between who he'd once been and who he'd since become. But the moment he'd stepped foot back in that cottage, he felt things coming alive in him that had been dormant long enough to fool him.

No matter how much time passes, or how hard you scrub your flesh, mind and soul, you'll never be clean. You may find ways to live at times without feeding the things that hunger so desperately inside you, but you'll always be exactly what you've been since the day you met me. Always, Deacon…Always…

Lauren had no way of knowing he was doing her a favor. He was a disease, and he was sparing her, her son and that beautiful soul of a dog from a darkness they couldn't even begin to comprehend.

Once she'd reached the dunes without looking back, Deacon crossed the sand to the snack bar. The dark blue paint on the wood slats covering everything had chipped in places, and the wood was pitted and in rough shape, but they were otherwise nondescript.

Looking for clues, Deacon slowly circled the structure.

As he made his way around to the backside of the snack bar, and found what he'd gone looking for, Deacon froze. Painted onto the scarred wood was another symbol made with the same paint. The infinity sign below a double cross, it was known as the Leviathan Cross. An ancient symbol, it originally designated sulfur in alchemy, and in Asia was known as the Brimstone Symbol. In the 1960s, the Church of Satan adopted it as its emblem, and it had been associated with Satanism in many circles since.

Deacon stared at it as fresh sea air filled his lungs. He knew what it meant for others and cared little for their theatrical, melodramatic, mindlessly idiotic and ignorant foolishness. For him, for Fay, it had a deeper meaning, and he knew exactly what she was telling him by having left it behind.

Come to me and see…if it's what you choose…come to me and see…

SMOKE, IN CRIMSON

He wanted to forget, walk away, go back to the cottage, pack his things and return to his life, such as it was, leaving all these ghouls in their tombs where they belonged. He wanted nothing more, and deep down, though he knew it wasn't possible, he lied to himself a while, as he'd become wont to do, listening to the voice in his head assuring him he could beat this, that if he stopped giving in it would leave him alone.

But Deacon knew the truth. Much as he despised it—and himself—he was no more beyond its reach than he'd ever been. He reached for his cigarettes with shaking hands, focusing on one addiction in the hopes it might distract him from another.

Self-loathing washed over him in mighty waves, even as he got another cigarette going and greedily drew on it, inhaling maniacally again and again, as if no amount of smoke in his lungs, no degree of nicotine was sufficient.

Damn you, Fay, he thought. *And damn me.*

Somewhere in the chambers of his mind where she crouched in wait, watching with her smoldering eyes, Fay smiled through the darkness, crimson dripping from her lips.

For so long now, baby, for so very long now.

HOURS AFTER LEAVING THE Park Bench, they found themselves at Dana's, as Deacon knew they would. The girl, although drunker than she'd likely ever been in her short life, seemed dumbfounded by the cramped apartment. She'd left with them easily, if not somewhat eagerly, giggling and stumbling and pin-balling about between them as they stalked the streets before vanishing into the mounting darkness. Once there, the girl stood just inside the door, astonished.

"Oh my God," she said, stifling a laugh. "You guys actually *live* here?"

"It's a friend's place," Fay told her as Deacon closed and locked the door behind them. "She's out at the moment, but she'll be here soon."

"She must be, like, *super* poor or something!" the girl said, releasing a quick burst of laughter before scrunching her face into a scowl and bringing a hand to her little nose. "Gross, what is that awful smell?"

"Oh that?" Fay flashed her brightest smile. "That's just fear."

The girl cocked her head like a baffled kitten. "Huh?"

Later, when it was just the two of them lying in bed, Fay lit a cigarette, the back of her head resting on Deacon's bare chest. "That's why the world feels so different for me in winter," she said dreamily, raising and extending a leg and pointing her toes like a ballerina. "She died in winter."

She'd been talking for a minute or so about her mother's death.

SMOKE, IN CRIMSON

"Are you listening to me?"

"Of course," Deacon said softly. The apartment was quiet, except for their hushed voices and the occasional weeping coming from the bathroom. He didn't like hearing about Fay's mother, but he liked the sounds of that poor girl in the bathroom with Dana even less. "Go ahead."

"That's when he first came to me, when my mother was dying. I was just a kid."

"That's when *who* first came to you?"

Fay smiled coyly and exhaled a stream of smoke at the ceiling, bounced her leg a few times then turned her ankle back and forth, inspecting her toes. "I looked out my bedroom window one morning and he was standing there watching the house. He looked like a shadow out there in the snow, and it scared me at first, made me never want to go outside again. But then I didn't see him for a while, so when my mother got really bad I started going for long walks no matter how cold it was or how much snow there was. I had to get out of that house."

In that moment, Deacon understood the instinctual need to flee perhaps more than he ever had before. The whimpers coming from the bathroom were gutting him.

"I started to wonder if he'd ever really been there at all," Fay continued, "or if I'd just imagined him. Until one day, about a week after my mother died, there he was again, standing on a snowbank across the street, staring at me."

She explained that after that, although he kept his distance and never said a word, he'd walk along with her in the snow.

"He knew what my father was doing. I could sense it. He knew…everything."

As a siren sounded a few blocks away, Fay finally dropped her leg back to the bed and told Deacon how one night, after her father had fallen asleep, she went to the window and looked out.

"It was harder to see him in the dark," she said. "But he was there. So I snuck out and we went for a walk in the snow. That was the first time I heard his voice, the first time he actually spoke to me."

Deacon studied the cracks in the ceiling as Fay explained how the shadow told her that all who came before her were with him, and that one day, she would be with him too. When she told the story she shook her head, as if even she couldn't quite believe it, and then confessed she'd asked him where he came from, where he lived.

"*The corner of your eye,*" the shadow told her.

A chill coursed through Deacon's body.

"I asked him why he picked me. "*I didn't, child,*" he said. "But *you* can pick *me.*"

"Jesus."

"Not even close. Maybe it's a copout, but I've always believed my father sealed my fate. At least that's how I see it. I was just a confused and frightened and devastated kid, you know? All I had left was him. Where the hell else was I supposed to turn?"

Fay rolled over onto her stomach, the cigarette dangling from her lips, the rising smoke causing her to squint. "I never saw him again," she said. "But he was there. Watching, waiting, guiding."

From behind the bathroom door came Dana's deep, guttural laughter.

"And then, just like that," Fay continued, unfazed, "I didn't feel him around me anymore. He'd left his mark behind, but he was gone."

"His mark?"

"On me," she said distantly. "All the fuck over me."

"Who was he, Fay?" Deacon asked.

"Exactly who you think he was." She cupped his scrotum with one hand and began slowly masturbating him with the other. "Exactly who you're afraid he was."

Deacon's eyes met hers. She wasn't joking.

He tried to appear immune to such information—if that's in fact what it was—but either way, Fay was right, he *was* afraid.

More whimpering sounded from the bathroom.

Fay handed him the cigarette then slipped his limp cock between her lips.

Just then the bathroom door opened with a creak and Dana stepped into view, nude and grinning, her teeth and lips and breasts slick with blood, her eyes wild like the feral *thing* she'd become. Behind her on the filthy floor, the girl sat with her back against the sink, nude and trembling and bloody too, already gone. Who she'd been before was no more, and what was left in its place was something so foreign to her, like so many others, her mind had begun to crack and give way.

Deacon felt himself grow hard in Fay's mouth, though he wasn't even remotely aroused. In fact, he felt sick to his stomach. Looking away from Dana and the girl's teary, desperate eyes, he took a hard pull on the cigarette and focused instead on Fay.

BACK AT THE COTTAGE, visions of dark and dirty alleys in a city pummeled by torrential downpours, and deep forests concealing ancient stone temples shrouded in darkness and mist slithered through Deacon's head.

He had a couple shots of vodka in the hopes his hands might stop shaking before he had to force himself back out that door. He'd spent years dodging these things, but they were no longer avoidable. He had no choice.

To solve the mystery of what was happening here, he had to go back *there.*

But what could be left after all this time?

SMOKE, IN CRIMSON

"*The space between,*" Fay whispered to him from another place and time.

Deacon slammed shut his eyes, only to be greeted by flashes of his sister flying through the air, her body turning and twisting as much of what resided within her burst free in an explosive spray of blood, bone and viscera.

He opened his eyes to the beach and ocean beyond the tall windows. A part of him wished Fay really *had* walked out into those waves and disappeared beneath them. Another part wished he had the courage to do the same.

Suffering is joy.

"Fuck you," Deacon muttered, popping a handful of mushrooms he'd plucked from Fay's stash into his mouth. He smiled reflexively, humorlessly. Sometimes there was little difference between the dark and the light, but as far as he was concerned, Fay had been wrong about that all along. There was no joy in any of this for him.

All he'd ever wanted was peace.

CHAPTER **TEN**

AT A DRUGSTORE DOWNTOWN, Deacon purchased his roundtrip ticket, and although the bus was nearly empty, he sat in the bench seat at the very back, right near the aisle. From that position he could keep the rest of the bus in his line of vision, and if anyone approached him he'd see them coming. Other than city buses back in Utica, it had been quite a while since he'd ridden on one, but years ago these same commercial buses that ran through town every few hours were his main means of transportation to and from Boston, and he'd always chosen the last seat if available.

The steady, slight rocking motion of the bus made him sleepy, but Deacon refused to allow himself to drift off. Although none of the other six passengers onboard were even remotely threatening, he felt a strong instinctual need to remain alert nonetheless.

As his mind drifted, about twenty minutes or so into the hour-long ride, Deacon noticed movement in the middle of the bus. A little girl, perhaps nine or ten, slowly got out of her seat, said something to the woman she was with, presumably her mother, and then walked down the aisle toward him. Moving with uncertain balance, the little girl gripped the back of each seat as she maneuvered her way closer.

"Excuse me," she said in a sweet voice.

Deacon slid over a bit, to allow enough room for the girl to comfortably step through the door and into the bathroom to his right, but he never took his eyes from her. She reminded him of another little girl, one that still haunted his dreams and memories. One he'd struggled for years to forget.

As the little girl unlatched the bathroom door she smiled at Deacon before slipping inside. He couldn't be sure if he smiled back or not, he'd fallen into something akin to a trance of sorts, even as she closed the door behind her and vanished from sight.

Flashes of Dana came to him, standing at the bottom of those old rusted metal steps that led to her alley apartment, smiling up at him with her typical demonic glee. Holding her hand and standing next to her was a little girl in a beautiful yellow dress and black Patton leather Mary Jane shoes. Deacon's heart plummeted the moment he saw her, just standing there, confused but not yet frightened, as she should've been, her beautiful big blue eyes gazing up at him innocently, hopefully. Her hair was so blonde it was nearly white, razor-straight and hanging below her tiny shoulders, and in her free hand she clutched a little stuffed rabbit.

"Somebody got lost," Dana said, already drunk and slurring her words. "Found her all alone, wandering around the bus station, so I promised her we'd help find her momma. Say hello to our new friend, Mary."

Deacon slowly shook his head no.

"You can leave if you don't want to help. But we're coming up now."

"Take her back," he said, his voice shaking.

Dana ran her other hand over her shaved head. "Not happening."

"I said, *take her back.*"

Clearly amused, Dana stared at him with malevolent eyes. "Where's Fay?"

"Inside," Deacon said.

"Inside my place, is that what you mean? *My* place?"

"Dana—"

"You think you call the shots now?"

"Just take her back. *Please.* Take her back."

Dana began to laugh. It was a horrible sound.

The clicking of the door lock disengaging snapped Deacon back to the bus. As the past faded, he watched the little girl emerge from the bathroom, replacing the one in his memories as she slowly made her way back to her seat.

The world blurred through a sudden onslaught of tears. Struggling to prevent himself from openly weeping, Deacon quickly wiped his eyes and focused on the sound the rear tires of the bus made against the pavement outside, a strange and steady buzzing noise that echoed up from the floor panels at his feet.

He imagined himself pinned beneath those tires, spinning, flailing, further crushed and dismembered with each rotation, his gruesome remains dragged behind the bus as it barreled down the highway.

Embracing the carnage, Deacon fantasized about the relief that might bring, and as his tears subsided, he felt another wave of exhaustion wash over him. This time he allowed his eyes to slide closed.

As always, a private darkness awaited him. The demons scurried closer, their hideous jaws snapping and dripping blood and thick drools of saliva.

"The Devil's *never* asleep," Fay once told him. "He just pretends to be."

EVEN THROUGH THE TRIPPY lens the mushrooms provided, a lot had changed since Deacon had last been to Boston. Years before, the buses dropped riders at the Greyhound station on Saint James Avenue, near Arlington Street and not

SMOKE, IN CRIMSON

far from Copley Square. Now it took them directly to South Station, a large and bustling transportation hub.

Several taxis were parked out front, so he climbed into the one at the head of the line and gave the driver his destination. It was about an eight-minute ride, and as the cab weaved its way through the city, Deacon gazed out the window in awe. Boston had once been like a second home to him, but it all looked so different now.

When they reached Saint James, and he stepped from the taxi into a gentle rain, Deacon realized the grimy old Greyhound station was long gone, replaced at some earlier point with a twelve-story office complex. Stunned, he stared at the building as waves of memories, one after the next, crashed all around him.

He'd been through that small station so many times, either catching buses coming in or going out of the city, he'd become far more familiar with it than he'd ever wanted to be. Deacon remembered the horrible smell of the place, and how even half a block away the nauseating stench of urine from the basement restrooms wafted up to street level. He remembered the rows of dilapidated plastic chairs bolted to the worn tile floors, some of them equipped with little built-in televisions with scratched screens and tinny speakers patrons could watch for ten-minute intervals after inserting a quarter in the pay slot. He remembered the customer service desk, and how in all the times

141

he'd been there, day or night, he'd never seen a single person manning it. He remembered the battered old taxis parked out front, the rundown buses outside in the lot at the rear of the station, and how the fumes from their engines pushed through the dirty and pitted double glass doors. He remembered the Burger King attached to one side of the station, and how even the smells of broiling meats couldn't overpower the lingering stink of urine. Deacon remembered the people from every walk of life, the harried businesspeople, the sullen high school and college students, the tourists, the travelers, the homeless that used the station as a place to sleep, the conmen and the pickpockets, the Hare Krishnas and other cult members handing out their literature or milling about, the predators and their prey, the perverts and junkies and psychotics that prowled the place at all hours, the lost and the lonely, the cruisers, the pimps, the hookers and the occasional uniformed, overweight, months-from-retirement beat cops that would strut through now and then, bored and indifferent, swinging their nightsticks with one hand, the other resting on their holstered guns, keys and cuffs and other items on their belts jingling as they made their way from one end of the station to the other, giving those they felt needed it the evil eye while itching to beat someone into oblivion, but not in any official capacity because they weren't worth the paperwork.

SMOKE, IN CRIMSON

And Deacon remembered how on many weekdays, at certain points in the afternoon, the place was almost empty. Those were the same days the infamous bus station bathrooms were most active. To the left of the front entrance, down a set of filthy tile stairs and around a slight jog, the restrooms resided. The women's was hidden behind a wall of matching tile that had to be negotiated around and provided some privacy, but the men's room was afforded no such luxuries. It was just a large and unobscured opening leading to a long row of grotesquely unclean sinks, a mirror above them that ran the entire length of one wall, fogged by smears of various bodily fluids, scarred and battered toilet stalls against the back wall, and a row of stained and chipped urinals along the other. There always seemed to be a lone and oblivious maintenance man shuffling about, emptying the trash bins or mopping up piss and shit, yet the bathroom floor was perpetually wet in certain areas, sticky in others, and always littered with wads of toilet paper and assorted trash. The bathrooms were far filthier than the station upstairs, and the smell of urine was so profound it was difficult not to gag. Even after being in there for a minute or two, the stench was not something one got used to. In fact, it seemed to get worse with each passing moment. And down there, in the bowels of that station, there was no law or order or even rules, except for those dispensed by the patrons themselves. The police never went down there unless they absolutely had to, and everyone knew it. Once you descended those stairs you were on your own.

Ignoring the rain, Deacon studied the office building that had taken the station's place. There was no trace of the past left here. It was as if these old stomping grounds had never been there at all and were merely a figment of his imagination. Time was often such an extraordinary and strangely fickle construct. Sentimental as it was ruthless, it harbored no middle ground. It left you with everything. Or it left you with nothing at all.

The Park Bench had been located half a block away and across the street, but it too was gone. Another office building stood in its place. How much office space did this little avenue in the city need? All the individuality—the grit, the danger—was gone.

Maybe that was best, maybe not. Deacon didn't much care either way. He hadn't come for the new, cleaner, more generic version of things. He'd come for the ghosts.

Did you really think you'd find a city frozen in time? Is that what you expected?

In his mind, Deacon saw a much younger version of himself pass by on the street. So thin—too thin—in worn jeans, a t-shirt, battered leather jacket and scuffed boots. His hair mussed, eyes saddled with heavy dark bags and his face pale and sunken, an earring in the shape of a dagger swinging from the lobe of his left ear, he hurried across the street to the bus station, glancing about as if afraid he'd been followed.

No, Deacon thought. *Not followed*, seen. *Noticed...*

DEACON STALKED BACK AND forth by the door, hands clenched into fists and a cigarette dangling from his mouth. Fay stood in the doorway to the bathroom in a tank top and panties, disheveled and only recently awakened, dull eyes slowly panning back and forth between Deacon and Dana.

"Easy," she said softly.

Dana, sitting on the edge of the bed with a bloody stuffed rabbit in her hands, grinned like an imbecile.

Fay stared at her, expressionless. They hadn't spoken in days.

The grin slowly faded. "If you don't like the way I hunt, then maybe it's time the golden boy started pulling his weight. How's that sound?"

Fay crossed the small room, her bare feet padding along the dirty old floor. "Hey," she said softly, sweetly, taking Deacon's hands in hers. "Everything's going to be all right. Forget about the rest. It's over now."

"After tonight," Deacon said, his rage barely contained, "I'm out. I'm done."

"Yeah," Dana said, rolling her eyes. "Because that's how it works."

"Fuck you!"

Dana flipped him off. "You're no better, no different than me, Deacon."

"I'm nothing like you," he growled through gritted teeth.

"Sure. You keep telling yourself that."

"Look at me," Fay said, and Deacon did. "She's right. It's time."

"Did you hear what I just said?"

"Yes, I heard you."

"Then why the hell would I go?"

Fay gently plucked the cigarette from his lips. "Because," she said, taking a slow drag then exhaling through her nose. "I'm asking you to."

"I leave now I may not come back."

Fay returned the cigarette to his mouth and gazed deep into his eyes the way only she could. She said nothing more. She didn't have to.

"Fine," Deacon said through a heavy sigh, and then, making sure he'd made eye contact with Dana added, "I'll make sure it's a *woman*."

"No," Dana said, eyes widening excitedly. "No, I want a *man* this time."

Deacon turned to Fay for help, but instead, she gave a

quick little nod, sauntered back into the bathroom and quietly closed the door.

Cackling with laughter, Dana took hold of the bloody toy rabbit's arm and made a shooing motion. "Run along now, we're waiting."

Minutes later Deacon was hurrying down the stairs and out of the alley. Near midnight, the colorful lights of nearby Chinatown burned bright, but the streets were mostly empty, the city relatively quiet. He'd hoped he might be able to find someone on the street, but the odds of that seemed low. There were always the parks, the Boston Commons, he might be able to find someone there, someone looking for someone like him, but he decided to go where he knew his efforts would not be wasted.

Hands in his jacket pockets and head down, he made his way through the city, putting off what he knew was inevitable, crossing through the theater district, passing by the Park Plaza Hotel, and eventually reaching Saint James Avenue. It was a relatively warm night, and by the time he found himself crossing to the bus station, he was dripping with perspiration.

Once through the doors, his heart hammering his chest, he hesitated and lit a cigarette, hands shaking. He knew what was waiting for him down those nearby steps, but he'd never done this before. Dozens of scenarios and conversations coursed through his mind as he quickly smoked the cigarette. The station was mostly empty, but for a few homeless people sleeping in the plastic chairs.

As he dropped the cigarette to the floor and crushed it out with the tip of his boot, the mangled filter reminded him why he couldn't do what he most wanted, which was to go and sit in one of those chairs, ride out the night and wait for the first bus out of there.

Nicotine was no longer his only addiction.

Deacon felt sick to his stomach, couldn't get his hands to stop shaking, and he was now sweating profusely. He looked around again. There was no one here he could settle on. He had to hunt. He'd become no different than those pitiful junkies stumbling around, trying to hide their ticks, looking to score, *needing* to score, their entire existences whittled down to chasing the next fix.

The horrible stench of urine wafted up the stairs, as if to taunt him.

"Hey, man."

Startled, he spun around and saw a huge homeless man standing next to him. Well over six-feet and weighing three hundred pounds or more, the man towered over Deacon, a beefy hand held out before him. "You got a quarter?"

"What?" His head was spinning.

"A quarter," the man said, pointing to a nearby row of seats with the little built-in televisions. "I want to watch TV before I go to sleep. Can you help me out, boss?"

SMOKE, IN CRIMSON

Deacon reached into his pocket, came back with two quarters and a dime, and dropped all three into the man's waiting hand.

"*Nice*," the homeless man said, then lumbered away, leaving the stink of body odor in his wake.

Deacon closed his eyes, drew a series of deep breaths then turned and, opening his eyes, approached the stairs. He couldn't see the bathrooms from there, but he could smell them.

He ran his hands through his hair, pushing it off of his forehead and away from his face. They came back slick with perspiration, so he wiped them on his jeans and watched the shadows at the base of the steps a while.

He pictured Fay and Dana waiting for him in that awful place. He pictured the stuffed rabbit and the blood stains spattered across it. And he pictured that little girl's trusting eyes and how he wanted to save her.

You're no better, no different than me, Deacon.

With Dana's voice ringing in his ears, down the steps he went.

CHAPTER **ELEVEN**

THE OFFICE BUILDING WHERE The Park Bench had once stood was a small, squat, unimaginative little structure with tinted windows. Deacon moved through the rain, studying it first from across the street and then at closer range. There was nothing that indicated the old bar had ever been there, so he stepped off the curb and stood at the mouth of an alley that ran behind the building. From what he could see, nothing out of the ordinary awaited him there, a few fire escapes, a set of large dumpsters and an old homeless man sitting in a doorway trying to use the slight overhang as shelter from the rain.

Deacon entered the alley anyway.

When he was within a few feet of the homeless man, their eyes met. Filthy and dressed in several layers of disgusting clothing, the man—perhaps seventy or so—stared at him with sorrowful bloodshot eyes, his face covered in gray stubble and framed by long, thick segments of unruly white hair that reminded Deacon of dead snakes. The man adjusted his position but didn't stand. His feet were wrapped in newspapers held in place with duct tape, and his hands were mangled with arthritis, the nails like talons and caked with grime.

Deacon looked to the rear wall of the building. There was an emergency exit door that emptied into the alley, and to the right of it was a cluster of spray-painted graffiti decorating the otherwise empty space. From the varied styles and colors, the graffiti had obviously been painted at different times over the years, and by more than one person, but amidst the squiggly lines and other nonsensical markings, something more stood out.

Though badly faded, a crude rendition of the Leviathan Cross had been painted near the bottom of the wall. It appeared to have been left there a long while ago.

Behind him, a shuffling sound broke Deacon's concentration.

The homeless man was shifting his feet back and forth and laughing quietly, but his laughter quickly became a gurgling sound and then a hacking wet cough. Finally, he spat a ball of brown phlegm into a nearby puddle, wiped his mouth with the back of his hand then offered a nearly toothless smile.

Leveling a dead stare at him, Deacon took a step closer.

SMOKE, IN CRIMSON

"I don't mean no harm." The man's smile vanished, replaced with a look of abject terror. "I—I'm just an old fool is all."

Deacon knew this man was many things, but a fool was not among them.

There was wisdom in that old, deeply-lined, slowly dying face. Like many of the homeless across the city, he often noticed what others did not, and saw not only the shadows, but those things that moved within them. The horrific things suddenly swimming in Deacon's eyes were not new to the man. He'd seen them before in others, and understood what they meant. With that dawning came the realization that within those dark eyes there resided something profoundly deadly. What stood before him could be as much predatory wild animal, as it was man.

Turning away, the old man gazed deeper into the alley, as if something in the distance had caught his eye. His entire body shivered, but not from the cold. "Don't mean no harm," he muttered. "I don't—don't mean nobody no harm."

Deacon walked away, back across Saint James Avenue, and then headed for Chinatown. The rain picked up, falling harder now, like bullets.

HE SAW HIM THE moment he stepped into the restroom.

No more than sixteen or seventeen, he was dressed in chinos, loafers, and a barracuda jacket, the collar flipped up. Tall and thin, with a light complexion, light brown hair cut short and meticulously styled, he possessed the kind of innocent face that was vaguely handsome but easily forgettable. Standing nervously by the bank of sinks, lingering there purposely and taking an inordinate amount of time to dry his hands with a scrap of industrial brown paper towel he'd yanked from a nearby dispenser, he shot Deacon a quick sideways glance.

As Deacon moved closer, he saw that there was one other man in the bathroom over by the urinals. Unlike the teenager, he looked directly at Deacon, but tried to appear nonchalant in doing so. Early thirties, with a moon face and a chubby, soft build, he was clad in a pair of nondescript pants, a striped shirt and sneakers.

Deacon turned to the sinks, ran the water in one and pushed his hands under the stream. In the filthy mirror, he saw the teenager offer a subtle smile then slide closer, still drying his hands with the paper towel.

"Hi," the kid said softly.

"Run."

"What?"

Deacon slowly turned his head, finally making eye contact. *"Run."*

SMOKE, IN CRIMSON

The boy dropped the towel and quickly scurried off, disappearing up the steps to the bus station.

Still bent over the sink, Deacon found the other man's reflection in the mirror.

As he continued looking Deacon's way, he began to masturbate.

Deacon finished washing his hands then made his way across the wet and sticky floor to the urinals. Standing before the one directly next to the man, he pulled his cock free, making sure he was far enough away from the urinal to remain in full view.

The man licked his palm then continued masturbating.

Deacon turned back to the urinal, pretended to pee then stroked himself, trying to get hard. He couldn't, so he angled a bit away from the man so it wouldn't be obvious that he was having trouble.

And then he felt a hand on his shoulder.

Deacon forced a smile. "Hey."

The man cocked his head toward one of the nearby toilet stalls.

"I've got a place," Deacon said.

"Fuck that, we're here now."

Deacon flushed the urinal and turned a bit so the man could see him again. "It's a five-minute walk, nobody else there."

The man, still staring at Deacon's cock, licked his lips. "I ain't no faggot."

"Yeah, me either."

"I don't go for none of that kissing or fucking queer shit."

"It's cool," Deacon assured him. "But it'll be better there. Don't have to worry about cops, and it's private, I live alone."

The man was hesitant but clearly thinking about it.

"We can take our time." Deacon gave his cock a couple quick strokes then slid it back into his pants and zipped up. "Do whatever we want."

"Five-minute walk you said?"

"Less if we hurry."

"I don't need no fucking problems," the man said, breathing heavily. "I got a wife at home, know what I mean? Just looking for some fun."

Deacon glanced at the man's member then turned and walked out of the bathroom and up the steps to the bus station. Trembling and lightheaded, his stomach in knots, he fumbled his cigarettes from his jacket and managed to get one going.

Smoking greedily, he waited.

And as he knew he would, seconds later, the man slowly emerged from the shadows below, climbing the stairs toward him with an excited smile on his face.

SMOKE, IN CRIMSON

ON THE OUTSKIRTS OF Chinatown, Deacon found himself in another alley, this one more familiar, standing at the base of the same rusted metal stairs that led to what had once been Dana's apartment.

A small ankh, about the size of a disposable cigarette lighter, was spray-painted onto the pavement at the foot of the staircase. Although no such marker had existed there in the days he frequented this place, it was not freshly drawn either, as it was so badly faded Deacon nearly missed it.

The rain steadily pinging off the metal was so loud in the small alley it should've been distracting, if not startling, but a sudden montage of images, horrifying and vicious, flashed before his mind's eye, pulling him under and into darkness. Deacon knew that was going to happen but had convinced himself he was sufficiently prepared for it.

He wasn't.

His fingers found the small green stone he always carried in his pocket. He rubbed it a moment then cautiously ascended the staircase. It felt shaky and far less structurally sound than in years past, so he was grateful to reach the landing without incident. A battered old door stood before him. He'd seen it waiting for him in his nightmares for years. A large red X was posted on it now, indicating to first responders that the building was no longer safe to enter, and a tattered paper alongside it announced the building had been condemned several years prior and left to rot. Deacon never knew who owned the property, but it had evidently become nothing more than a tax write-off, forgotten and long-abandoned.

Or so it appeared.

Echoes of evil swirled around him, a residual haunting left in the wake of all the horror that had occurred in those two little rooms. But there was something more. Not all the remnants of nightmares within these walls were ghosts.

There was something far more current at work here. He was sure of it.

Deacon tried the door. It was locked. He took a quick look back at the alley below to make sure no one else was around, and then slammed the door with his shoulder. The entire staircase wobbled from the force, but his first attempt cracked the doorframe. His second split it, and the door swung open.

A terrible smell wafted out. Deacon recognized it immediately. Something had died in there, and whatever it was, the corpse was still present and decomposing.

The rain and clouds had prematurely darkened the day, leaving the interior of the apartment thick with shadows. There wasn't enough light to clearly see inside, so Deacon dug his phone from his pocket and activated the flashlight feature. Using his other hand to cover his nose and mouth, he stepped into the main room.

SMOKE, IN CRIMSON

Ankle-deep trash covered the floor. The walls, vandalized and badly damaged, had also been painted with crude satanic imagery. There was no longer any furniture, but an old box spring was leaned against one wall. The bathroom door had been ripped from its hinges and lay to the left of the doorway in two jagged pieces.

The rancid smell grew stronger.

Another step into the apartment revealed the source.

The carcasses and entrails of three plump rats were strewn across the cracked tiles of the bathroom floor. The animals had been torn to pieces, ripped from limb to limb before being partially devoured. A pentagram and 666 drawn in their blood had been finger-painted on the nearby wall. More blood smears streaked the floor and the sides of the same cast iron clawfoot bathtub that had been there years ago. It was now filled with trash, debris, used and discarded drug paraphernalia, and some sort of gelatinous-looking black fluid.

Seeing that tub and all the memories it conjured sent a shiver through Deacon so violent it felt like his entire body was being throttled. And then his ears began to ring with distant screams and frantic pleas for help, for mercy.

It was horrifying the things people promised when frightened beyond anything they previously considered possible, the deals they were willing to strike, the things they freely offered and accepted without protest or further provocation, the things they were willing to do, to give up, to give away if only they could find their way to some sort—any sort—of reprieve. Though he wished he didn't, Deacon understood that all too well.

He also knew what this scene represented.

The graffiti was purely for show, to scare away some and to amuse others. The state of the place meant no one had actually resided or done anything of any significance there in a very long time. But the rats, and the way in which they had been so savagely slaughtered, indicated that this condemned old building hadn't been entirely vacant for as long as it initially appeared.

Deacon switched the flashlight off, and with a hand still pressed over his nose and mouth, looked back out the open front door he'd damaged. The rain was falling in sheets now, more aggressively, causing an even greater racket as it pummeled the metal steps.

As Deacon watched the rain, momentarily mesmerized and lost in the horror of his memories, above him, cradled in the thick shadows along the ceiling, something came awake. Silently, it unfolded itself and separated from the darkness, hanging there like a massive predatory insect.

By the time Deacon sensed its presence, it was too late.

It was already dropping down on top of him.

SMOKE, IN CRIMSON

THE MAN'S SCREAMS ECHOED through the darkness. The disbelief, the realization of what was really happening to him, the pleading and gasping, the writhing and struggling, the cries to God, his mother, and finally, somebody—*anybody*, the tears and incoherent ramblings, the thrashing, and those gruesome, spine-chilling screams. When all of that finally ceased, as always, what remained was labored breathing, quiet whimpering, and a strange gurgling sound.

And then, silence, eerie and empty. Somehow, that was often worse.

"Are you all right?"

Deacon opened his eyes. The ceiling fan spun above them in the near-dark of the bedroom. He no longer answered that when people asked, even Fay. *Especially Fay.* There seemed little point. It was rhetorical now. Perhaps it always had been. "I like it better here," he said softly.

"Is it the cottage you prefer or that it's only the two of us here?"

"Yes."

Fay snuggled closer, her head on his chest.

"We should just stay here," he suggested.

"It's less dangerous in the city."

"We could be careful."

"What about Dana?"

"Fuck Dana."

"Been there, done that."

"I thought she was going to the desert."

"She is."

"When?"

"In time."

Deacon stroked her hair. It was thick, like straw, but soft. "We could stop."

"*You* could stop."

"So could you."

"It's too late for me."

"No, it isn't."

"And what makes you so sure of that?"

"You're still...you."

Fay stayed quiet, but looked up into his eyes as if in search of something. "I wish I'd known you when my mother was dying."

Deacon did too, but he said nothing.

"Maybe if I'd known you that day I looked out the window and saw the man watching the house I wouldn't have gone with him. Maybe I wouldn't have talked to him, listened to him."

The phone on the nightstand began to ring but Fay made no move to answer. Instead, she held him tighter. After a moment he reached over her and snatched the phone from its cradle.

"Hello?"

"*Deacon*, is that you?"

SMOKE, IN CRIMSON

Gina. He recognized her voice too. "Yeah," he said quietly.

"I suppose she's there with you."

"Well, yeah. It's her place, not mine."

"Jesus, are you two in bed? Is she lying right next to you?"

"Gina—"

"*Is* she? Answer me!"

Deacon handed the phone to Fay. She took it, sat up and swung her feet around to the floor. "Gina?" she said, and then spoke so softly Deacon couldn't make out exactly what she was saying even a foot or so away. After a moment, she hung the phone up but remained sitting on the edge of the bed, her nude body painted in alternating stripes of shadow and moonlight spilling through the window blinds.

"She's drunk again," Fay finally said.

"Gina's my sister. I love her. I have to find a way to make this right."

"She thinks she's been betrayed."

"Hasn't she?"

"You saved her life. She just doesn't know it yet."

It was true, their being together had spared Gina his fate, but it had still come at a terrible cost. Deacon missed his sister. He missed their bond. She was the only true family he had left, the only one who could bring him back from this brink.

Fay stood up and faced him, hands on her hips. Her labia, still swollen and red from fucking, like a wound, looked as if it had been violently turned inside out. Her breasts, full and firm, glistening with sweat and crisscrossed with scars, the nipples erect, cradled the silver ankh that dangled between them. "She said she's going to rehab."

"Good," Deacon said.

"For the booze and a pill problem she's apparently developed. Little place up in the mountains of Vermont, she said."

"When will she be back?"

"When she's better, I guess."

"She thinks if she gets better she'll be able to convince you to—"

"I know. She doesn't understand the truth."

No, she doesn't, Deacon thought. *I'm not even sure I do.*

The man he'd picked up at the bus station weeks before was back in his head. His expression equal parts fear, confusion and embarrassment as he gawked at Deacon with disbelief, like he still hoped he might rescue him from this madness somehow. His body, pudgy and pale, was quivering and stripped nude, stretchmarks along his belly and sides like scars slashed deep into his flesh. Big sloppy bare feet slipped in the blood along the cold floor, drooping breasts jiggling as he lumbered about, pleading all the while to be left alone as Dana effortlessly pulled him down from behind and crawled on top of him, mounting him, laughing at his weakness. The realization in the man's horrified eyes that submission was his only option, would be forever seared into Deacon's brain.

"We have to stop."

Fay looked at the floor.

"I said *we have to stop.*"

"I heard you." She turned and walked out of the room, leaving him alone with the demons—their demons—slithering up from under the bed and crawling along the walls to lord over him like the hideous nightmares they were.

IT LANDED ON HIS shoulders and skittered down onto his back like a giant spider, its appendages clamping across his ribs and neck, its weight nearly toppling Deacon backwards. At the last second he was able to brace himself, and, remaining upright, reached back, grabbed the back of its head and executed a snapmare, flipping it over his shoulder and down onto the floor.

Deacon staggered forward as the thing crashed onto its back, trash flying into the air on either side of it. But as quickly as it hit the floor, it regained its feet and spun toward him, arms outstretched, clawed hands poised to attack, its slimy, hairless face and slick sinewy body covered in a sheen of blood that made it look like its leathery skin had been sliced away in sheets. It cocked its head, baffled by Deacon's presence, its black eyes wide, no longer completely human.

It sniffed the air, shook its head then sniffed again. Slowly, it assumed a less threatening posture, sank back onto its haunches and bowed submissively.

Both knew what they were looking at, and both knew who was more powerful.

Deacon pawed at the back of his neck, wiped away the slime it had left behind then flicked it onto the floor between them in a long wet string.

The thing backed into the corner.

He'd seen these hopeless causes before, those so far in and so far gone they began to change not just emotionally, mentally and spiritually, but physically. The longer and deeper in, the less human they became. This one was right on the precipice.

Freaks like that had no choice but to stick to the shadows, and were never far from the hives they served, as they were wholly dependent upon them for their survival.

Its presence here meant Deacon was close.

"Where is it?" he demanded.

As a black tongue emerged from its mouth and licked at the thick mucus covering its lips, the thing pointed a clawed finger at the floor.

Deacon knew what it was telling him. His answer was in the basement. He was aware of the entrance behind the

SMOKE, IN CRIMSON

metal staircase, had been years before as well, but he'd never been down there.

Now there'd be no avoiding it.

As the aberration folded itself into a fetal position, partially disappearing into the shadows and garbage, Deacon turned his back on it as a final show of dominance. He lit a cigarette and smoked it to the filter in silence, steeling himself for what was to come.

Then, a man condemned, he walked back out into the rain.

CHAPTER **TWELVE**

THE LIGHT WAS CHANGING, shifting, the shadows growing longer, the natural colors of the world drifting around him like clouds, many brighter than they should've been, others more muted than normal. Dark shapes stalked his peripheral vision, lurking there, just out of reach of reason or understanding. But Deacon needed no explanations. He knew what they were. He knew where he was.

People think drugs turn their brains off...

Fay's words hung in his mind as he descended the rickety staircase then stood beneath it. The open stairs provided little shelter from what had become a heavy rain, which poured through them and gushed along the pavement to the alley in narrow rivulets, but Deacon remained unaffected. He was focused on the battered black door behind the base of the staircase.

They're wrong...

He moved closer, took hold of a rusted silver handle, and pulled.

Their brains are turned off to begin with...

The door refused to budge, so he yanked the handle harder. It gave a bit, the bottom scraping the pavement loudly enough for him to hear it over the driving rain.

Drugs truly turn their brains on for the first time...

A third try slid the door far enough for him to fit through the opening.

Deacon hesitated. A strange red light spilled from within the basement, along with another terrible stench.

They don't realize it, but that's why they can be so dangerous...

Although it was even worse than the smell upstairs, this time Deacon made no move to cover his nose or mouth. Instead, he drew a deep breath of it and slipped inside.

They don't recognize being awake because they're conditioned to being asleep...

Red...everything was draped in a glowing red light that was at once disarming and disturbing. Like a haze, it hung in the stale air, coating the darkness and distorting the shadows.

They mistake one for the other...

Deacon wiped rain from his eyes, his fingertips leaving odd trails of sparkling light in their wake, which dissipated as they were absorbed into the sea of red.

Blindness for sight...

SMOKE, IN CRIMSON

Things huddled, crouched along the cement walls, watching him. Some scurried off, disappearing into the red mist like shelled bugs beneath an overturned stone running from a sudden intrusion of light and fresh air.

Lies for truth...

In the center of the basement, the strongest of the group sat slumped in what was left of a once plush but now old and tattered chair. With a razor-thin but sinewy build, and bright blond stringy hair that hung well below his shoulders, he wore only a pair of scarred black leather pants; his chest and feet bare. Numerous tattoos covered his torso, most crude and amateurish. At first glance many were so small they looked more like scars, a series of old wounds perhaps caused by the fine point of a very sharp knife.

Dark for light...

Pentagrams painted in black blood adorned the cheeks of his otherwise haggard, sallow face, and two females sat on the floor on either side of him—one middle-aged, the other much younger—both hanging on him like the disciples they were.

In the brilliant red light, Deacon couldn't make out much else, but he knew there were several others there in addition to those he was able to see. He could smell them, sense them scuttling about nearby.

Rain spattered against a small, filthy window on what was the wall of the basement to his right, but in that peculiar moment it looked impossibly far away. He studied it a moment, waiting until the perspective changed and corrected itself.

Strange dark shadows cut the red, approaching Deacon from either side. He ignored them, waited for the realization to arrive. As it did, those that had surrounded him slowly backed away and out of sight.

The disaster in the chair casually scratched his chin with a long, brittle fingernail. His hands were small, but the fingers long and tapered, almost delicate, except for the bloodstains and scars. His blue eyes were coated in a thin milky sheen similar to the look of cataracts, and as his head lolled to the side they fell on Deacon with disinterest. "Look what the rain has brought us," he said in a dreamy, slurred voice, a slight smile parting his thin lips to reveal beige teeth caked with blood distinguishable even through the thick red haze. Those on the floor on either side of him rubbed his lean, leather-clad thighs. "And it's as stoned as I am."

"You know why I'm here." Deacon's speech, slower than normal, distorted into a significantly deeper, foreign tone. "Where is she?"

"This isn't about her. It's *of* her." As if only then realizing it was there, he gently stroked the ends of his blond locks with an odd and curious fascination. "It's just one of her nightmares. And this one's all yours. She's in the midst of it right now." His cloudy eyes blinked slow and reptilian-like. *"We're* in the midst of it right now."

The women on either side of him rose to their feet. Their eyes were milky as well, faces drawn. Nude, they gazed at Deacon with an eerily familiar longing, moist hands touching his face, their fingers running delicately up and down the length of his cheeks like slayers petting disabled quarry moments before devouring it.

Something deep inside Deacon stirred. He'd kept it at bay for so long he thought he'd mastered it. But it all came alive in him the moment they laid their hands on him.

A touch of wickedness...of evil...

"Addiction," the blond freak said with a demonic grin. "Ain't it a motherfucker?"

Without realizing it, Deacon slid his hands around the women's waists. Their flesh was hot and slick, slippery but soft, pliable. He turned his head and licked the older woman's neck. It tasted of salt and the beefy nectar of raw meat. With the tip of his tongue, he could feel her diseased blood rushing through her veins in time with the slow but insistent beat of her heart.

This time the voice in Deacon's head was his own, reminding him that *he* was the one to be feared in this wretched den of forsaken souls.

It's all a mindfuck, baby...

Deacon's eyes rolled back in his head, and he fell away to darkness.

FAY HURRIED INTO THE room, crossing through the kitchen before flopping down on the couch. She leaned over the coffee table and inhaled a long line of coke. Sniffling, and then rubbing her nose with manic repetition, her eyes darted about, stopping on Deacon only long enough to offer a suspicious squint, as if she couldn't quite place him.

Across from her, Deacon stretched out on the couch where he'd earlier collapsed in a drug-fueled, drunken heap. Pushing his cotton shorts aside so he could comfortably scratch his balls, he noticed the beach and ocean beyond the windows behind her, and how infuriatingly bright the sun was. "Fuck time is it?"

"I don't know. Daytime."

"Yeah, no shit." Deacon chuckled and drunkenly reached for his drink on the coffee table between them. "But what time is it?"

"Who cares?" Fay snorted another line. Bolting upright, she shook her head, as if to dislodge something. "You worry about the most insignificant shit."

Deacon sipped his drink with more difficulty than seemed reasonable. All he could remember at that point was they'd been locked away in this cottage partying and having sex for days. Booze, pot, hash, mushrooms, windowpane LSD, cocaine, speed, codeine, he'd lost track, but every time

SMOKE, IN CRIMSON

he and Fay went on one of their binges—*quests*, as Fay called them—there always seemed to be an endless supply.

"Seems like it was night just a few minutes ago," he mumbled.

Fay stabbed an accusatory finger at him. "You're fading."

Deacon vaguely remembered ordering pizza at one point, and late one night they'd had some Chinese food delivered, but he couldn't remember the last time he'd actually eaten. "I'm really hungry."

"You're drunk and stoned and tripping balls."

"So are you."

"Do some of this," Fay said, motioning to the pile of cocaine on the coffee table. "It'll set you back in motion."

"Motion sounds exhausting. Much as I've come to love coke, right now I'm content to exist as a sedentary blob. So if you don't mind, or even if you do, I'd rather not engage in any activity more strenuous than scratching my nuts."

Like a spring, Fay shot back to her feet. She'd had a white bikini on for days, but at some point the bottoms had disappeared and she was left with only the top, which was now peppered with various stains. "You think it's all a fucking joke," she said. "It's not. *We're* not."

Deacon studied her a moment, standing there swaying as if in an attempt to remain upright against a mighty wind. Hair mussed, eyes glazed, a bit of drool collected in the corners of her mouth, full breasts lifted and pushed together in the underwire bikini bra, her dark blonde pubic hair was littered with tiny flecks of toilet paper, the red polish on her toes was chipped and faded, and her fingertips were stained yellow and brown from nicotine.

That's what these binges do to us, he thought. *They reduce us to* this.

Pathetic drug addicts and alcoholics stumbling around a tomb disguised as a cottage, trading addictions—one for another—and searching for answers that eluded them every time. That's what they became in those bleary moments, those days and nights that all blurred together into a dust devil of hedonistic, over-the-top excess. And yet, it remained bizarrely liberating as well, because during those stints Deacon never felt more alive, more genuine, or closer to something at least resembling peace.

"You want to think we're magic, something special." He chuckled again, though he no longer found anything funny about their conversation. "There's no great mystery here, no hidden meaning or mind-expanding reality we're tapping into. We're junkies, Fay. That's all we are, junkies."

She snatched a bottle of whiskey from the coffee table and drank it down even though it was half full. A good deal of it ran down the front of her, but she either didn't notice or didn't care. "We *are* special, baby." She wiped her mouth with the back of her hand. "We *are* magic."

"Fine, magical junkies then, how's that?"

SMOKE, IN CRIMSON

Fay was clearly not amused, but looked more confused than angry.

"We should probably bathe," Deacon said. "When's the last time we showered?"

"Couple days, I think."

"We're starting to stink." Deacon struggled into a sitting position. As his feet hit the floor a wave of lightheadedness swept through him. "My armpits smell like a slowly rotting Italian sub."

Fay remained expressionless for several seconds, but when she finally processed what he'd said, she barked out a loud, bawdy laugh.

"And you have a shitload of little pieces of toilet paper stuck in your bush," he said. "What the fuck is that all about?"

Fay looked down at herself. "Holy shit, I do. It's actually kind of pretty, like it's been snowing. Snatch snow."

This time Deacon laughed. It eventually became a hacking cough he thought he'd counter by lighting a cigarette. "I'm used to finding those little balls of toilet paper lower and toward the back. That happens, but how the fuck did you get so many in front?"

Laughing, Fay pranced around before the tall windows like a nymph. "In the middle of summer it snows in the land of snatch! Who knew?"

Deacon laughed too, but the darkness quickly returned, as he knew it would, draping itself over his shoulders like a fucking shroud. He took a drag on his cigarette and powered down the remainder of his drink. His breath, heavy and hot, fogged up a portion of his glass. He considered the empty tumbler a moment, and then hurled it against the far wall.

It hit and shattered a foot or so from Fay. She stopped dancing, immediately mesmerized by the shards of broken glass all over the floor at her bare feet. "That's beautiful. There's something beautiful about that, isn't there? Isn't there, baby?"

"Jesus, you're so fucking pretentious sometimes. It doesn't matter how much we drink or take drugs or fuck or try to see beauty where there isn't any," Deacon said, his voice softer now. "It won't fix this. It won't fix *us*. It won't make any of this go away."

"I never promised it would."

"And it won't make any of this right."

"Right and wrong are subjective concepts."

"That's horseshit and you know it."

Fay smiled coyly. "You only challenge me when you're this fucked up."

"Maybe I should do it more often."

"Gina did, but then, you're not her."

"No, I'm not. But if we're going to discuss family, maybe you should tell me about your father."

"I already have."

"I don't mean like that."

SMOKE, IN CRIMSON

Careful to avoid the broken glass, Fay came closer, plucked the cigarette from Deacon's mouth and took a drag. "You want specific details, is that it? Or would that be too *pretentious?*"

"The shadow man you saw watching your house when you were a kid, he didn't appear until your mother was dying and *other things* with your father started to happen. That's why he came, wasn't it."

It wasn't a question, but with a sudden grimace, Fay nodded anyway, exhaling two thin streams of smoke from her nostrils.

"Are you looking into the past?" Deacon asked.

"No," she said sullenly. "It's looking into me."

"Where was your father when you'd see the shadow man watching your house?"

"I don't know, around."

"Was he asleep, Fay?"

"Maybe *I* was asleep. Maybe I'm asleep right now. Maybe you are too." "Answer me."

"Why does that matter?"

"You know why."

"But do *you?*"

"He chose you, the shadow man."

"Why don't you just say his name?"

"Why did he choose you? Of all the people in the world, why did he want you?"

"My poor Deacon," Fay said with a playful pout. "Always trying to find sense in things where there is none."

From the corner of his eye, something caught Deacon's attention. A black spider about the size of an eraser at the end of a pencil crawled across the wall then dropped to the floor, disappearing from sight. "Tell me."

"It's not us he wants. It's our dreams, our nightmares."

"What's happened to you, Fay? What's happening to me?"

"Let's drop more acid and take a shower, see where it leads us."

"To more nightmares," Deacon said, "where else?"

Fay offered a futile nod then sauntered into the kitchen and toward the bathroom.

The tears, the horror, the blood—always the god damn blood—they were all back in an explosion of depravity, a storm churning and growing stronger, deadlier.

Through his tears he saw Fay's bare ass. His eyes lifted, found hers. She'd stopped at the far end of the kitchen and was gazing back at him. "Come on, baby," she said, as if summoning a puppy. "Come. Come on."

Then, like a wisp of smoke, she was gone.

And so was he.

SMOKE, IN CRIMSON

DEACON DREAMED OF THE past.

When he was nine years old, his mother decided he should serve the parish as an altar boy, so she took him to the local Catholic Church they attended as a family every Sunday morning and turned him over to Father Sebastian, an older, kindly priest Deacon always liked. Tall and thin, he was a soft-spoken, gentle man with dark skin, thinning gray hair and sympathetic eyes. As Deacon's mother waited by the doors, Father Sebastian took Deacon aside and they sat together in one of the pews where he patiently explained what being an altar boy would entail and all that would be expected of him. He'd have to be reliable, and dependable and not only show up when he was scheduled, but competent in his role. He'd have to memorize all three versions of Mass, in both English and Latin, and he'd have to attend a training class for once a week for more than a month until he was ready to perform his duties for real.

For the next three years, Deacon served as an altar boy at both masses and for weddings, christenings and other church events. He learned his routines and cues and knew all the masses by heart, and for one hour or so, usually on Sundays, in that little church, beneath windows of stained-glass and the melancholy gaze of saints and the Virgin Mother, and the shadow of crucified Jesus on a large cross behind the altar, Deacon felt connected to God in a way he hadn't prior. His duties—making sure the water and wine was prepared and presented to the priest, ringing bells at the appropriate times, assisting in communion, tidying up the altar when everything was done—all of it made him feel a part of something good and positive.

And yet even then, Deacon began to sense something else.

Something approaching, circling him.

Something evil...

Just shy of his thirteenth birthday, Deacon decided it was time to do other things, so he stepped down. His mother was upset. His father didn't seem to care one way or the other. Gina thought the entire thing was a waste of time anyway and didn't have much else to say about it. And Father Sebastian told him he understood, thanked him, and gave him his blessing.

In the dream, Deacon and Father Sebastian were sitting in that same church, in the same pew, only he was a grown man and his mother was no longer with him. The altar behind them was empty except for a single young altar boy he didn't recognize, standing before the altar and staring at them with an expressionless face.

"Did you know, Father?" Deacon asked. "Did you know what was coming for me even then?"

"No. But you did. Didn't you?"

"I didn't mean for this to happen."

"I know you didn't. *God* knows you didn't. The Devil is a trickster."

SMOKE, IN CRIMSON

"Can I be forgiven, Father?"

"Of course, but that's not the question." Father Sebastian glanced at the doors to the church then shook his head. "Will you truly seek His forgiveness? And when it's granted, will you seek your own?"

"Isn't that why I'm here?" Deacon asked helplessly.

The priest slowly shook his head no. "Seeking and obtaining are not the same things, Deacon."

The previous silence of the church was interrupted by a quiet but insistent hissing sound, like the release of steam from a tea kettle just before it begins to whistle. And then something passed by the large stained-glass window to their left, something sudden and black, it surged forward then away with a sound of large, angrily flapping wings.

"You are not where you think you are," Father Sebastian said, his focus still locked on something over Deacon's shoulder.

Deacon turned and looked.

Just inside the doors stood Fay, nude, her wounds seeping blood and dripping across her bare flesh to the floor below.

"*Blasphemy,*" Father Sebastian whispered. Grimacing, he looked away.

On the altar, the boy began to shake, his entire body trembling, shaken by an invisible force. His face twisted in fear and his mouth dropped open, but no words came from him. Instead, his eyes turned dark crimson and began to bleed.

"Get out of here!" Deacon screamed, jumping to his feet.

When he looked again, Fay was gone.

You are not where you think you are.

The church was empty. Deacon was alone.

And in that moment, he knew he felt nothing. Desperately as he wanted to, *needed* to, Deacon felt nothing at all. Even God had left this place, it seemed.

Seeking and obtaining are not the same things.

And it was then that Deacon realized what he was feeling, and why.

The true sorrow, the worst agony in Hell, was not proximity to the Devil, but the distance of God.

Deacon stumbled from the pew and fell to his hands and knees before the altar.

The gulf, the desert between the two, is not of God, Deacon, but Man.

Horrible screeches tore through his skull. Gripping his head with his hands he fell forward, the pain beyond anything he'd ever felt.

Snapping awake, Deacon felt his legs kick out in front of him as he looked around frantically in an attempt to figure where he was and what was happening.

"Easy there, my friend," a man with a thick accent said from somewhere in front of him. "You are A-OK, yes?"

Deacon rubbed his eyes. Slowly, he began to remember. He was in the backseat of a cab barreling through the city.

SMOKE, IN CRIMSON

The driver was alternating between watching the road and looking in the rearview mirror at him. A pudgy, Middle Eastern man, he appeared somewhere between concerned, amused and annoyed.

"Yeah, I—I'm fine," Deacon said, clearing his throat.

"You fall asleep," the driver said. "Too much fun last night, now you pay, huh?"

Deacon pulled his jacket in tighter around him despite the oppressive heat in the car. He felt sick to his stomach, his eyes burned and a horrible taste coated his mouth. He ran a hand through his hair. It was wet with sweat. "How much longer?" he asked. He'd lost all sense of time.

"Five minutes, my friend. Traffic is not too much shitty today."

The nightmares continued to slither through Deacon's mind like the snakes they were. His nausea grew worse. Hoping for a distraction, he gazed out the grimy window to his right.

The rain had stopped but a veil of gray still hung over the city.

Seven minutes later the cab lurched to a stop on a quiet side street in Mattapan. Located in the southwest region of Boston and neighboring Dorchester, with a population of over thirty-six thousand and known for its largely Caribbean and African American roots, it was home to several parks, boardwalks, a beautiful bird sanctuary, diverse restaurants, shops and cultural centers. And in certain sections, it was also one of the more dangerous neighborhoods in the city, particularly after dark.

This was one of them.

After paying the driver, Deacon stood on the corner and watched the taxi disappear as it turned at the top of the block.

The street was short and narrow, with only four modest, rundown one-story houses, each with tiny front yards fenced off with chain link. Three were boarded up and had been abandoned some time ago. The one closest to the corner—boxy, with chipped white paint and the only mowed yard—still appeared to be lived in. It was remarkable how similar it looked these years later, but Deacon had no way of knowing if the person he'd come looking for was there as well.

Until he saw the black Harley-Davidson motorcycle parked in the driveway. Monstrous and polished to a high-gloss, it looked like some sort of war machine.

With an equal amount of relief and apprehension, Deacon approached the house, his memories from within those walls crashing down on him for the first time in years.

Locked in the dingy bedroom in back, the shades drawn, darkness all around, his convulsing body strapped down, the begging and horror, the *need*, the sickness and mayhem, the frantic bargains with God, the Devil, himself,

SMOKE, IN CRIMSON

and finally—days later, utterly exhausted and lying in his own urine, vomit and excrement—the release. Even then Deacon knew he could never be free, not entirely, but he'd dragged himself out of Hell in the hopes of getting as close to peace as someone like him could.

And it all happened inside that dilapidated little house. He'd not been there since.

Shrugging off a sudden shiver that began at the base of his neck and fanned out across his shoulders, Deacon took a look around to make sure he was still alone on the street, and then headed for the front door.

CHAPTER **THIRTEEN**

YELLOW LIGHT SPILLED FROM behind the slowly opening door, followed by a thick vine of twisting smoke and the harsh aroma of cheap cigars. Some things never changed, and for once, Deacon found that comforting.

From the shadows and smoke inside, stepped Felix Enki. "*Shit,*" he said in a familiar gravelly baritone. "You must be shining me on."

Slump shouldered and pale, Deacon offered no response.

Poking his bulbous, bald, shiny head out the doorway, Felix looked up then down the street. Standing six-six and weighing nearly three hundred pounds, very little of it fat, for a man his age, which had to be somewhere in his late sixties to early seventies, Felix was in remarkable shape. His beard was still long, full and bushy, hanging six inches or so below his chin, and although it had turned entirely gray since the last time Deacon had seen him, it suited him and contrasted nicely with his dark brown skin.

Apparently satisfied that Deacon had come alone, Felix swung the door open wider. Barefoot and dressed in an ankle-length, leopard print silk robe, the big man looked Deacon over without a hint of subtlety. "The runner stumbles."

Deacon couldn't think of a response worth voicing.

"Come on then." Felix motioned for him to come inside with his right hand, which was when Deacon realized he was holding a pump shotgun with a pistol grip in his left, down against the side of his leg. "Or are you waiting on an *official* invite?"

Deacon nodded guiltily.

"Old habits die hard." Felix chomped his cigar with a repulsive squishy sound.

"Yeah, something like that, I guess."

Felix raised the shotgun, hesitating with the barrel pointed directly at Deacon's chest for a second or two before laying it back across his shoulder. "In that case," he said evenly. "Won't you come in?"

Deacon stepped directly into a living room.

As Felix closed the door behind him, Deacon took in his surroundings. The house looked exactly as it had years ago. An enormous black leather sectional took up an entire wall. A framed painting of an African woman surrounded by stars and reaching for the moon hung behind it. A plush black leather chair was opposite it, the wall outfitted with open wood shelves behind lighted glass cases and

SMOKE, IN CRIMSON

stocked with various antique books and pieces of ancient art—mostly vases and sculptures. In the corner was a stereo system consisting of numerous components stacked atop one another, their blue display lights twinkling in a rack of dark wood and smoked glass. Small speakers were still installed near the ceiling in all four corners of the room, and between the sectional and chair was a familiar rectangular solid wood coffee table that also served as a subwoofer. The kitchen was just off the living room, toward the back of the house, and a fully stocked bar with two crossed samurai swords and several ornamental African and Asian knives displayed behind it separated both rooms from a hallway leading to two bedrooms and a bathroom.

His silk robe whispering as he moved, Felix made his way to the sectional and sat down, the shotgun in his lap. Through the cigar smoke, he pointed to the chair.

"It's like time stood still here," Deacon said, the dated but pristine thick white carpet beneath his feet slowing his stride. "Still got the shag too, huh?"

Felix remained quiet but watched intently as Deacon slowly lowered himself into the chair across from him. A Marvin Gaye tune played softly through the speakers.

"It's good to see you, Felix."

"No it's not."

Deacon eyed the shotgun balanced across Felix's knees. "Still in the game?"

A dead stare.

"You don't really think you need that firepower with me, do you?"

"I don't know, Deacon. Do I?"

"Aren't we friends anymore?"

"Is that what you thought we were, *friends*?"

"You saved my life."

"I saved a lot of lives over the years, ended quite a few too. What's your point?"

They both let that sit there a while. "Do they still fear you, Felix?"

"I'm an old man."

Deacon returned the dead stare with one of his own.

"And who are *they*? Place across the street turned into a crack house a while back. I put an end to that shit quick, it was a motherfucking bloodbath. So yeah, dealers, crack-heads, gangbangers old enough to know better, *they* fear me. That who you mean?"

"Why are you playing games with me?"

"Why are you here?"

Bile bubbled up into the bottom of Deacon's throat, reminding him he was still sick to his stomach. The awful smell of the cigar only made it worse. "I need your help."

"Is that a fact?"

Deacon nodded. It seemed unnecessarily warm in the room. Odd, since his memories of this place did not sync with that. He remembered it being deathly cold in that second bedroom the entire time he was there, so cold he could see his breath.

"There's not as many as there used to be." Felix adjusted his position on the sectional a bit. "But this new breed, they're younger, full of themselves. Seen too many movies, played too many video games, think they're invincible. Used to be there was shame, guilt, uncertainty, fear, a deep *need* for contrition. Not anymore."

"There's no helping them?"

"They don't want help. They want war."

And when they do, Deacon thought, *you still give it to them don't you?*

They stayed silent a while, listened to Marvin Gaye.

"Fay's gone missing," Deacon finally said. "I'm trying to find her."

"I should've put that cunt down when I had the chance. She's a fucking disease."

"You think I don't know that?"

"Then what the hell are you doing? I heard you'd almost made it, had yourself a good situation in New York, living right, doing your thing and getting by fine."

Deacon remembered the quiet of his studio apartment, his job at the diner, the sense of security routine and honest work provided. He also recalled being adrift in loneliness, and a life of self-imposed isolation. "It wasn't all good, Felix."

"No? Was it better than the night I brought you here?" Felix plucked the cigar from his mouth. "Was it better before you felt the need to come back to get clean again?"

Deacon rubbed his stomach. "I'll be all right."

"Keep telling yourself that, maybe it'll stick this time."

"That's not the kind of help I need."

"Yes it is. It's not the kind of help you *want*."

"I thought maybe you'd heard something."

"Like what?"

"Like where Fay is and what this is all about."

"Why the *fuck* would I know any of that?"

"Because you've got eyes and ears everywhere, that's why."

"That was a long time ago," Felix said, stuffing the cigar back into the corner of his mouth. "I don't offer second chances these days. Didn't you hear what I said? They don't want them. I'm not in the savior business anymore." Felix gave the shotgun an affectionate pat. "Strictly an exterminator now."

"Does that include me?"

"We'll have to wait and see how things play out."

A sharp pain spiked deep in Deacon's gut, as tentacles of cigar smoke broke free from the cloud filling the space between them, curling and spiraling through the air with wraithlike elegance. Hands tremoring, he dug cigarettes and a lighter from his jacket pocket, then shook a cigarette free from the pack and placed it between his lips. "I…"

SMOKE, IN CRIMSON

"Light it," Felix told him. "Go on, fire it up and smoke the motherfucker right down to the filter. Savor every drag. It'll be the last one you get for a while."

Once the tremor passed, Deacon quickly lit the cigarette before the next one hit. He knew what was coming, and though he'd sworn he would never put himself through that horror again, there he was, right back under Felix's vigilant gaze. All of Deacon's promises—even those he'd made to himself—were meaningless now, perhaps they always had been, and although it made no logical sense, he knew better than most that digressions such as these swam in much deeper waters. "How long?" he asked quietly.

"Last time took near a week, but you were a lot worse than you are now," Felix reminded him. "Only smart move you made was to get your sorry ass here quick as you did. This go-round, assuming you survive it, we're looking at a day, two at most."

Terrifying memories of what had taken place in that room strobed in Deacon's head like the continual flash of a camera. "I got to figure out what Fay's doing and—"

"*Deacon*," Felix said, silencing him. "We'll talk about it on the other side."

He couldn't be certain, but Deacon thought he'd heard a hint of compassion in Felix's otherwise stern tone. Tears welled in his eyes. "I'm so fucking ashamed, man."

"You know who Procopius was?"

Deacon shook his head no as he wiped his tears.

"He was a Greek cat, a scholar in the sixth century, probably the most reliable of the Byzantine military historians." With a muffled grunt, Felix rose to his feet. "He once said, '*A man without shame stops at no vice.*' There's a lot of bad juju in you, man, but that shame that's carving you right down to your soul is what's gonna save your life."

Deacon took a final drag on his cigarette, crushed it in an onyx ashtray on the coffee table and pushed himself to his feet. Legs shaking, he remained where he was, but like a feral animal cornered, he *needed* to run, and knew he couldn't fight it off for long.

Reaching into the front of his robe, Felix pulled free a large gold cross he was wearing around his neck, let it fall against his broad chest then cocked his head to the side, indicating the nearby hallway.

With Marvin Gaye singing about mercy from the speakers above him, Deacon slowly made his way from the room.

A FEW YEARS PRIOR, unaware that this would be her last day on Earth, sixty some odd miles north of Miami, in the small seaside city of Lake Worth Beach, Gina watched the sun slowly rise from the lone window in her room. She'd recently completed her latest stint in rehab. Given options,

SMOKE, IN CRIMSON

on this, her third attempt, she chose to seek treatment far from home in Florida, and once she'd made it through the program, decided to remain there a while instead of returning to Massachusetts. After everything she'd been through, she planned to do whatever she could to continue her sobriety, including being in no hurry to go home. In fact, if she could avoid it altogether, even better. Carrying only a small suitcase packed with clothes and a few personal items, Gina found a room for rent over a gas station near the beach. It took almost all of her savings, but she paid for a month in advance. The idea was to get her Florida nursing license and find a job. Then she could support herself and stay as long as she liked. Gina loved the warm weather and relaxed pace, and for the first time, dared to see a future that included the possibility of genuine happiness and some semblance of normalcy. There was nothing back home but sorrow and bad memories, and heartbreaking as that was, she knew where it would lead.

Gina had been warned about the power of those memories, and the best ways to contend with them. Rehab didn't make them go away, and no amount of subsequent therapy would either, but she *could* control her reactions to such things, and that's what she was working on. Despite her anger and pain, she also felt guilt, among other things, at having introduced her brother to Fay in the first place. There were times that morning when Gina allowed thoughts and memories of Deacon to linger in her mind, and the sense of sorrow it produced was nearly overwhelming. She missed her brother dearly but could no longer trust him, not as long as he was mixed up with Fay and under her spell. Together, they'd betrayed her, and Gina believed Fay had targeted Deacon from the moment she saw him.

I know what you are, Fay, Gina thought. *What you really are.*

She'd had her suspicions, insane as they were, but she couldn't tell anyone. Not anyone in rehab, not her therapist, no one. Who would believe such a thing?

They'd all think I was crazy.

There were days Gina wondered if perhaps she was. Her relationship with Fay hadn't gone far enough for her to be certain. The only thing she knew for sure was that Fay was evil, and if anyone was around her long enough that evil started to influence them too. She *had* known her long enough to experience that, and she'd paid a terrible price for such knowledge, one she was still paying in guilt and torment even then. She'd fallen so far with Fay, lost her mind, really, that there had come a point where Gina was willing to do anything—*anything*—not to be without her, and that madness, that evil had nearly destroyed her physically, emotionally, mentally, even spiritually.

Especially spiritually, Gina thought. *That was your plan, your target all along.*

SMOKE, IN CRIMSON

The result, total destruction…*annihilation*…

Gina realized that now. She also knew that after all this time Deacon was likely drowning in that evil, and it was at least partly her fault.

As the beauty of the sunrise distracted her, Gina remembered Deacon as a little boy, so innocent and wide-eyed, filled with wonder over every little thing, always seeing beyond the surface world, deeper into those important and poignant areas so many—even those much older—consistently missed.

Why then, when he'd been a bit older, hadn't Deacon seen right through Fay?

In answer, Fay came to her next. Those wild, frightening eyes, full mouth open ever-so-slightly, lips wet, hair mussed, her nude body like some plaything forged in the perverse sexual fantasies of a deviant madman, it all came together to produce something neither she nor her brother could defend themselves against.

Sometime earlier, Fay had succumbed to something as well, something that to her had been equally, if not more, darkly powerful and overwhelming. And if Fay couldn't combat such evil, what chance did Deacon or she have?

We were doomed from the start, little brother.

Even then, after so much time apart and with so many miles between them, she felt Fay's power over her. A rush of warmth that began between Gina's legs fanned out across her pelvis, flowed up into her belly and filled her breasts. Trembling, she did her best to drive the sensations away and focus instead on Deacon.

Although Gina wasn't in a position to do much of anything at that point, despite everything that had happened, a part of her still felt the need to rescue her brother. At a minimum, she had to try. But she'd learned in rehab that before she could be of use to others she had to get herself back on track first. The goal was to secure her mental and emotional stability, maintain her sobriety and establish a safe environment in which she could flourish. Maybe *then* she could see if there was anything left of Deacon to salvage. Waiting was a risk, of course, but one she had to take. If it meant her brother was lost to her forever, so be it. This was her chance, *her* turn at happiness and self-sufficiency, and she'd gone through Hell to get it. Nothing was going to derail her. Not this time.

As Fay and Deacon mercifully faded from her mind, Gina threw the lone sheet covering her aside. She studied her bare legs and feet stretched out before her, then her belly and breasts, shoulders, arms. She'd already lost the few pounds she gained in rehab, and had also managed a nice tan since coming to Florida. She actually felt good about her appearance lately, what a welcome change.

Maybe later I'll walk down to the drugstore on the corner and buy some nail polish, do my toes in something bright and festive to celebrate new beginnings.

SMOKE, IN CRIMSON

Since kicking drugs, alcohol and even cigarettes, Gina had come to rely on her coffee. She drank more of it than she should have, but compared to the things she could be ingesting, in the overall scheme of things, coffee seemed relatively harmless.

She'd been frequenting a small coffee shop across the street, stopping in every morning and then usually once again in the early afternoon. They opened quite early, so Gina threw on a pair of shorts and a top and decided to go get an extra-large breakfast blend with milk and three sugars. Maybe she'd even get a muffin.

As she headed out, skipping down the stairs to the street, she took in the beautiful day blooming all around her, so certain this was the first of many that awaited her.

But then, Gina had no way of knowing that in a matter of minutes she'd be dead.

THE ROOM WAS THE same as Deacon remembered it. No lights or fixtures, it was empty except for an old dirty mattress on the floor against the back wall. Two lengths of chain attached to a square of steel riveted to the wall behind it hung across the head of the mattress, thick man-acles at the end of each. The lone window was boarded up from the inside and covered with black cloth. The floor was bare, heavily scarred wood, the walls and ceiling stained, scratched and void of any paint or wallpaper. As before, it remained the only part of Felix's house that was unkempt.

Deacon stood at the foot of the grimy mattress. He'd smelled it the moment Felix swung open both sets of doors, a nauseating combination of perspiration, urine, vomit, and a feral odor reminiscent of the kind wild animals sometimes leave behind. He'd experienced it before, but until that moment, he had convinced himself it would be forever relegated to his darkest, most deeply buried memories.

The remnants of his high from the mushrooms still tingled in his temples, but this was no dream or hallucination, not entirely anyway. At that point, it didn't much matter.

"Go on," Felix said, motioning to the mattress. "You know the drill."

Deacon removed and handed over his jacket, belt, shoes, cigarettes, lighter and jewelry. Much as he hated to part with it, he gave Felix the stone in his pocket as well. "Jesus, Fe," he said, wincing and blocking his nose as the stench from mattress wafted up at him in another wave. "Would it kill you to clean this fucking thing now and then?"

"You've already laid down in filth, little late for cleanliness."

Deacon looked back at the doors to the room. There were two, an interior and an exterior. The former metal, the latter wood. Both were extra thick and outfitted

SMOKE, IN CRIMSON

with so many locks it would've been comical had they not been so necessary. Although it was highly unlikely, in the event he somehow broke free from the chains, those doors were the last line of defense and the only thing preventing him from escape.

With pain shooting across in abdomen in slashing arcs, Deacon doubled over and dropped down onto the edge of the mattress. "Hurry up before I change my mind."

Felix left with Deacon's belongings but returned seconds later and grabbed hold of the shackles, rattling the chains.

Deacon drew a deep breath, hung his head then held his hands out before him.

Felix snapped closed a manacle on either wrist then released the chains. They fell with a thud onto the mattress. With a heavy sigh he left the room a second time, only to return again with a big plastic bowl of ice water and a large white bucket. He placed both on the floor a foot or so from the mattress.

The length of the chains would allow Deacon to stand and even move around a bit, while he still had the strength, though only about three feet or so from the mattress. Raising his head, he looked at the manacles and chains, felt their coldness, their weight.

"You'll be out of your head soon enough," Felix said, motioning to the bucket. "But remember, when this is over, if you're not dead and I haven't put your ass down, whatever mess you make in here you're cleaning the fuck up. I'm not your god damn maid, feel me?"

Deacon looked up at the big man. "See you on the flip."

Felix dropped a hand onto Deacon's shoulder, gave it a squeeze, then turned and walked back to the doorway. "Night's falling," he said in a deep melodious voice that was somehow soothing and menacing all at once. *"Bonam fortunam, viator..."*

Good luck, traveler, in Latin.

And with that, Felix was gone.

The interior door closed behind him, snuffing out all light. A series of locks engaged, one after the next, followed by the slam of the outer door. It was a cold, brutal, final sound.

Not long after, the whispers began.

Deacon was by himself in the darkness, but he was no longer alone.

A FEW YEARS PRIOR, in Lake Worth Beach, Florida, not long after dawn...

The oversized pickup barreled along the otherwise empty beachside road. Behind the wheel, Wyatt Davis, a fortysomething warehouse worker, was on his way home from an all-night drunk. He'd spent the better part of the evening at a local bar, and then went to a friend and

SMOKE, IN CRIMSON

coworker's house where he partied until the wee hours. After passing out on the couch, he snapped awake only a couple hours later with a pounding headache and a horrible case of diarrhea. Once the runs settled, despite still being drunk and stoned, and having had less than three hours of sleep, Wyatt decided to head for home. Halfway there, the cramps kicked in again, so he gunned it, speeding through the quiet streets in a desperate attempt to make it to his bungalow in time.

Bleary-eyed, he leaned on the wheel and shot through town like a comet, nearly rounding the corner to the beach road on two wheels. He never saw the young woman coming out of the coffee shop. Never noticed how she sipped coffee from a large Styrofoam cup as she stepped off the curb and into what had been an empty street when she'd glanced both ways just seconds before.

By the time he did see her, she was in the middle of the road. Apparently having heard the screech of tires as he turned the corner, by the time the woman turned toward the sound, Wyatt had nearly reached her.

As it registered in his hazy mind that someone had walked out in front of his truck, Wyatt slammed the brakes and jerked the wheel, but it was too late.

Later, in his nightmares, he remembered flashes of the woman's face, and the look of terror just seconds before impact, as she turned and looked back in the direction she'd come. But mostly, it was that awful *thud* that haunted Wyatt. The sound of his truck smashing into her with such force it nearly passed right through her, firing her body away and into the air, literally blowing open her chest and abdomen, sending her internal organs exploding into the air in a rain of blood, bone and body parts.

He remembered her shattered, already dead body flying through the air, landing on the cement and cartwheeling before tumbling to a stop near the opposite curb perhaps sixty feet in the distance, and how everything was seen as if from a merry-go-round, as his truck spun out in circle after circle, a curtain of thick black blood sluicing along the windshield, the front of his truck spattered with viscera.

Her body a savaged and mangled husk, Gina lay dead in the gutter, pieces of a Styrofoam cup of coffee still clutched in one broken, mutilated hand.

Later, Wyatt would be arrested and convicted. He would be sentenced to ten years in prison but would only serve three before being paroled due to good behavior.

A year later, on a dark and rainy Saturday night, during what authorities determined to be a botched robbery attempt, he would be found dead in an alley behind a bar where he'd gone to smoke a joint and urinate. His throat had been slashed so deeply and violently Wyatt Davis was nearly decapitated.

His killer was never found.

SMOKE, IN CRIMSON

IN DARKNESS, TIME CEASED to exist.

Deacon had no way of knowing how long it had been since Felix locked him in, he only knew it felt like he'd been lying on that filthy mattress breathing in its stink for an eternity, the weight of the chains and the pinch of the manacles a constant reminder of his captivity.

Like ink spilled and running across black parchment, the darkness became liquid, slowly roiling about in barely discernable black clouds. The whispers continued, circling him with greater ferocity now, their volume rising then falling, only to rise again before morphing into distorted growls and garbled soliloquies spoken in an urgent, ancient, alien tongue. The temperature in the room had dropped dramatically and to the point where Deacon could see his breath escaping him in long misty plumes.

Flat on his back, he attempted to sit up, but dizziness prevented him from getting far. As he flopped back down, disturbing and making worse the stench from the mattress, Deacon struggled against the chains even though he knew such attempts were pointless. Fear was rising, and with it the instinctual need for flight.

"Let me out!" he called, his voice already strained and raw and echoing in the small dark room. "Felix! Let me out! I—I have to get out of here! Let me out!"

Deacon closed his eyes, concentrated on his breathing and tried to slow it down.

It suddenly felt as if thousands of insects were scurrying across his skin. The sensation began along the nape of his neck but spread quickly, rushing down his spine then exploding out around his ribs, chest and into his abdomen. Writhing about, he frantically tried to sweep them away with his manacled hands, but his reach was limited and the feeling was already spreading into his legs and feet.

Within seconds, it felt as if those same insects were *inside* him as well, scuttling about and attempting to force their way free.

Deacon screamed for Felix again, but he knew full well there would be no reply, much less rescue. As he thrashed about on the mattress, the visions began. He'd been anticipating their arrival, so he opened his eyes wide as he could, straining to see something—anything—else in the darkness. His terror rose. So too did his rage. At first it supplemented his fear, but he knew if he let it take over it could also be his best weapon against it.

From deep inside him, it suddenly felt as if the insects had begun to *eat* their way out. He could feel their shelled bodies clicking and scurrying through his gut. He could *hear* them chewing.

Flogging about violently, Deacon screamed. From his peripheral vision came countless talon-like fingers, gnarled

SMOKE, IN CRIMSON

and pale, lunging out on either side of him to scratch and maul his flesh. His throat raw and his body weak, he fought back the terror and pain, staring hopelessly at the ceiling and the darkness churning all around him.

Gradually, the phantom clawed hands receded, and the feel of insects crawling on him and eating their way free of his insides lessened.

But there then came a palpable shift in the room which brought with it the unmistakable sensation that another presence had joined him.

Something primal and unholy, something horrifying...

Deacon lie there a moment, body motionless and eyes wide and darting about.

There...to his left...a black protean shape emerged from the darkness, separating from it though still largely cloaked within it.

This was something new. He had not experienced it last time.

A vaguely humanoid form, it seemed to move with the darkness as if it were an actual part of it. Deacon strained to make out further detail, but it was apparently a kind of molten substance because it kept morphing and dissolving into itself, which made the thing impossible to discern clearly.

I looked out my bedroom window one morning...

"Get—Get away," Deacon said breathlessly, his voice raspy and raw from screaming. "Get the fuck away!"

...and he was standing there watching the house...

The blackness—a void—moved over him now, surging overhead.

He looked like a shadow out there in the snow...

But then a pinpoint of light that seemed far off, too far to be accurate, emerged. It looked miles away. Slowly, as the form blended in and out of focus alongside Deacon, the pinpoint began to move. Erratically at first, like the dot from a laser pointer wiggling about, it moved frantically, sweeping back and forth along the ceiling, clearly under conscious control.

I started to wonder if he'd ever really been there at all...

Slowly, the light drew closer, growing in size as it did so and expanding like a star burning in an otherwise empty night sky.

Until one day, about a week after my mother died, there he was again...

Somewhere close, Deacon heard hideously cruel laughter.

...standing on a snowbank across the street, staring at me...

The light, an eye now—a red eye—exploded before him, becoming a river of fire that flowed overhead, dripping embers and bubbling like lava.

It was harder to see him in the dark...but he was there...

Before him, the river became a landscape, stretched out as far as Deacon could see. His heart hammered his

SMOKE, IN CRIMSON

chest so violently, and his throat so constricted he could barely draw a full breath. It was as if he had been transported to some primordial place and time, light-years from that terrible little room.

I asked him where he came from, where he lived...

Giant masses of rock, pools of fire, everything burning, bubbling, boiling, like the dawn of time, it all played out before him. But he didn't just see this alien world, he *felt* it, smelled it even, heat from huge spires of fire exploding from the sandy, rocky ground, shooting up into a burning sky of red-hot clouds rolling and tumbling and passing overhead at incredible, impossible speeds.

The corner of your eye, the shadow told me...

Burning—the skin on his back was burning—the pain unbearable.

"Help me!" Deacon tried to sit up. "Help me, get it—get it off!"

I never saw him again...

Everything exploded in a spray of fire, and then the blackness abruptly returned, plunging the room back into total darkness. He was again trapped in the void, and along with it came an eerie, short-lived silence.

But he was there. Watching, waiting, guiding...

Deacon heard his heart thudding again, each intake and exhale of breath rushing through his ears in thunderous surges, the chains and manacles rattling nearby.

As grunting sounds swirled around him in the dark, accompanied by the growls of things no longer human, the black form dissipated, coming apart and blowing away like a sand structure slowly dissolving in a heavy wind.

His body began to convulse, twisting and flaying against the old mattress with such violence Deacon lost all control of himself, a ragdoll throttled mercilessly by unseen hands.

He closed his eyes, felt a tear break free and roll the length of his cheek.

In the darkness of his mind, a thick fog curled ominously around ancient stone temples in snakelike tendrils, drifting along the floor of a forest dark and vast. Deacon saw a primitive form of himself running with animal-like speed and agility, darting effortlessly through the trees in the cold night air, his senses heightened beyond those of a human being, his *need* greater than anything he could govern or even truly comprehend. He could feel the blood pulsing through his veins, and up ahead, the smell of his doomed prey called to him with the seductive power of a siren.

Terrible pain erupted deep in Deacon's gut. His eyes popped open and his legs shot up as if from an electric shock, his knees hitting his chest as he turned onto his left side. The pain was so horrific he began to gag, and eventually vomit, his entire body convulsing throughout.

SMOKE, IN CRIMSON

"Oh, God," he groaned, spitting remnants of whatever he'd thrown up from his mouth. "God, please—help me, you've got to help me, I can't—"

A stabbing pain worse than the others took his breath away, left him doubled up on the mattress, shaking and writhing in agony. Although he was freezing, a thick sweat broke out across his entire body, drenching him from head to toe within seconds. As delirium took hold, his mind blurred. Nothing made sense. Deacon could no longer see and just barely hear, but he could *feel*. In that terrible darkness all he knew was crippling pain, waves of it that caused him to lose control of his bodily functions. He didn't want to close his eyes because he knew the things he'd see, but the pain became so great he did it reflexively.

Muttering incoherently, his eyes slid shut, bringing him to that forest and that same version of himself smashing his prey with a large rock. Grunting, he crushed its skull then straddled its still quivering body, lapping blood from the shattered skull before tearing into one of its legs, ripping free a chunk of meat and spitting it into the darkness.

Blood covering his face and chest, he shrieked at the heavens, no longer man but beast, feeding, drinking, swallowing, ingesting, *becoming*—

"Get me out get me out get me out!" Deacon cried, opening his eyes to the darkness and struggling to free himself from the chains. "I need it—Felix!—get me out!"

Another wave of pain struck, and Deacon's screams became irrepressible wails.

"Why are you hiding, you sonofabitch?" he said, his words slurred as he searched the darkness for the form he'd seen earlier. "I know you're here, show yourself. I'll do whatever you want, just get me out of here, please, I—get me the fuck out of here!"

But now, Deacon truly *was* alone.

He screamed in agony, rage, confusion, shame and horror. When he could no longer gather the strength, he became a groveling, weeping mass, reduced to something that barely resembled anything human.

Eventually, complete exhaustion allowed sleep to finally arrive, but Deacon silently prayed it was death that had come for him instead.

In a way, it had.

CHAPTER **FOURTEEN**

LIKE A DEEP-SEA DIVER slowly rising toward shafts of sunlight and the surface of an otherwise dark ocean, Deacon gradually came awake. It felt as if he'd been worked over with a baseball bat, and a headache pulsed along the lower back of his skull. Everything was blurred, his eyes thick with some sort of clear, jelly-like glop, and his mouth was so dry he had trouble swallowing. Managing to raise a hand, he wiped his eyes. In doing so, he realized the manacles had been removed, the chains left on the floor nearby.

Slick with perspiration, Deacon wanted to sit up but was still too weak. He reached for the bowl of water, most of which had spilled, but didn't have the strength to lift it. Groggily, he lolled his head to the side. Both doors to the room were open, the light beyond them explaining why he was no longer in darkness.

GREG F. GIFUNE

Deacon faded in and out of consciousness a couple times before coming awake to see Felix standing over him, a cigar jammed in the corner of his mouth and his fierce eyes glaring down at him. From the other room came the vocal stylings of Al Green.

"Here," Felix said, crouching and pressing an open plastic bottle of water to Deacon's lips. "Small sips, or you'll throw it up, and there's already enough of your vomit in here, you nasty bastard."

The water was tepid but just about the best thing Deacon had ever tasted. He was still taking sips when Felix took the bottle away and placed it on the floor within reach. "It'll be there when you're strong enough to drink it yourself," he said. "Stay away from the water bowl, though, you blew serious chunks in it. Got to give it to you, that was some mighty impressive projectile vomiting. We're talking *The Exorcist* level shit." The big man placed a hand on Deacon's forehead. "Your fever broke a few hours ago. Long as it stays gone you'll be all right."

"How long have I been here?" Deacon's voice was so weak it was barely audible. "How...long..."

"Forty-eight hours," Felix told him, returning to his feet.

Two days, Deacon thought. *I have to get out of here, I can't be gone from the cottage this long or I could—*

"You'll be back on your feet soon," Felix said. "Then you're cleaning up the disgusting stinking mess you made in here, you repugnant-ass motherfucker."

SMOKE, IN CRIMSON

"I got to..." Deacon struggled to sit up but couldn't do it.

"Rest," Felix said, moving away. "It's not over until I say it is."

The doors closed then locked, and Deacon drifted back into unconsciousness.

DURING THE ORDEAL OF the last two days, Fay had been suspiciously absent. While she hovered in the background, not once had she stepped directly into Deacon's thoughts, or appeared in his horrific visions. But now, there she was.

In his dream, or whatever it was playing out in his mind once he'd passed out, all he could discern in the darkness was her pale face and blonde hair protruding from a sea of black, her sullen eyes watching him.

Things moved in those liquid eyes, primordial and deadly, and yet, when Deacon looked long enough, he witnessed innocence and vulnerability in them as well. Perhaps those things weren't as far off as Deacon suspected. Perhaps they all existed within Fay simultaneously, none of it destroyed or replaced but simply overpowered, shuffled, reorganized to form a more efficient machine.

Her whispers echoed all around him in the darkness, as if they'd both been locked away in some ancient tomb, but no matter how hard he strained to listen—to hear—he couldn't make out anything she was saying.

Through the darkness, light...light from her eyes but born of the things within them. Brighter and brighter still, nearly blinding, the light swallowed Fay, *absorbed* her then exploded into red, rushing by and on all sides of him, turning and twisting and folding into itself again and again.

As it fell away in spirals, the light revealed a desert below. He knew instinctually that these were the beginning times, the earliest times, and as a violent desert wind blew across that red sky, the sands shifted and slithered as if alive.

Deacon struggled to awaken, but he was flying, soaring like a bird over the vast desert. He was certain it was empty until, below, at the summit of one dune in particular, there stood a stationary figure. Dressed all in black, and wearing a broad hat, its head was bowed and its arms were at its sides. Contrasting with the scorched red world, the figure did not look up.

Yet Deacon knew it was aware of him.

Who was he, Fay?

Ethereal music made by ancient instruments of wood and bone played from somewhere far away, carried on the winds.

Exactly who you think he was.

Like a reed, the figure swayed, the tails of its black coat billowing as it raised a hand to the black hat on its head for fear the winds might dislodge it.

SMOKE, IN CRIMSON

Exactly who you're afraid he was.

Alive in the land of the dead, Deacon waited, watching.

The red light is greater than time and substance.

Still holding its hat, the figure began to walk, its strides long and purposeful along the thick and heavy sand.

It dwells in a realm where all things are possible.

Deacon watched it move down one dune and up the next.

Anything...everything...

The red world flickered, like a candle nearly extinguished, and in that strange and frightening moment, Fay's whispers returned, as did her touch—he could feel her—but all he could see was the dark figure striding across endless mountains of sand, moving faster now, more powerfully.

As the sky turned to fire, the figure stopped suddenly, spread wide its arms like some giant bat, and slowly lifted its head to the burning heavens.

It had no face. Where one should have been was an empty black void, like an endless expanse of deep, dead, starless space.

Don't you know by now, baby? There is no death, not for us.

LATER, WHEN DEACON CAME awake and had regained some strength, Felix presented him with a mop, plastic gloves, Febreze, a big bottle of bleach and some rags. Wearily, Deacon cleaned the area, emptied the buckets into the bathroom sink and toilet then finally left the room for what he assured himself was the last time. He'd made that promise once before, of course, yet here he was. Regardless, same as the previous time, Deacon meant and believed it. If there was to be any chance at success, he had no other choice.

After a long hot shower and a breakfast of eggs, sausage, bacon, potatoes, toast and several mugs of hot coffee, Deacon began to feel like himself again. His strength was back, as was his focus. Once the dishes were washed and put away, he and Felix sat down in the living room to talk. It was late afternoon, but could've been any time. In Felix's place it was hard to be sure. "Fay's dreaming," Deacon told him as lights from the equalizer bounced along with an Ohio Players tune. "She's still dreaming right now."

"Is that what you think this is?" Felix had changed into black leather pants, boots and a black silk shirt open nearly to his navel. The giant gold cross still hung around his neck. "*Her* dreams?"

"Nightmares…" Deacon winced, sitting forward on the couch. "I'm tangled up in them. Like a god damn web."

"Maybe she *is* dreaming, but this isn't about her nightmares. It's about yours."

Deacon couldn't help wonder if there was much difference anymore.

SMOKE, IN CRIMSON

"Just go home, Deacon," Felix said. "It's the smart move."

"I thought I *was* home."

"No. That town's not your home, not anymore. Go back to New York, or go somewhere else—anywhere else—and make *that* your home. Just get as far away from here as possible. Let the nightmares be, and live whatever life you got left."

"What about Fay?"

"For Christ's sake, you think she's the only piece of ass on the planet?" Felix shook his head, leaned forward and snatched his cigar stub from the ashtray. "She's done, man, *done*. There's no coming back for her, hasn't been for a long time. You got to let her be, man, walk the fuck away while you still can."

"I wish it was that easy."

"It is. It's the rest that's hard." Felix stuffed the cigar into the corner of his mouth. "I know she's got a hold on you, but you broke free."

"Did I, though? Look where I am."

"Once you knock the monkey off your back you can't ever let the motherfucker ride again. You know that."

"I went back to the old place," Deacon told him. "There's a nest there."

"Good to know."

"That's it?"

Felix sighed heavily. "Look, you were in trouble and I helped you out. Fuck more you want from me?"

"Information," Deacon said.

"Go ahead."

"That was Dana's place."

"Yeah, a million years ago."

"Last I knew she was going to the desert."

Felix nodded. "That's where it should've ended for her."

"*Should've*? When was this?"

"While back, after you bailed," Felix said, looking bored. "She had a clique out in the desert in New Mexico, middle of nowhere. She was living there with the rest in a mobile home she inherited from her mother. Nobody was gonna hear screams out that far. Should've seen this place, man, there were chimes made of human bone everywhere, rain-catcher barrels full of blood, and more graves in the sand than anybody's ever gonna know for sure. You could feel the evil crawling on your skin a mile out."

"Sounds like you were there yourself."

"I was."

Deacon let the silence alone for a while.

"She ran her mouth too much about where she was headed, so even tracking her across the country wasn't hard," Felix continued a moment later. "The bitch was real strong by then. I took some damage but put her tribe down. Dumped them in the trailer and set the whole thing on fire. Then I sat there and licked my wounds, cracked a few beers and watched the motherfucker burn. It was beautiful."

SMOKE, IN **CRIMSON**

"But Dana got out?"

"She wasn't there when I hit them," Felix explained. "Maybe somebody tipped her off, maybe it was instinct. Either way, she left her minions to die."

"You knew where Fay was all these years. Why didn't you do the same to her?"

Felix didn't answer right away. On the stereo, Earth, Wind & Fire replaced The Ohio Players. "I scoped out your little love shack for a while," he said.

"But never moved on it?"

"You're still breathing aren't you?"

His answer genuinely surprised Deacon. "You telling me you held back because I was there with her?"

"Yeah, Deacon, that's what I'm telling you."

"And once I was gone? What stopped you then?"

"I got busy with shit closer to home. Fay was on the list. Still is."

"Why wasn't I?"

"I figured maybe you were salvageable." Felix plucked the cigar stub from his mouth and studied it a moment. "Your problem is you're living in the past. You think as powerful as Fay is now she'd be hanging around that old shithole of Dana's?"

"In a way, she led me there."

"Only place that bitch led you was right to my doorstep."

"Do you know where she is?"

"No, but I know where she's not." Felix set the cigar back in the ashtray then sat back. "Let me ask you something. What's your plan if you do find her?"

It was a good question, and a fair one, but Deacon didn't have much of an answer. "I don't know," he said quietly. "I want to put a stop to this, but—"

"You want to put a stop to *this*? Or you want to put a stop to *her*?"

Deacon sat forward and rubbed his eyes. "I don't know, maybe the both of us."

Music filled the silence between them for what seemed a long time. Eventually, Felix rose from his chair and walked over to one of the bookshelves. He seemed to be scanning the titles, but rather than select a book, he turned back and faced Deacon.

"In the western part of the state," Felix said, "way back in the woodlands, there's these abandoned ruins of an asylum that was shut down in the early 1960s. There are three or four buildings on the grounds, and the whole area's cordoned off, condemned. See, back in the day, this place was known for its inhumane treatment of patients, and when it came out that they were doing government-backed experiments on some of them that included torture, dosing them with huge levels of radiation and pumping them full of experimental drugs, the dump was finally shut down. A bunch of alleged *investigations* followed, but nobody gave a shit about some poor locked away mental patients, so none of that ever amounted to shit. Over the years the facility and the atrocities committed there were forgotten, lost in time. The place sat abandoned for decades, became the kind of spooky attraction teenagers hung around at night and partied in, told ghost stories, got laid, whatever. But that all stopped a year ago, and word is, for a while at least, that place wasn't quite as abandoned as people thought. There were unexplained disappearances, people and pets, and the local cops found some strange altars and rings of stone out in the woods where rituals had been performed. Then the remains of a couple homeless guys were found ripped to shreds in the forest not far from there. The official report was an animal attack of some kind, but that's bullshit. A few months ago, stories started drifting across the state to those in the know, stories about black vans in the woods and around the old asylum grounds, stories about the crazies inside. I've heard tell there's as many as thirty of these fuckers, real powerful super predators. Word is they left those woods some time ago and been hunting across the state, up into New Hampshire, even in parts of Maine. They've been leaving a lot of death in their wake, but they're hard to track because they're always on the move. To the sheep they're just a myth, one more ghost story to scare the kiddies, yeah? But those of us that know what actually goes on in this so-called reality of ours understand they're a whole lot more than that."

"Where did these fuckers come from?" Deacon asked.

Felix shrugged. "Hell?"

"I didn't ask where they were going."

"There hasn't been solid intel on that yet, but I heard from a few trusted sources it started with the survivors of a nest somewhere out west headed up by a crazy-powerful bitch with a real taste for black magic, death and destruction. Sound familiar?"

Deacon's gut clenched. "Christ."

"Dana's not what you knew, not anymore. She's way worse. She's...something else now. Once she had solid numbers they hit the road to stay undetected. Supposedly they crisscrossed the country a few times, picking up steam and bringing more into her fold to increase their numbers and power. They ran with the worst of the worst, I'm talking the darkest of the darkest groups out there, man, and it just made them—and her—stronger and stronger. When things got heavy, the remnants of their rituals were being found, and the disappearances and bodies started piling up, so they fled the west and relocated here. They found those old asylum grounds out in the woods and used them as a place to nest awhile. They're like fucking cockroaches. They always find a place to hide, but never too far. They're always close, among us, yeah? You just don't see them. Until you do. Flip the lights on and there they are, scattering. Once the remains of those bodies were found

SMOKE, IN CRIMSON

they were on the move again, this time sticking to New England. Eventually, when it gets too dangerous, they'll move on from here too. But it's clear there's another reason Dana's back, and it's got you and Fay written all over it. Unfinished business, nothing like it, yeah?"

Deacon ran a hand through his hair. "You're sure about all this?"

"Can't verify every detail just yet, but it makes sense and it's as good a story as any. Regardless, I get the chance, down they go. I'm not gonna miss that cunt twice."

"Or anybody else that gets in your way?"

"Stay the fuck out of it and you'll have nothing to worry about."

"What about Fay?"

Felix, stone-faced, said nothing.

Deacon rose to his feet. The small house was making him feel claustrophobic. He was almost himself again, but after what he'd been through it would take a few days before he was fully recovered physically and emotionally. "Are you saying Fay's running with them now?" he asked, pacing. "Is that it?"

"I always liked you, Deacon, always had a soft spot for you. But sweet Jesus you never were too fucking bright. It's like you lived the life and all you saw was Fay. Some days I'm not even sure you even truly saw her. No, I don't think she's running with them, you stupid bastard. I think she's running *from* them. But Fay's doing it her way, the way one as powerful as she is always does, by tracking those that are tracking her and waiting for her opening. This isn't about teaming up. It's about settling old scores and the consolidation of power through black magic and blood. You're right in the fucking middle of it and don't even realize it."

"Dana and Fay were friends," Deacon said. "They were tight."

"Yeah, then you showed up."

"It was the three of us at her old place and all across this city."

"Dana was in love with her too."

"So?"

"So who'd Fay end up with, genius?"

"Me."

"Right," Felix said, drawing the word out for emphasis. "Dana got cast aside. She wanted Fay, wanted it to be the two of them out in that desert."

Dana's mother has a little place out in the middle of nowhere in New Mexico.

"She wanted it to be her and Fay doing that black magic under the sun."

Dana's going to crash there a while...said I'm welcome to come stay with her as long as I want.

"Fay took a pass. First to be with you, but by the time you were out of the picture Dana was riding those highways with her crew, living the life, hunting and unstoppable. She came back for her, Deacon, and Fay took a pass again."

"Jesus," Deacon said, rattled as the realization took hold of him. "Fay was trying to get clean. That's why she wanted me to come back for her. Without me she had no chance."

"She doesn't have any chance period. Fay's been gone since she was a kid. Get that through your *fucking* head, man. She didn't lure you back here to help her get clean. She knows that's not a possibility for her and hasn't been in years."

"Okay, you've got all the answers, why did she bring me back then?"

"She didn't. Dana used her black magic to do it."

"Why? If it's Fay she wants what's that got to do with me? What the hell am I to Dana after all these years?"

"For Christ's sake, Deacon," Felix said, shaking his head with disbelief and pity. "You're the god damn *bait*."

CHAPTER **FIFTEEN**

THE FIRE CRACKLED AND popped as Felix dropped another piece of wood into the pit on the small stone patio that essentially constituted his backyard. A six-foot cement wall with curls of barbed wire running along the top had been constructed along the back of the property, providing both privacy and security. Deacon stood a few feet from the fire pit, watching a column of smoke rise into the gray sky. It was a chilly afternoon, and the crisp fresh air felt good in his lungs and against his face. Darkness was a few hours off.

"They desecrated Gina's grave, broke the stone clean in two," Deacon said. "She and Fay were...*close* for a while, but Gina never even met Dana, so why her?"

"The defilement has to take place under a particular phase of the moon, and the dirt's supposed to come from the grave of a person that knew and loved the target." Felix gazed into the fire before them and frowned. "Sorry to have to ask this, but did your sister die violently?"

"She was hit and killed by a drunk driver."

"The violence helps bring more power to the spells, makes the magic even darker. Your sister was the perfect candidate to get to you or Fay, even both of you. Was there anything left behind on the grave like booze, money or personal items, trinkets?"

"A key," Deacon said. "But Fay left that."

"How do you know for sure?"

Deacon lit a cigarette then explained about the box hidden in the wall, and the items he found inside it, including Fay's phone and the video she left on it.

"The candle was black?" Felix asked.

"Yeah, and Fay's name was scratched into the base, but in real small letters. I almost missed it. I was focused on the video, figured the rest was a bunch of nonsense."

"You said there were pieces of glass in the box."

"Yes, from a mirror."

"And there was dirt from your sister's grave in the box too?"

"There was some dirt, and the pieces of mirror were caked with dirt, but I have no way of knowing if it came from Gina's grave. All I know is ever since I opened that box I haven't felt right. Everything's been a little *off*, and it's been harder to think clearly."

SMOKE, IN CRIMSON

Felix grabbed an iron rod that leaned against the fire pit and rearranged the burning wood. The fire crackled and again sent a shower of sparks into the air before calming. "Did the dirt in the box have any unusual colorings, a yellow tint, maybe?"

"No, it just looked like dirt."

"Considering the reaction you had to it there's a good chance Goofer dust was mixed in with the dirt from Gina's grave."

"What the fuck is *Goofer dust*?"

"A hexing powder used in hoodoo. It originated in the Congo but it's used in circles here too. You don't find it much this far north, though, more in the southeastern part of the country. Dana likely incorporated it into her magic in her travels."

"What does it do?"

"Breaks your mind down little by little, drives a wedge between you and everyone else, especially people you're close to. Isolates you, slowly drives you crazy. Extended exposure can lead to death. This is heavy duty shit we're talking about here, she's not fucking around." Felix knocked over another log, and as the fire grew stronger, he put the rod aside. "The black candle you mentioned, did it look like it had been buried and dug up?"

"It's possible," Deacon said. "Everything in the box was dirty."

"Was the candle white on the bottom, or all black?"

"All black."

"Okay. You know what a spell box is, right?"

"Yeah, Fay had it for years. It has to do with casting spells."

"Reversing them too," Felix explained.

"Far as I knew all she ever used it for was a jewelry box. Dana was always more about black magic and witchcraft than we were. I know Fay dabbled in it, but she told me her interest in it was more as a piece of a larger puzzle. I didn't know much about it. I still don't."

Felix began to pace over by the back door. "You said Gina's stone was damaged. Was the dirt in front of your sister's grave disturbed too?"

"Yes."

"The black candle and broken mirror pieces were planted there. If you bury the black candle with the name of your target—your enemy—inscribed on it, along with pieces of a broken mirror, whatever evil is intended for you will be reflected back on them. My guess is Fay suspected something had been buried when the grave was desecrated, and she was right."

"So she dug up the box and removed it. Does that break the spell or something?"

"I don't know for sure. But I can tell you this. Dana felt the need to go to all the trouble of laying down a spell to protect herself from Fay. She wanted to be sure that whatever

SMOKE, IN CRIMSON

Fay came after her with would be deflected and reflected back on her." Felix folded his thick arms across his chest. "Obviously Dana thought it was a way to protect herself in case things didn't go her way. What ought to worry you is the fact that she felt the need to do that in the first place."

"Maybe Dana's not as strong as you seem to think she is after all," Deacon said.

Felix's dark eyes found him. "Or maybe Fay's become far more powerful than either of us realized."

Those words hit hard, and Deacon went quiet. He stared at the fire, lost in it.

"You need to get out of the city, go back to that cottage," Felix said a moment later. "Throw that box in the ocean— or better yet, *burn* the motherfucker—then gather up your shit and get as far away from there as possible. Leave this to them, man. Just because they made you a pawn doesn't mean you have to play their sick game. You're way over your head and out of your league on this one, trust me. Get the fuck out of Dodge while it's still possible. Go someplace else, start over again."

Deacon forced his eyes from the flames and looked at Felix. "I owe you, man," he said softly. "Thank you."

"You don't owe me shit. Just don't be there when this goes down, because I can't promise if I'm there too I won't smoke you along with the rest, you dig?"

"I dig."

"This is it, Deacon. There won't be any more chances. *This*," Felix said, thumping his chest with a fist. "This is the life you got left."

Deacon could think of nothing more to say. His old friend was right, and they both knew it.

The rest was darkness and lies.

PART
TWO

"Your blood was always whispering, even if you didn't want to listen."

—Tom Piccirilli, *November Mourns*

CHAPTER **SIXTEEN**

THE OCEAN BROUGHT HIM back. Once again, Deacon found himself on the sand, the wind in his hair as he watched waves steadily roll into shore. The rain had stopped but it was still gray and overcast, with a chill in the air that signaled harsher weather would soon follow in the coming weeks and months. But for now, there was something tranquil and oddly comforting about the wind and ocean sounds, and returning to that modest stretch of beach he knew so well. Such moments of reflection caused Deacon to wonder if he'd ever really left this place at all, until his sour stomach and painful joints and muscles reminded him that the ordeal of the last few days could have easily ended with his destruction.

With Felix's words of wisdom replaying in his head, Deacon turned his back to the sea winds and trekked across the sand then up the dunes. At their summit, he clearly saw not only Lauren's cottage nearby, but the same rundown tow truck he'd seen a few days ago was parked diagonally across the street from it. Albert sat behind the wheel, devouring a sandwich as he watched the cottage.

Deacon made sure he crossed directly in front of the truck so he'd draw Albert's attention, and when he did and their eyes met, he saw the man chuckle with amusement.

Exhausted and wanting nothing more than to get back to Fay's cottage and rest a while, Deacon forced himself to stop and glare at him until Albert's expression became one more closely associated with annoyance.

He rolled his window down. "What?" he asked, still chomping bites of sandwich and chewing noisily. "This is a public road. I ain't doin' nothin'."

Deacon continued to stare.

Albert tossed what remained of his sandwich out the window, and complaining bitterly, started his truck. As he pulled away he flipped Deacon the finger then sped off along the beach road.

Once the tow truck was out of sight, Deacon continued on his way, glancing at Lauren's place as he went. It looked dark and as if no one was home, yet that clearly hadn't discouraged Albert.

It's not my problem, he thought. *It can't be, I have my own things to—*

Something in Deacon's peripheral vision caught his attention. In the distance, Stevie was standing out in front

SMOKE, IN CRIMSON

of Fay's cottage, leaned against his cruiser with his arms folded across his chest.

Great, now I get to deal with this fucking guy.

He considered going the other way but Stevie had already seen him and offered a tentative wave. Deacon walked on, not acknowledging him until he got within a few feet.

"Hi," Stevie said, pushing away from the cruiser.

"What's up? There something wrong?"

"Came by a couple times but you haven't been here for a few days."

"Okay, and?"

"Where you been?"

"Why do you think that's any of your business?"

"God Almighty, why are you always such an asshole?"

"Look, man, I've had a long couple days and I'm tired."

"Yeah, looks like it."

"Then be a pal and give me a break, huh? Fuck do you want?"

"Unbelievable." Stevie sighed and shook his head. "I was just checking on you."

"That's very sweet, but I'm fine. Did you go inside?"

"I don't have keys to the place, but I did look through the windows to make sure you weren't there and, well, let's go with *incapacitated*. I expected you'd be here until something broke with Fay."

"We all have to deal with disappointments in life, Stevie."

"Look, wiseass, Mr. Dillon let you stay here because he—"

"You're here on his behalf, is that it?"

"No, I—"

"Then it's none of your concern."

"You're supposed to be here in case Fay comes back or makes contact. We both know Mr. Dillon isn't letting you stay here so you can use the place like some sort of flophouse whenever you feel like it."

"So you weren't checking on me, you were checking *up* on me. What a stunner."

"Maybe for once in your life you could try to be responsible and actually follow through on something you agreed to. Maybe even lay off the hooch and drugs for two minutes and be dependable. How's that sound? That sound like a plan to you?"

"Did you just say *hooch*? What are you, a hundred years old?" Deacon couldn't prevent a slight laugh. It beat crying. "Stevie, listen to me. I'm really tired, so I'm going inside to get some rest. My arrangement is with *Lance*. Stay out of it."

"If you think I'm about to watch you take advantage of him and this situation—"

"Don't you have anything better to do? Right this second, I bet somewhere in this town someone's littering. A kid's probably shoplifting a candy bar. It's an out of control crime spree. Go do your job, such as it is."

"At least I have one."

SMOKE, IN **CRIMSON**

"Yes, annoying the fuck out of me apparently."

Stevie took a step to the side, placing himself between Deacon and the back door. "Seriously, have you found out anything more, anything at all?"

"No, but I *can* confirm you're still a fucking clown." Deacon lit a cigarette. "Whatever I was up to, am up to or will be up to in the future, I'll discuss directly with Lance. Just like Fay, it has nothing to do with you. Get that through your head. The whole love-struck pining thing is embarrassing beyond belief at your age."

"You're one to talk."

"Jesus, do you really think my situation with Fay is anything like yours? You've got a wife and kids at home, try acting like it."

Stevie took a step closer. "Careful," he said evenly.

"Careful isn't really my thing."

"Don't talk about my family."

"Only one I'm talking about is you."

"I mean it, Deacon. Watch your mouth."

"You watch it. It's about to say something. Ready? Watching? *Fuck off.*"

Hands on hips, Stevie turned away. "Why do you hate me?" he said so quietly it was barely audible above the sound of the wind. "What did I ever do to you?"

"You hassled me constantly, treated me like shit. And all because I was with Fay and you weren't. It wasn't my fault she wanted me and didn't want you, Stevie, but you took it out on me for years. You're still doing it." A sudden wave of guilt shook and weakened Deacon's anger. "The worst part is you'll *never* know how lucky you are to have what you do *instead* of her. I don't hate you, man, I never did. I feel sorry for you."

Stevie spun back around and pointed a finger at Deacon. "Fay and I are *friends*! I'm a happily married man with a family. I've always cared about her, but in a purely platonic way. I look out for her and—"

"Stevie," Deacon said. "You want to look out for somebody? Go talk to Albert, the guy that works at the gas station and drives the tow truck. He's been stalking Lauren Petty—or whatever her name is now—and giving her son a hard time."

"Lauren DiCicco?" he asked, pointing in the direction of her cottage.

"Yeah, that's it. You want to do some good? Go talk to that pile of shit Albert and set his ass straight." Deacon took a couple quick drags on his cigarette, dropped it to the ground and stepped on it. "Don't worry about me or what I'm up to. Go worry about him instead."

"I'll look into it, but regarding this other business—"

"There is no other business. If anything happens or I hear anything, you and Lance will be the first to know." Deacon hesitated near the back porch. "Okay?"

SMOKE, IN CRIMSON

Rather than reply, Stevie sauntered back to the cruiser, got in and drove off.

🔥

SUMMER WAS OVER. EXCEPT for assorted stragglers, the tourists had gone home and the area had returned to that curious period of time after the hotter months were gone but fall had not yet arrived.

Two little girls in neon swimsuits wandered along the shoreline. No more than seven or eight, they padded through the moist sand giggling and talking, oblivious to the gentle waves licking their bare feet.

With a joint dangling from his lips, Deacon watched them from the windows overlooking the beach until they became ambiguous colored dots on an otherwise empty horizon. Sipping his vodka, he wondered who those girls might one day become. There were so many experiences out there lying in wait with the power to either destroy or recreate them as women. The idea that such innocents could already be doomed in many ways seemed the epitome of evil.

Horrible visions haunted him, there in the cottage, relentless and obscene.

"What are you staring at?"

Deacon turned. Fay stood in the kitchen, arms folded across her breasts. Clad in nothing more than an old sweatshirt of his, though busty, at first glance Fay's petite frame and hair chopped short reminded him of a young boy. Visions of their earlier lovemaking flooded his mind. He remembered her first in the most vulnerable and trusting position—eyes wide, legs spread, ankles high, delicate toes pointed like a ballerina—but found himself wishing those pictures conjured different emotions in him.

Things were changing. *He* was changing. Irreparably he hoped.

Rather than answer her question Deacon said, "I didn't realize you were awake."

Fay continued to stand there with her arms crossed; a demanding, determined look on her face. It was time for a joust. Combat without contact, argument without anger, life without breath. That's what things had come to in recent weeks. They both knew Deacon was drifting, struggling, but neither had any idea what to do about it. They hadn't fully arrived at that reality yet. They were still too busy creating their own.

A tracer of anguish lingered in the air like a foul odor. Deacon considered his options. He chose silence.

Along the backside of the property, on the street, a trash truck rumbled by, filling the silence for him and throttling the cottage in the process. Glassware and other items rattled and shook until it had gone.

"I hate those fucking things," Fay muttered.

SMOKE, IN CRIMSON

Deacon, on the other hand, found it difficult to hide his amusement. Was there anything filthier than garbage trucks? Certainly never associated with romance or intrigue, they instead served as inelegant and jarring metaphors indicative of the hollow, dark, violently unclean dreams that haunted them both.

Fay sauntered into the room with the confident stride of the predator she was, fully aware that her sudden presence was both disturbing and turning him on. She plucked the joint from Deacon's mouth, took a deep hit and smiled ever-so-slightly, a spider atop her web grinning at her favorite fly.

Like them, the cottage had developed a deciduous air. Similar to the horns of certain animals that fell away during particular seasons or stages of development, only to remerge stronger and more powerful, their life together was in constant flux. It was nothing new really, even tucked away in their alleged hideaway, burrowing deep into each other and the darkness between them. Perhaps it was just more blatant now.

Ice cubes clinked in Deacon's glass, and he was grateful that at least for the time being, his thoughts were his own.

"You look yummy without any clothes on," Fay said, floating over to the couch and taking the joint with her. "Giving a free show today?"

"That's your thing. I was just being careless, I guess." Deacon retreated from the windows to a wicker chair and sat down. As he crossed his legs he noticed the small fine hairs that ran from his lower calf to upper thigh. Against the backdrop of his tanned skin, they made him feel like a great fuzzy peach. "Besides, there's no one out there anyway."

Settled on the couch, Fay sat back, leaving her legs open as if mistakenly.

Deacon looked to the tall windows again, but could feel her eyes tickling the back of his neck. He took a swallow of vodka. It burned his throat. He was convinced the sensation was imagined. Liquor could no longer harm him. He was immune, a cockroach reinventing itself in the residue of progressively lethal toxins, each one targeted at a new, more resilient generation.

There was only one addiction that could destroy him now.

"You're slipping away," she said.

"I'm tired, Fay. I shouldn't be so tired. I'm a young man."

She took a long pull on the joint. "Not anymore."

"What do you want from me? What else could I possibly give you?"

"The truth," Fay said, coughing out a cloud of smoke.

"I've never lied to you."

"You're lying right now." She took another hit. "You want to run. Even after everything we've been through, all we've accomplished, you want to run."

"*Accomplished*, are you insane?"

Fay threw her head back and laughed her bawdy laugh.

SMOKE, IN CRIMSON

It soon morphed into another cough, which lasted so long Deacon held out his drink as an offering. She rose from the couch, went to him and took a couple sips. As she handed the glass back, she leaned closer, her crotch near the side of Deacon's face. "How could I be anything *but* insane?" She returned the joint to his mouth. "We're powerful, but it slowly eats at our minds and transforms them into something else. It's both a gift and a price we pay."

"It's only one of the prices we pay," he reminded her, sliding his hand around onto her bare ass. Although he very much wanted to leave his hand there, to continue to cup and squeeze each sculpted half and to allow his fingers to slide between them and eventually inside her, something stopped him. "And it's no gift."

Taking his chin in her hand, Fay gently lifted it until their eyes met. "Yes, baby, it is," she whispered. "It allows us to see and hear and think and do *amazing* things. You can't even begin to comprehend how powerful we'll be one day, the extraordinary things we'll experience and the countless lives we'll live. The world is ours."

Laughing aloud for the first time in days, he slapped her ass and powered down the remainder of his drink.

Fay arched an eyebrow. "Are you laughing at me?"

"As fast as I can.

She showcased her sexiest pout.

"We're not gods, Fay. We never will be."

"Given the right circumstances, we all are."

Deacon raised his empty glass. "Here's to the politics of language."

"You prefer to think of us as machines? It's easier for you that way, I suppose."

"Not machines," he said softly. A thin line of sweat collected in his hair caused it to itch. As he scratched, almost absently, he visualized dozens of ravenous insects devouring his scalp. "Just big lumbering apes that somewhere along the line convinced ourselves we're something greater."

"And you call *me* pretentious?" Fay pulled away. "You're stoned."

"So are you."

"Leave then," she told him, as if daring him to do so. "Go ahead."

Squinting through the ever-growing cloud of smoke, and the montage of pictures clogging his mind's eye, Deacon finally located her in the kitchen. Leaned against the kitchen table, Fay defiantly pulled the sweatshirt off and tossed it aside. Like always, his eyes were drawn to the scars first. Her breasts were littered with them. She told others the same lie she'd initially told him, that she'd had a breast reduction as a teenager performed by an incompetent plastic surgeon her father took her to, and that the scars were a constant reminder of a botched job, nothing more.

SMOKE, IN CRIMSON

As was usually the case with Fay, the reality was much worse.

He looked away from the scars and settled on her eyes, realizing they'd suddenly taken on a different appearance, no longer sleepy and stoned, but fierce and deadly. In that moment, in her complete nudity, she looked more creature than human, more dangerous than sexy, yet somehow still impossibly erotic.

"Do you think I'd stop you?" she asked. "I'd never force you to stay with me, you know that."

"You mean even though you *could*, is that it?"

"Yes," she answered in a cold, quiet tone. "Even though I could."

He closed his eyes and saw her plunging the blade into the bodies of countless strangers again and again, the spray of blood spattering her nude body, her mouth and chin and throat coated with it, eyes wild as she rode the corpse, breasts bouncing, viscera flying, pussy grinding.

God help me.

"Little late for that, baby."

Deacon opened his eyes. He'd have sworn he heard Fay utter those words, but she'd already slipped from sight. The kitchen was empty, his sweatshirt on the floor the only indication she'd been there at all.

As a single tear rolled the length of his cheek, for reasons he wasn't entirely sure of, Deacon thought about those little girls again, happily walking the beach in their bright swimsuits. That innocence…he'd known it once… hadn't he?

No answer came.

Rather than wipe his face, Deacon let the tear remain, and in the deafening silence of the cottage, finished the joint the same way he began it.

Alone.

ONCE INSIDE THE COTTAGE, a quick look around revealed no one had been there in Deacon's absence. Nothing had been touched or moved, and the only remnants of recent occupation were his own. Like the time capsule it was, his history here with and without Fay stood still, undisturbed until his return.

Deacon stood in the kitchen, taking it all in.

Empty alcohol bottles, the ashtray brimming with cigarette butts and roaches, the spell box and its contents on the table, the wall phone on the counter exactly where he'd left it, the gaping hole in the sheetrock a reminder of the mess he'd made uncovering it.

The woodstove had of course gone cold, which left the cottage quite chilly, so Deacon loaded it with wood and got it going as quickly as he could.

SMOKE, IN CRIMSON

Once the fire was raging and he'd gathered all the spent bottles and trash and thrown them away, he emptied the ashtray then sat at the table and checked his phone.

One missed call and one new voicemail, both assigned to Lance Dillon.

According to the timestamp the call was placed the night before. Rather than listen to it Deacon focused on the last unopened bottle of vodka before him as his mind drifted to Fay's nearby drug stash. As always, both whispered assurances everything would be fine, all he had to do was trust them.

Deacon lit a cigarette instead. As he pulled the smoke deep into his lungs, he felt his nerves settle. Exhaling through his nose, he defiantly stared at the bottle. Their battle of wills had resumed.

Need was often a horrible thing…

All you have to do is pour and drink, relief in two simple steps.

A lonely thing…

Leaving his phone on the table, Deacon hit the speaker then pushed away from the table. As the voicemail played, he gathered his things and stuffed them back into his knapsack.

"Deacon, hi, it's Lance. I'm just touching base to see if you need anything else or if you've procured any *leads*, as it were. Sadly, I've heard nothing more since we last spoke, and as I'm sure you can understand I'm worried out of my mind at this point. I mean, there should've been some word from Fay by now, don't you think? How difficult is it in today's day and age to make a quick call or send a text, an email, something—anything—it just doesn't make sense to me that she'd stay away without any contact for this amount of time. At any rate, I'll be in the office or out on work projects throughout the day, but please call me back should you have any further needs. Obviously if you hear or learn anything more, please contact me right away, day or night, regardless of the time. I just..." Lance's voice caught in his throat. "I just want to know my little girl is all right, Deacon. I *need* to know she's all right."

The call ended.

Deacon hit the speaker button, deleted the voicemail then tossed his knapsack on the chair and eyed the table. He'd already made the decision to leave. Felix was right. There was nothing for him here but pain and destruction. The only thing he was still mulling over in his head was whether or not to leave his findings displayed on the kitchen table for Lance to discover and decipher on his own, or if he should put it all back in the wall and hide it away again.

He picked up Fay's phone, held it in his hand a moment.

They're coming...

The only option that made any sense was to get the hell out of this town and never look back. He'd promised himself that once before, and nearly made it. This time there would

SMOKE, IN CRIMSON

be no turning back, no returns, no—as Felix put it—*stumbles*, not from this runner. Whatever showdown Fay and whatever was left of Dana had instore for each other was their business, not his, and no amount of hauntings were going to drag him into the middle of it.

Deacon slipped her phone into his jacket pocket. He'd leave the rest for Lance, let him sort it out and try to make sense of it on his own.

The only other bit of business he needed to attend to was Gina's grave, but there wasn't anything he could do about it at that point. He didn't have the funds to get the stone fixed or removed, but maybe at some point down the road, once he reestablished himself somewhere and had a job, he could eventually save enough to get it taken care of.

He could feel his sister watching him from the deep shadows in his mind.

Run, little brother.

Memories of life before all this came to him. They always arrived at the strangest times, and were rarely anything profound in and of themselves. Instead, they seemed to be nothing more than insignificant moments from a distant, blurred past: a quick vision of him with Gina and their parents at the dinner table, silverware clicking against plates in the otherwise silent room, as if in code, playing in the yard with his plastic toy soldiers and the way the grass felt against his bare feet and between his toes, riding on the back of Gina's bicycle before he had his own, his sister pedaling furiously as they sped through town on their way to the general store to pick up something for their mother or to get a few pieces of candy or maybe a comic book, the way the breeze felt in his hair, against his face as they glided along, and how in those surreal moments he'd never been so free. It was as if somehow, he and Gina had become other people, carefree and alive in ways they rarely experienced. In those wonderful and exhilarating snippets of time when it was just the two of them and that bicycle and the town flying by all around them, it was as if nothing could stop them, interfere or even slow them down.

Were we ever really that happy, Gina?

Sometimes we were. I'm sure of it.

But the rest of the time, what then?

It was sorrow, only we never realized it.

Are you sure we didn't?

We had nothing to compare it to. We thought it was normal.

Maybe it was. Maybe it is.

Maybe so, little brother, but it doesn't matter, not anymore.

I think it matters more than we want to admit. Why is it so hard most days for me to remember our lives then? Why can't I remember Mom and Dad more clearly?

Mom and Dad—

SMOKE, IN CRIMSON

Their faces, I—sometimes I can't see their faces no matter how hard I try.

Can you still see mine?

"Yes," Deacon said aloud, though he was still staring at the table. "I sometimes feel you around me, but I never feel them. I wish I could, I—"

Do you? Do you really?

They made mistakes. They weren't perfect but they tried, they—

Our lives are our own, Deacon.

What have I done? What the fuck have I done?

You're no martyr, little brother. Not yet.

What's my excuse then? There was no strange shadow man watching our house, waiting to lead me astray.

We didn't need the Devil in a cloak. We had Fay waiting for us.

She's just a lost soul, too damaged to find her way back in the dark.

No, Deacon, Fay is the dark now…and so are you.

Fay once said he needed to be cautious regarding internal dialogues. Sometimes people chalked them up to having conversations with themselves, she explained, while others believed it was guardian angels or deceased loved ones attempting to guide them.

"But that voice in your head?" Fay told him. "It usually isn't who you think it is."

They're coming…

Deacon grabbed his phone and hit Lance's number. It went straight to voicemail.

"Lance Dillon here, leave your message and I'll be back in touch."

Rather than leave a message, Deacon disconnected the call. He knew his number would show up on Lance's phone as a missed call. When Lance called back he'd answer and tell him he was out, already gone and there was nothing more he could do. Or maybe he wouldn't answer at all. Maybe he'd slip away like he always did. No goodbyes or explanations, just a straight-up vanishing act, a fucking ghost slipping into the mist from which he'd come.

Angrily, Deacon snatched the bottle of vodka from the table and jammed it into his knapsack. Rubbing the stone in his pocket with his free hand, he took a hard drag on his cigarette and drifted over to the tall windows. The beach was deserted.

He pictured himself walking into the wind out there, trudging along the sand, his knapsack slung over his shoulder and this nightmare in his rearview. But first, he needed sleep.

One more night, he thought. *Then first thing in the morning I'm gone.*

For a moment he thought it might be best if he hunkered down in the dunes as he had his first night back in town, but that wind was cold and raw and the comforting

SMOKE, IN **CRIMSON**

heat already pulsing off the woodstove convinced him otherwise. He next considered the bedroom. Enticing as flopping down on that bed and curling up under the blankets was, Deacon didn't want to step foot in that room ever again, much less try to sleep there, so he quickly dismissed that option as well.

After another drag on his cigarette, he put it out in the ashtray on the coffee table then sunk down onto the couch. The horrors of the last few days seemed to come through the walls, up through the floor and down from the ceiling, engulfing him from every direction like the bad dreams they were.

It's just one of her nightmares, and this one's all yours.

The horrible cellar in Boston flashed across his mind's eye...

She's in the midst of it right now.

That freak's cloudy, reptilian eyes gazing up at him through the darkness...

We're *in the midst of it right now.*

"Wake up, Fay," Deacon whispered.

He was afraid, because he knew all too well what was waiting for him, but he could no longer keep the exhaustion at bay. Sliding onto his side, Deacon stretched out on the couch, and unable to prevent his eyes from closing, let the darkness take him.

CHAPTER **SEVENTEEN**

IN THE MIDMORNING LIGHT of a new day, a lone boy ran along the beach, his dog galloping beside him as the two played and pranced across the sand, solitary figures on a long, otherwise desolate, windy stretch of shoreline. A choppy ocean roiled beneath an ominous canopy of black clouds, the white-capped waves crashing shore as seagulls squawked, soaring overhead and occasionally dropping down to the surf. Gliding toward their destinations, wings spread wide as they tilted back and forth, they rode the cold winds in a constant struggle with the elements.

A ways down the beach, near the stone jetty, a teenage couple emerged from the road, stepping down onto the sand and watching the water. The girl's head rested on the boy's shoulder, her arms wrapped tightly around his midsection. The boy had an arm around her waist, his hand stuffed deep into the back pocket of her jeans. Although the girl appeared

GREG F. GIFUNE

to be hopelessly in love, she was in fact only smitten. The boy was truly in love, but tried to hide it behind a tough guy veneer he'd been taught was manly. In a year or so, she would break his heart and move on, but in that moment their union seemed indestructible. In time, she would come to regret losing him, and realize that many men were not like him, not as thoughtful and loving and loyal. She would have a life with someone she learned to love and a family that sustained her, though for the remainder of her years she would secretly yearn for that wonderful boyfriend from her high school years and always consider leaving him the biggest mistake of her life. After a lengthy and painful period, the boy would find someone new, someone he could also love and who loved him back, but he would spend his life wondering about the girl, whatever became of her, and what might have been. Even decades later, as a happily long-married father and grandfather, he would sometimes think of her and that day on the beach they watched the ocean as a storm rolled in. For the rest of his life, a part of him would miss her. A part of him would love her. And while both would have long and involved lives apart from each other, nothing could ever recreate the way they felt in that exact moment in time. They would never again be so carefree, or know anything like the peace that filled them that day.

The rain moved in, gently at first, sweeping about in a misty spray before becoming a downpour. Visions of the

SMOKE, IN CRIMSON

beach dissolved, though the world still looked and felt like a dream, an old film projected across a faded screen, even after Deacon awakened flat on his back on the couch. He blinked, rubbed his eyes then watched the ceiling blend into focus. Raindrops drummed the roof and tapped at the windowpanes as occasional gusts of wind shook the cottage, but he was warm and comfortable beneath the heavy blankets. Deacon loved awakening to the sound of rain, he had since he was a young child. It was one of the few times he felt something akin to serenity. Pulling the blankets in tighter around him, he yawned and fantasized about lounging there all day.

The night before he'd come awake on the back porch, soaked to the bone and huddled beneath his jacket, his knapsack used as a makeshift pillow. He never meant to wind up there but was drunk, stoned and tripping, and after becoming disoriented in the storm, stumbled onto the porch in the middle of the night. Some time later he was discovered by Larry the dog, whose cold wet nose and sloppy tongue shocked Deacon from unconsciousness. The first thing he saw was that long nose and those big soulful eyes as Larry's tail wagged and thumped the nearby wall. It was then that he noticed Lauren standing in the doorway, her face riddled with concern, confusion and trepidation.

"Deacon?" she asked. "Do you have any idea what time it is? What are you doing? How long have you been out here?"

Embarrassed and exhausted, he tried to leave but could barely stand on his own, so Lauren insisted he come inside. He'd been there since, sleeping it off on her couch, straight through the night until now, the following morning.

A relentless need to urinate forced him up from under the blankets. He was still in his clothes and his knapsack was on the floor near the foot of the couch, his jacket draped across it. Deacon groggily swung his feet around to the floor. His socks were still on but his boots had been left alongside the couch. Rather than stand he leaned over far enough to reach his jacket, snatched it up then went through the pockets until he found his cigarettes and lighter. He shook a cigarette free.

"What are you doing?"

Suddenly Henry was moving though the kitchen into the front room, stopping just a few feet short of the couch. The layout of their cottage was nearly identical to Fay's place. "Morning," Deacon said in a raspy voice. "I was just gonna have a smoke."

The little boy folded his arms across his chest. "Gross."

"You're right, it's a filthy habit."

"Then how come you do it?"

Christ. "It's not too smart, is it?"

"You better do that outside. My mom won't like you doing that in here."

Deacon nodded, took the cigarette from his mouth and returned it to the pack.

SMOKE, IN CRIMSON

"How long are you gonna sleep on our couch for?" Henry asked.

"I didn't mean to—I mean—I just wound up here last night is all."

Henry frowned.

"You think it'd be all right if I used your bathroom?" Deacon asked. "I got to pee so bad I can taste it."

Though it was clear he was trying not to laugh, Henry said, "You can do that outside too."

Deacon casually looked over his shoulder as rain spattered against the windows. "Awful nasty out there."

Henry's serious face returned. "So?"

"Okay, pal." Deacon sighed and reached for his boots. "Your house, your rules."

The boy seemed impressed with this assessment. Slowly, he moved a bit closer. "Mom said you were sick but you don't look sick to me. You just look weird."

"Good to know, thanks." Deacon pulled on his boots.

"Are you drunk?"

"No."

"Were you drunk before?"

"Last night, I guess. Look, I don't think we should be—"

"Are you a druggie?"

"What? I don't—what does that mean?"

"Like you don't know," Henry scoffed. "Drugs and alcohol are bad for you."

"Yeah, just say no, right? Do they still say that? *Just say no*?"

"What are you talking about?"

Deacon stifled a yawn. "I just mean you should stay away from them."

"I do," Henry said. "You should stay away from them."

Fuck. Deacon rubbed his eyes. A slight headache was already setting in behind them and his neck was stiff and sore. "So where's your mom at?"

Arms still folded across his chest, Henry remained silent, apparently unsure if he should answer the question or not. "On her phone talking to work," he finally said. "She's taking the day off because *you're* here."

"She doesn't have to do that. I'll be out of your way this morning."

"You're leaving? You mean back to the other cottage?"

"No, I'm leaving town."

"Why?"

"You don't want hear about it. Listen, about that bathroom—"

"Are you coming back or leaving for good?"

"For good, Henry, I'm leaving for good."

The boy dropped his arms to his sides. "Yeah," he said. "That's what I figured."

He didn't have a lot of experience with kids, but Deacon was baffled. One minute Henry was upset with him for even

SMOKE, IN CRIMSON

being there and the next seemed disappointed he was leaving. Unsure of what to say, he was grateful when he saw Lauren emerge from the hallway and cross through the kitchen into the front room.

Dressed comfortably in faded jeans, a sweatshirt and slipper socks, she offered a guarded smile. "Hey."

Riddled with embarrassment, Deacon forced a smile of his own. "Hi."

"Henry, would you go feed Larry, please? He's been sitting over by his bowl for the last half hour waiting for breakfast."

His eyes still trained on Deacon, the boy shuffled off to the kitchen.

"Are you okay?" Lauren asked once her son had gone.

Deacon pushed himself to his feet. "I'm so sorry I wandered over here in the dark, I didn't really know where I was with the storm and all and—"

"Tough night, I take it?"

"A difficult few days, actually, thanks for taking me in."

"I couldn't very well leave you out there in the storm."

They held each other's gaze a moment. "Henry said you were calling in to work," Deacon said, snapping the spell. "You don't have to do that. I'll be out of here in—"

"It's no big deal." Lauren absently hooked a strand of auburn hair behind her ear. "I've got some personal days I need to take before the end of the year or I lose them."

"Doesn't Henry have school?"

"I'm keeping him home today," she explained. "He woke up last night when I brought you inside. In such a small space it's hard to be quiet sometimes, and it was really late so, what the hell, I decided we'd both take the day off."

Deacon nodded guiltily. "If I could just use your bathroom real quick I'll get myself together and be out of here in a few minutes."

Lauren hesitated. "I heard you tell Henry just now you're leaving town."

"That's where I was headed last night."

"Given your condition it's a miracle you made it as far as you did." Her pale blue eyes continued searching his. "Want to talk about it?"

"There's nothing to talk about. I'm just a disaster."

"Something tells me it's a whole lot more complicated than that."

"Sweet, funny, smart *and* perceptive," Deacon said, shuffling his feet. "How are you single again?"

Lauren playfully rolled her eyes and nibbled her lower lip. "I *know*, right?"

"Sorry, but I really have to use your bathroom."

"Yeah, you've got that whole pee-pee dance thing going on." She jerked a thumb toward the hallway on the far side of the kitchen. "Down the hall on the right."

"Thanks," he said, starting in that direction.

SMOKE, IN CRIMSON

"You don't have to leave this morning if you don't want to. That storm's still going strong. If you'd rather not go back to Fay's place for some reason you're welcome to stay here a while. You can at least wait until the weather clears."

"Every time I see you it seems all I do is say thanks and sorry."

"I could do some awkward flirting and make an ass of myself again if that'll make you feel better. Apparently I'm really good at it. Who knew?"

With a smile, Deacon pointed toward the hallway. "I really need to…"

"There's aspirin in the medicine cabinet," she said, stepping out of his way.

Seconds later Deacon stood staring at himself in the bathroom mirror. Horribly pale, hair a tangled mess, eyes glazed, bloodshot and saddled with black bags, he looked even worse than he felt. After a long pee he splashed cold water on his face, grabbed the tube of toothpaste on the counter, squirted some on his finger and quickly brushed it over his teeth, gums and tongue. After rinsing with a small paper cup from a dispenser next to the sink, he grabbed the aspirin from the cabinet, swallowed three then had another look at his reflection.

You look like you're dying.

He combed his hair with his fingers as best he could then pulled it all back into a ponytail and fastened it with a rubber band he found on his wrist.

Leave them alone.

He drew a deep breath then slowly exhaled. His chest wheezed like a chew toy.

They can't save you. She *can't save you.*

When Deacon left the bathroom, he found Lauren making breakfast. He stepped out onto the porch, quickly smoked a cigarette then joined her in the kitchen.

"Hungry?" she asked. "Pancakes sound good?"

"Think I'll stick to coffee this morning, but thanks."

"Sit." Lauren motioned to the table. "How do you take it?"

"Black," he said, sliding a chair out from the table. "No sugar."

"Rugged."

"That's me." He slowly sank down onto the chair.

"Sure you're not hungry?" Lauren poured him a mug and set it before him. "Some hot food in your stomach might do you some good."

"Maybe later," he said, gripping the mug with both hands. The warmth felt good. He brought the steaming mug closer so he could feel it against his face, and then took a sip. It felt even better going down. "That might be the best cup of coffee I've ever had."

Larry, having finished his breakfast, scampered over to Deacon, rested his chin on his leg and looked up at him lovingly.

SMOKE, IN CRIMSON

"Larry likes you," Lauren said as she continued preparing breakfast.

Deacon gently scratched the dog's head. "I have a feeling he likes everybody."

"Not Albert," Henry said as he returned to the kitchen and slid into the chair next to Deacon's. Larry curled up at their feet. "Just about everybody else though."

"Speaking of Albert, Officer Avado stopped by yesterday," Lauren said. "He told us he'd spoken to you and you'd told him about the trouble we were having."

"I hope that was all right," Deacon said. "I've known Stevie for years."

"Of course, it's just an awkward situation because apparently, technically, Albert hasn't broken any laws yet." Lauren got something from the refrigerator then returned to the stove. "Being a nuisance is annoying but not necessarily a crime."

"I just thought he could have a chat with the guy, get him to leave you two alone."

"He said he'd have a talk with him. I guess he just wanted to hear exactly what had happened first, but he assured me Albert wouldn't be any more trouble after he spoke to him." She poured pancake batter into a skillet then grabbed a spatula from one of the drawers. "And he told Henry how to handle things from now on too, didn't he, Henry."

"Yup, I'm supposed to tell him if he bothers me my mom's calling the police."

"Good." Deacon gave Henry a quick wink.

"I thought Deacon was gonna beat him up the other day," Henry said, laughing lightly. "That would be funny."

"No, we use our words," Lauren said. "Not violence."

"Yeah but sometimes—"

"Henry, we've been over this. There's nothing funny about violence. Besides, violence is for weak people, smart people use their intellect. *No violence.*"

Henry looked at Deacon and shook his head like that was about the dumbest thing he'd ever heard. Sipping his coffee, Deacon leaned closer. "It would've probably been pretty funny."

"What about Dad?" Henry asked suddenly.

"What about him?"

"He used violence. He was a soldier."

Lauren took a plate down from the cupboard. "He was at war, that's different."

"How come it's different?"

"Sweetie, it just is," Lauren said, sliding a stack of pancakes onto the plate.

"Deacon, do you think it's different?" Henry asked.

Deacon sat back and drank his coffee. "I'm gonna stay clear of this one if you don't mind, pal."

Lauren slid the plate onto Henry's place, along with a small tub of butter and a bottle of syrup. "Eat your breakfast."

SMOKE, IN CRIMSON

As she turned back to the stove she gave Deacon a playful smirk.

Awful as he felt at that moment, there was something sweet about being there with them. Foreign though welcome territory, it was a life Deacon had never known and likely never would. Watching that little boy eat his pancakes, his loyal dog fast asleep at his feet while Lauren lovingly prepared her son's breakfast before joining them at the table to enjoy her own, he'd never felt such a connection to something he knew virtually nothing about. But soon, the guilt returned, as he knew it would.

You don't belong here.

"Do you play Xbox?" Henry asked rather suddenly.

"You mean like video games? I never have, no."

This seemed beyond Henry's comprehension. "You never played Xbox *ever?*"

Deacon had another swallow of coffee. "Nope, never have."

Laughing, Henry continued devouring his pancakes. "That's unbelievable!"

Lauren smiled at Deacon knowingly. "Well maybe after breakfast you can show Deacon yours and see what he thinks."

"I can teach you how to play if you want," Henry said. "Do you like basketball?"

"Sure, but I don't know if I'll be here, I…" When he saw the disappointment on the boy's face, Deacon looked to Lauren. She did her best to suppress a smile and raised her eyebrows as if to say: *Well?* "All right, I'm in," he told Henry. "But you've got to promise to go easy on me."

"Okay, but only at first though." Henry smiled mischievously. "Then I get to crush you."

Feigning shock, Deacon looked to Lauren as he pointed at her son. "Wait, what?"

Laughing, Lauren leaned to her side, playfully bumping shoulders with Henry.

"Xbox," Deacon muttered. "All right then."

CURLED UP IN A nearby chair with a novel, Lauren watched Deacon and Henry on the couch, Larry sound asleep between them as they played Xbox. She knew Deacon was horribly hungover, and she was touched that he'd taken the time to play games with her son. What she assumed would be a few minutes had become several hours, and Deacon actually seemed to be enjoying himself and not in such a hurry to leave. A usually quiet and solitary boy, Henry didn't have many friends and it often took him long periods of time to warm up to people he didn't know. But there was something different about Deacon, and the way her son was drawn to him so quickly. She hadn't seen Henry so happy and talkative in a very long time.

SMOKE, IN CRIMSON

There was also something noticeably different about the way Henry played and interacted with Deacon specifically. Lauren had spent countless hours playing video games with him too, though for her they were a labor of love. She never particularly enjoyed them. They were just a way to spend some time together. To a certain degree Deacon was likely doing the same, playing more for Henry's sake than his own, but it was Henry she focused on, his gleeful abandon. Lauren wasn't sure she'd ever seen him like that, except perhaps when he played with Larry on the beach.

At one point Henry caught her watching. She gave a little wave. He waved back, his face alight with a smile as he returned his attention to the game. "Three-pointer!"

"And nothing but net," Deacon said, shaking his head. "You're mopping the floor with me again. I'm really bad at this."

"It's okay. I wasn't very good when I first started either. You'll get better."

Lauren pretended to read her book, but she couldn't take her eyes from them. She and her husband had never enjoyed such moments, Henry was too young and Ron died too soon, but she'd imagined them, hoped for them, and wondered if Henry had too. Could he long for something he'd never known? She was convinced now that he had.

And maybe the same was true for Deacon.

GREG F. GIFUNE

BY MIDAFTERNOON THEY'D PLAYED numerous games and split a frozen pizza. The storm had lessened, but the rain continued to fall. Needing a break, Deacon waited until Henry won another game then stood up to stretch his legs and step outside to have a cigarette.

"You're already better than you were when we started," Henry said.

"I'm only losing by a little now instead of a lot."

Lauren closed her novel and let it rest in her lap. "That's enough for now, Deacon's probably had enough Xbox basketball to last him a lifetime."

"That's okay," Henry said, motioning to the cabinet the TV sat atop. "I've got some other games too. We can try them out tomorrow if you want."

"I wish I could, but I'm gonna have to head out tonight, Henry."

Henry's smile vanished. "Why?"

"Sweetie," Lauren said. "Deacon has other things he has to do."

"Do you *have* to go?" Henry asked.

"Yeah, pal, I should get going," Deacon said softly. "Sorry."

"You could stay longer if you wanted to," Henry said, looking to his mother. "Couldn't he, Mom? If he wanted to couldn't he stay longer?"

SMOKE, IN CRIMSON

"It's all right with me, but that's up to Deacon." Lauren hesitated a moment then turned to Deacon. "It's really no trouble. You're welcome to stay."

"Will you?" Henry asked, bouncing on the balls of his feet. "Will you stay?"

Deacon looked from Lauren to Henry then back to Lauren. "You sure it's okay?"

"Of course," Lauren said with a smile. "It's fine. We'd like you to stay."

"Yeah," Henry added.

"If you're sure it's no trouble," Deacon said, shrugging self-consciously. "I could stay one more night."

"Yes!" Henry said, beaming.

"Then it's settled," Lauren said. "I'll make up the couch properly after dinner."

"Great." Deacon motioned to the back door. "I need to step outside a minute."

Once out on the porch and greeted by a welcome burst of cold air, Deacon stood beneath the overhang near the door, a curtain of rain blurring and separating him from the beach beyond. The change in temperature cleared his head, snapped him back, and as he lit a cigarette and greedily took several drags, he was baffled by how he'd managed to lose himself so thoroughly over the course of the last few hours. He couldn't remember a time when his demons had remained dormant and quiet that long. It wasn't until he and Henry stopped playing and Deacon again focused on where he was and what was taking place that he felt the apprehension rising in him again. More miraculously, in all that time, despite the fact that Fay's cottage was within sight, he hadn't so much as looked in that direction or concerned himself with it, her, or their past. Deacon had never before experienced anything like it, certainly not to that degree, and it was accompanied both by a sense of relief, and what could only be described as *happiness*. It was almost as if he'd been set free from himself, Fay, and all that had taken place, and since those things were already slowly creeping back, maybe *almost* was the best he could hope for.

What are you doing?

Deacon smoked his cigarette, ignoring the cold.

You need to get out of here.

He watched the rain gushing from the eaves.

You'll bring them down with you.

The nearby dunes reminded him of the things he'd found on the beach, the jetty.

They're coming.

His head filled with the horrors in Boston and the nightmares in the cottage.

You're the bait.

His headache was back, this time in the back of his skull. A part of him wanted to step off the porch and wander away in the rain.

SMOKE, IN CRIMSON

Run. You can't protect them.

To find his way back to Fay's and to have a drink, several drinks, and—

You can't even protect yourself.

Deacon heard the door behind him open, followed by the sound of Henry's voice. "Mom's making dinner in a while and she wants to know if you like broccoli. I think it's disgusting. Not as bad as cauliflower but—"

Deacon feigned a little laugh. "Sure," he said without looking back. "I like broccoli just fine."

"Okay." Henry sighed. "I'll tell her."

"Be right in, pal."

When he heard the door close Deacon cleared his throat and wiped his eyes.

What the hell is the matter with me?

He knew it would be so easy to step through that wall of water and disappear into the coming darkness, to just run and never look back. But maybe, if he allowed it, going back inside to the people waiting for him would be even easier.

You're a disease, baby. We're *a disease.*

Deacon concentrated, doing his best to silence the whispers in his head.

What do you think you're going to do, live a normal life and play house with that clueless bitch and her kid? Is that it? Do you really believe that's still possible for you?

"Fuck you," he muttered.

They're coming.

Finished with his cigarette, Deacon flicked it out into the rain, watching as it was devoured by the downpour. And then, before he could change his mind, he defiantly walked back into the cottage.

Unnoticed in the distance, blurred and distorted by the rain, a dark form slogged along the beach, its deep guttural laughter riding the wind.

CHAPTER **EIGHTEEN**

LATER, AFTER DINNER WAS eaten and the dishes done, after a family-friendly movie together and sharing a big bowl of buttered popcorn, after Henry had taken a bath and changed into his pajamas, Deacon found himself at the kitchen table with Lauren having a cup of tea. Outside, the rain continued to pour in the darkness.

Deacon sipped his tea, remembering just moments before when Henry had gone to bed. He'd kissed and hugged his mother goodnight, and then, standing awkwardly next to Deacon, said goodnight.

"See you tomorrow, pal," Deacon said, offering him a fist to bump.

Instead, the boy leaned in and hugged him. Shocked, Deacon froze.

"Night," Henry said softly.

Slowly, Deacon wrapped his arms around Henry's small frame and hugged him. Fighting back emotion, he held the child with care as if fearful he might otherwise hurt him. "Goodnight, Henry."

Once he'd gone, Lauren shook her head in disbelief and smiled fondly, her eyes glistening with tears. "Well, that's a first."

Deacon nodded, flushed. "Yeah, I—I wasn't expecting that."

"Sorry to get so weepy." She laughed self-consciously as she wiped her eyes. "I've just never seen him do that with anyone besides me."

"Don't be sorry." Deacon reached across the table and gave her hand a quick pat. "He's a great kid."

"You're so good with him."

Deacon shrugged, looked down into his cup of tea.

"No really, you are," she said. "I don't date much, and to be honest there's only been two times when things got to a point where I felt it was time for them to meet my son. I'm very particular about who I allow around him."

Good, Deacon thought.

"In both cases they were really nice guys, but Henry didn't take to them at all. One tried really hard, I felt so bad, but Henry never came around." Lauren sipped her tea. "Being a single mom can make it difficult to have a social life sometimes, especially when your child has never bonded with anyone other than his mother and his dog."

"Doesn't he have any friends?"

SMOKE, IN CRIMSON

"Couple kids at school but nothing serious. Henry's always been kind of a loner."

"Maybe he sees the same in me."

Lauren cocked her head as if that had not previously occurred to her. "Maybe so," she said with an air of sadness. "Whatever the reason, it's wonderful to see."

"It was a nice day."

"Yes, it was."

Deacon could think of nothing more to say, so he sipped his tea as an excuse.

"We've been through a lot," Lauren said. "But then, hasn't everyone?"

"In one way or another, yes."

"It's been difficult for Henry to not have his dad. He was only four when Ron—my husband—was killed, so he doesn't really have much in the way of memories of him, sadly. I try to keep him alive with stories and photos but…" Lauren sighed, both hands clutching her teacup. "Anyway, it hasn't been easy for him. Or me."

The regret in her voice—the sorrow, the loneliness—was heart wrenching.

Unlike you, she and her son deserve better.

Deacon tried to imagine a world where he was the kind of man that could step in and make their lives complete. Taking Henry to ball games and the movies, teaching him things, being a good father to the boy, and a faithful husband to Lauren, a partner she could depend on that loved and respected her and worked day and night alongside her so they could all have a better life.

The last thing they need is you, *stop lying to yourself.*

He looked up from his tea directly into Lauren's smiling, hopeful face, and it all slipped away through his fingers like the sands along the dunes.

"So," she said, breaking the silence. "What are your plans?"

"I'm leaving town tomorrow, this time for good."

Lauren seemed to have a response but was having a hard time voicing it. Finally she said, "No chance you might want to stick around for a while?"

If you only knew how desperately I wish I could.

"I'm sorry," he said.

"Don't be, I'm sure you have your reasons." She smiled but it failed to mask her disappointment. "Has there been anything more on Fay, any word?"

Deacon shook his head no and had more tea.

"I hope you don't mind me saying but she's kind of a strange woman."

You have no idea.

"She could be," he said. "But her life is her own. I have myself to worry about."

The silence between them returned. Sounds of an unrelenting rain filled the gap.

SMOKE, IN CRIMSON

"Would you like another cup of tea?" Lauren eventually asked.

"No, I'm fine. Thanks though, it's really nice."

"It's supposed to be relaxing." She stood and moved closer to his chair. "Want to sit in the other room a while?"

He looked up at her.

Don't do it.

"Sure." Before he realized what he was doing he'd reached out and gently put a hand on her wrist.

Looking him in the eye, Lauren leaned over and kissed him. Deacon stood up and pulled her to him, still holding her wrist with one hand. They kissed again and stumbled away from the table a bit before righting themselves, and as they parted he gazed into her unblinking, desperate eyes. He felt her body tremble against his.

"Maybe we should stop," he whispered.

"No," she whispered back. "I—"

They kissed passionately, long and hard and deep.

You're killing her, don't you see? You're damning *her.*

Lauren's hands ran from his ass to his lower back to his shoulders blades. As the kiss ended, they stood holding each other, breathlessly locked in an intense stare.

You're damning them both.

As shadows played across the kitchen, the only light coming from a small bulb on the stove, Deacon released her then sank back down into his chair. Lauren remained where she was, standing over him and looking like she wasn't sure what to do next.

Somewhere very far away, Deacon could hear Fay's laughter. But she wasn't mocking him or being cruel. It was a shrewd laugh, as helpless as it was mournful, one she knew he'd understand and feel to the very depths of his being.

"Nights are the worst," Lauren said quietly. "I just thought maybe we didn't have to be quite so lonely on this one."

Deacon couldn't look at her. "I want it too, Lauren, but it's not a good idea."

"Right now I really don't care if it's a good idea or not."

"I know," he said, fiddling with his teacup. "But you don't want this, not really."

"I'm a grown woman, let me worry about what I do or don't want."

"You don't understand."

"What's so wrong about comforting each other, even if only for a little while?"

Nothing...everything...

"I'm sorry."

"Yeah, me too, Deacon," Lauren whispered, moving toward the darkness of the hallway. "More than you know."

He looked up again, still searching for the right words, but she was already gone.

SMOKE, IN CRIMSON

A LONE TRAIN SLID through the night, traversing the cityscape like a sentient being. As if the result of some strange magic, it twisted its way across Boston, its ghostlike appearance belying the fact that it was under human control.

On what turned out to be his last night in the city, Deacon eventually returned to The Park Bench, as he did most Saturdays after dark. He didn't have to worry about Fay and Dana joining him, they were busy with a fresh mark that would keep them busy for the next twelve hours or so. This was a lucky break, of course, because it meant there would be no one to stand in his way. There was also no turning back. Not from this night. There could be no in-between, maybes or what-ifs. Not anymore. It was too late for all that. The war between damnation and resurrection was older than time, but he no longer had the strength to fight it.

It was all about survival now.

The plan was to put enough money aside for a one-way bus ticket to wherever. He'd drink away almost all the rest at a series of bars, ending with The Park Bench, and then stumble over to the bus station and spend the night with the other lost souls there until the buses out of town started running again in the morning. Then he'd just go. No grand announcements, no warning. There one minute, vanished the next. Departed, like a dream.

Like the dead.

Deacon didn't know exactly where he was going or where he might end up. He'd see how far his funds could get him then figure it out in the morning at the ticket desk. Not that it much mattered anyway. As long as he got as far from there as he could, he stood a chance. A slim chance, certainly, but a chance nonetheless.

Later that night, after the bars closed and the city had gone quiet, rather than waiting at the bus station as he'd intended, Deacon instead found himself on a train. He and a woman named Wilma Malloy he'd met at The Park Bench were the only two occupants of their car, and at that hour, perhaps the entire train. Despite having just met, they hit it off immediately, drank and conversed for hours like old friends, smoked some dope in the alley behind the bar and did what coke they had between them. Now, on the public train—the T as it was called in Boston—they sat on worn bench seats across from each other and silently stared at nothing, as if in a shared trance. The old train, rocking and squeaking and groaning as it went, slithered through a city feigning sleep, rolling toward their ultimate destination, a neighborhood where Wilma lived known as Jamaica Plain. As the train made its way through the darkness, the lights in the car eerily blinked on and off in timed intervals, creating a periodic strobe-like effect that along with his stoned and drunken state left Deacon even more disoriented.

SMOKE, IN CRIMSON

After about thirty minutes, the train pulled into their stop. He and Wilma remained where they were a moment, and then Wilma suddenly seemed to remember where she was. With a shake of her head and a wry smile, she rose to her feet.

"Such as it is," she said, wobbling. "This is our stop."

The doors opened with a *whoosh*. Night seeped in, but since the lights in the car remained on until the train pulled out, Deacon was able to see Wilma more clearly under conditions far brighter than The Park Bench. The woman struck him as a little older and even slighter of build than she appeared to be at the bar. She wore black suede boots with silver spike heels and a long gray leather trench coat, buttoned closed, the collar turned up. Her short platinum blonde hair, combed straight back in a severe manner and hooked behind her ears framed a stoic, rather angular face, the jawline well defined. The artificial light accentuated her pale flesh as well as the black liner and shade on her eyes. Glazed and weary from too many drinks and drugs, there was also something more in those eyes, a profound and permanent damage that only resulted from extreme trauma.

She brought a long, blood-red fingernail to her lips, which were painted to match, and delicately scratched the corner of her mouth. A series of plastic bangles on her wrist clacked together noisily as she did so. "If you've changed your mind I understand," she said softly. "These things happen."

You don't have to do this.

Deacon suddenly felt like if he didn't get up from his seat he was going to pitch forward and face-plant right there on the train. "No," he said, his voice strangely hollow in the otherwise empty car. "I haven't changed my mind."

Apparently satisfied with his response, Wilma spun on her spike heels and tottered away, managing to get herself from the car to the platform without tipping over.

You can stop this.

Deacon struggled to his feet and stumbled after her. The night was cold and still, the starless sky black as onyx but the moon full and bright. He was immediately struck by the drop in temperature, the brutality of the cold as their breath escaped them in steady columns of cloudlike bursts. The city lay before them, a twinkling, oblivious panorama of night. A sea of apartment buildings and other structures of varied architectural styles and time periods separated them from downtown, reminding him of the distance they'd traveled. To the right was a string of commercial properties, a small park, and a cemetery surrounded by a spiked wrought iron fence.

As their train pulled away, joining a few others now rattling along on elevated tracks crisscrossing the city proper and beyond, Deacon wondered if this was how

SMOKE, IN CRIMSON

he'd always remember this place: ominously quiet and surreal, otherworldly and dreamlike in its darkness. Or was it just the drugs and alcohol at work, the exhaustion, the nightmares, his appalling need and the inescapable lore of night?

Arm-in-arm, he and Wilma negotiated the treacherous metal stairs to the street below. Once they'd arrived safely, she led him along the empty, quiet street, through the commercial section before turning the block. Soon, they came upon some old Victorian houses and two small, nondescript apartment buildings.

Can you feel it moving in her? Rushing, pumping steadily from her heart?

"You're shivering," Wilma said; her arm still locked in his.

"I'm cold."

"It's there." She pointed with her free hand to a three-story building on the far corner. "I'm afraid it's nothing special, but it *is* warm, quiet, and we'll be safe there."

There's no such thing.

Though neither was steady on their feet, Deacon clung to her as they walked on. Wilma smelled vaguely of cigarettes, Jameson and a subtle perfume. He tried to imagine who this woman was and what her life entailed. What were her dreams like?

She can't rescue you, not from yourself.

Heels clicking pavement, Wilma led him to the door of the building then pulled a small, slim handbag from her coat pocket and opened it. "The good news is we're here," she said, extracting a ring of keys from her purse. "The bad news is I live on the third floor and there's no elevator, so the adventure continues."

Precariously climbing a series of dark and dusty staircases, they eventually reached the third floor. The door to Wilma's apartment, which was at the end of a narrow hallway, was littered with little dents and nicks, the black paint chipped in numerous spots.

Once inside, rather than turn on a light, Wilma drifted to the wall to their right and pulled back a curtain to reveal a large glass slider that overlooked the city. As moonlight spilled in, it illuminated a tiny balcony on the other side of the glass, and provided just enough light in the otherwise dark apartment for Deacon to see where he was.

"The lighting in here can be rather harsh," Wilma said, moving away into the darker part of the apartment and out of sight. "The last thing we need is the place lit up like some tacky, over-the-top stadium."

Stay in the dark, it's where you belong.

With his back against the closed door, Deacon focused his bleary eyes as best he could. Through the shadows and limited light, a worn and scarred hardwood floor, a badly chipped plaster ceiling and walls featuring a couple small paintings but otherwise bare slowly took shape before him.

SMOKE, IN CRIMSON

You don't have to do this. Just run.

A flame cut the darkness, the pool of light it provided widening as Wilma bent over a dated coffee table and lit two thick candles. She moved a bit unsteadily to a mantle on the other wall that sat above an old bricked-over fireplace painted white, and lit a series of small candles in an ornate, antique candelabra.

The additional flickering light spread deeper into the room, exposing a vintage, late 19th century Victorian sofa and a mismatched antique armchair, the coffee table between them, and a small kitchen in the back part of the apartment that looked like something out of the 1960s.

"Voila!" Wilma said, striking a quick comical pose.

Deacon felt himself smile despite the whispers in his head.

She unbuttoned her coat then hung it on a freestanding coatrack just inside the door to Deacon's left. "You can put your jacket here if you'd like."

He hadn't noticed the coatrack until just then. "Thanks," Deacon said, removing his jacket. "You were right. It is quiet here."

A little too quiet, isn't it?

"No one bothers me and it's affordable." Wilma flitted away to the kitchen, only to return a moment later with two small crystal tumblers and a bottle of rye. "It's not the best neighborhood, but it'll do for now."

You can be quiet if you have to be.

As Deacon strode deeper into the apartment, something in the corner of his eye caught his attention. He turned and looked in the direction of the kitchen, and a small half wall that separated the two rooms.

Startled, he froze in mid-step.

A group of people were peering at him over the wall, as if crouched behind it to hide the rest of their bodies. The silhouettes of six or seven heads all positioned in a line were barely discernable in the shadows and candlelight but unmistakable.

Wilma, realizing what he'd seen, threw her head back and laughed.

As Deacon better focused, he realized it was simply a string of Styrofoam heads with an assortment of wigs on them. "Jesus," he said breathlessly. "I thought…"

In the walls, old pipes creaked and moaned then fell silent.

Go now before it's too late.

"My apologies for laughing, love," she said, still chuckling as she set the glasses on the coffee table and poured them each a drink. "I should've warned you about the girls. I never stopped to think about what they must look like in the dark."

As Deacon drew closer, he saw her without her long coat for the first time. Clad in a tight black skirt and a fishnet blouse with a black bra beneath, combined with the knee-high spike-heeled boots, Wilma could've passed for the lead singer of some quasi punk band. "It's okay," he said. "They just startled me."

"Of course they did, poor thing. And to think I almost put a pot of coffee on. Let's be grateful I came to my senses and fetched this aged rye instead." Wilma handed him a drink then lightly tapped his glass with hers. "To being startled by candlelight."

As Deacon took a long sip of his drink, he attempted subtlety, but after a closer look he realized her hair, while masterfully styled and initially quite convincing, was a wig as well. "With a new friend," he added.

Leave her alone. You don't want to hurt her…but you will.

"How lovely," Wilma said. Taking a quick drink, she motioned to the couch. "Sit, be comfortable. I'll be back in a jiff, but I have *got* to get these boots off. Sexy as they may be, they're hard enough to walk in sober never mind in this condition. Right now staying even relatively upright in these things is becoming a challenge. I feel like the Leaning Tower of Pisa."

"Don't worry about it," Deacon said, laughing dutifully as he lowered himself onto the couch. "Go do what you need to do."

Alone in the shadows and moonlight, Deacon had another sip of rye. An old iron radiator rattled and shook on the nearby wall, releasing additional heat into the already warm apartment. It felt good but made him sleepy, so when he noticed an ashtray on the coffee table alongside a small stack of worn magazines, he quickly lit a cigarette and took a few drags. He sat up straighter on the sofa. Although a rigid and fairly uncomfortable piece of furniture, its lack of luxury allowed him to feel more present in the moment and aware of his surroundings. Senses sharpened since his nightmare began came to life as his eyes scanned the room. There was an odd sense of familiarity there. Not that he'd been in this place before, he hadn't. It was something more.

Maybe these scenes were all beginning to blend one into the next to the point that he could no longer effectively differentiate one from another. No beginning, no end, ice melting and refreezing in a continuous cycle of evolving darkness and light, a whirlwind of misery, ecstasy, dominance, submission, survival and death.

Do it. Quickly, and be done with it.

He finished his drink. Wilma had left the bottle behind on the coffee table, so Deacon poured himself another. As moonbeams bled through the glass slider, creeping across the scarred wood floor, the shadows elongated, accommodating the intrusion. He had come to learn that darkness either devoured light or fled from it. On this night it chose the latter.

For now...

Moonlight caught the silver frame of a small, faded photograph positioned on the coffee table, drawing Deacon's attention. Trapped in the photo, two disheveled little boys of perhaps nine or ten stared back at him from some distant past, one with an unruly mop of brown locks and a big smile, the other, the older of the two, more reserved but smiling as well, a kickball held in his arms. A regal looking cat sitting next to them had looked directly at the camera when the photograph was taken, and behind the trio was the partial view of a modest rural home and some shrubbery.

The longer Deacon gazed at the photograph the more convinced he became that something was off about it. Both boys looked to be pretending, their happiness forced, perhaps in an effort to placate whoever was behind the camera. The cat was the only participant that struck him as genuine.

"That's my little brother Dignon and me with our cat Homer."

Deacon followed the sound of her voice to the darkness at the edge of the kitchen. Wilma emerged wearing an ankle-length silk robe spattered with black and white patterns that reminded him of inkblot Rorschach tests. Barefoot, she padded through the shadows and into the moonlight, a gold ankle bracelet on one leg outfitted with tiny bells jingling with each step.

"It was a long time ago," she added, joining him near the sofa.

Don't listen, it just makes it harder.

"Dig died not long after that photograph was taken."

Deacon took a drag on his cigarette. "I'm so sorry."

"Thank you." Wilma retrieved her drink from the coffee table. "He was such a special little boy. An amazing storyteller, a lover of film and books even at such a young age, he really was quite something. If it weren't for Dignon I wouldn't be alive today."

Bring her closer and do it.

"What happened to him?" Deacon asked defiantly.

"It's a sad story," Wilma said, sipping her drink.

"Is there any other kind?"

"Now and then, though they're few and far between, I'll give you that. Our mother died giving birth to Dignon, so we lived with our father. He was a very sick man, abusive, angry and ugly. My brother died in my arms in a horrible little crawlspace in our basement where our father often liked to leave us."

"I'm sorry," Deacon said again. "No child should have to go through that."

"And yet so many do."

Do it. Now, while she's distracted by the past.

"I'd have traded places with him if I could have." Wilma sat next to him on the sofa, one leg curled beneath her and the other stretched out straight, her foot on the floor. "As you can see, I was still pretending to be *William* in those days. So, in a way, I died too. Unlike Dig, I had the opportunity to be reborn."

SMOKE, IN CRIMSON

In Deacon's cluttered and drunken mind it all fell into place as it should have earlier. "Well then," he said, raising his glass awkwardly. "Here's to being Wilma."

Slowly, a smile surfaced. "Amen," she said, raising her glass as well. "You're an interesting soul, Deacon."

"Not really."

"As you well know, much like the sorrow it leaves in its wake, those of us who have experienced true horror can recognize it in others." Wilma threw back the rest of her drink in a single gulp then put her glass down on the coffee table and produced a small pipe and a plastic bag of marijuana from her robe pocket. "We *sense* it, don't we?"

Bleed her. Now, do it now.

Deacon squeezed his eyes shut, hoping to silence the whispers, but it only made him dizzy. "What else do you sense about me?" he asked, opening his eyes to find her packing the pipe.

Wilma placed the plastic bag on the table then realized she'd forgotten a lighter. Deacon handed her his. "You're haunted," she said, drawing several drags of smoke into her lungs. "Tormented and faced with what I assume are extremely serious dilemmas. There's an innate sweetness to you, but you strike me as something of a dichotomy as well because there's also an unmistakable violence just beneath the surface, a fury. *Rage* even. Yet, you don't want to hurt me. I don't think you want to hurt anyone."

Show her.

"How can you be sure?"

"Unfortunately, women have to develop certain skills of detection early on in life." Wilma exhaled a cloud of smoke before handing Deacon the pipe and lighter. "*Especially* women like me."

Deacon hit the pipe twice then held it out for her, but she waved it away so he placed it on the coffee table. "You think I'm harmless?"

Give in to it, feed *it, there's no other way.*

"We'd both like you to be," she said. "But no."

Head spinning, he poured them each another drink. "What then?"

"You're dangerous." Wilma fidgeted about until she found a more comfortable position. "I think given the right circumstances, *very* dangerous. But you're no sadist. You're capable of hurting people, you just despise doing it. Given a choice, you don't want to hurt anyone or anything, not if you can help it."

"What about *need*?" he asked, handing her a drink.

"You have yours of course, as we all do, but that's not one of them. Not yet, not completely." Wilma's eyes blinked slowly, tranquilly. She held her glass closer to her face and swirled the liquor around as if spellbound. "If your course isn't corrected soon that's going to change though, isn't it? You're right down to the wire. Decisions must be made, sides must be chosen. Lines must be drawn."

SMOKE, IN CRIMSON

"You're a wise woman."

"Survival's a cagey business, love." Wilma had another sip of rye. "We're all time travelers, trapped in a web of dreams and memories we can never be certain are even our own, forever lost to those channels of time in which we swim. All of our experiences, thoughts and fears unfold at once and without warning, while we cling so desperately to ancient concepts of deliverance and damnation. And the tighter we hold on, the clearer it becomes that all we really know for sure is that those two fates are separated by the most delicate of threads."

"This is obviously really good pot," Deacon said, smiling more easily than before. "You're laying down some trippy shit, but you're not wrong."

"No, I'm not, despite how pretentiously this maudlin version of me insists on phrasing it."

"*Poetic*," Deacon said. "Not pretentious."

"You're far too kind." Wilma put an elbow on the back of the sofa then let her chin rest on it. "And you *are* kind, aren't you?"

Shaken by a sudden rush of guilt, Deacon stared into his drink. "Not always."

"No, not always. No one is."

"Why did you invite me here?" he asked.

"Why did you come? Are you here to destroy me? Are you an assassin?"

"I'm a hunter."

"Aren't we all?"

"Not really."

"I know what you are," Wilma told him. "And I know what you're not."

Deacon's eyes lifted, found hers in the candle and moonlight. "No," he said just above a whisper. "You don't."

Cut it loose. Unleash it.

"It's all right, you know," she said. "You're safe here."

But you're not.

He powered down the remainder of his drink. His head whirled and his stomach grumbled as he put the glass down and reached again for the pipe. Using the lighter he took two more deep hits then returned it to the coffee table. "I have to…go."

"It's very late, love. God only knows what's out there in the dark."

You know, don't you, Deacon. You know what's out there in the dark.

In his mind he saw her running, staggering, falling in a spray of blood and bile, her eyes imploring him to stop, unable to believe he was capable of doing the things he was doing to her. And then, with eyes of fire and a hideously feral grin, her lips and teeth stained with blood, Fay filled his head as he knew she eventually would.

The only thing to fear is what's inside.

"Are you all right?" she asked.

SMOKE, IN CRIMSON

Deacon slowly shook his head. "No."

Things moved within the shadows. The eerily alien and unnerving screeches of mating cats suddenly echoed up through the darkness from a nearby alley. Nothing seemed right. Nothing seemed real. As the room spun, Deacon's heart felt like it was about to explode.

You can almost taste it, can't you?

"Wilma," he gasped, reaching for her.

She straightened her posture and let her glass rest on the table, her short blonde wig suddenly luminous in the faint light. "I won't scream," she said.

Trembling, Deacon gently cupped the side of her face. "I know."

"Easy, love. Easy."

He snapped shut his eyes and saw Fay on her back, arching her shoulders so she could thrust her breasts closer to him. As he tore the ankh from around her neck, she moaned and wiggled beneath him as if it had brought her to orgasm. Straddling her, and using the pointed end of the ankh, he slowly, meticulously added to the scars already painting her breasts. As blood ran, trickling, he thrust his cock inside her, lapping and biting at her belly and nipples while she bucked and took hold of his head, pushing his face closer, tighter against her and into the flow of blood. Her fingernails dug into the back of his neck as he pumped his cock deeper, barely able to breathe.

When Wilma's apartment reappeared before him, he realized his grip on her had gotten stronger. She stared at him with fear, and what could only have been pity.

Deacon shot to his feet and staggered into the pool of moonlight next to the sofa. Pain fired through his head like a dagger strike and he cried out, sank slowly to his knees and began to weep in a way he never had before.

Suddenly Wilma was there with him on the floor, her arms wrapped around him and her head against his shoulder. Rocking him slowly, tenderly, she whispered to him that it was all right, *he* was all right.

"I promise you it's still a choice. You're just a kid, can't be more than twenty."

"You have to let me go. I don't want to hurt you."

"Look at me." She gently took Deacon's face in her hands and lifted his head until they were looking into each other's eyes. "If it was beyond your power to control I'd already be dead or on my way to the same torment you're feeling."

He stared into her eyes, wanting, needing and hoping desperately that was true.

Slowly, Wilma kissed his forehead, pressing her lips against him for several seconds. And then she drew him closer and they reverted to the same two lost souls they'd been earlier, struggling to comfort each other in whatever ways they knew how, this time collapsed on an old wood

SMOKE, IN CRIMSON

floor in the moonlight, their nightmares twisting, turning and weaving together in the dead of night, becoming one.

Neither said another word, though Deacon remained in Wilma's arms for a very long time. Finally, as they separated, he saw that her wig had become mussed and off center when they'd embraced. Realizing it as well, Wilma self-consciously raised a hand to straighten it, but Deacon stopped her, carefully taking hold of her wrist and returning her hand to her lap. Then he straightened the wig for her, patting the hair down and combing it back into place with his fingers.

"Look at us," she said, laughing lightly. "We're quite the mess, aren't we, you and I? But we're going to be all right. In time, we're going to be just fine, you'll see."

"There's nothing wrong with you, Wilma," he told her. "You're already fine."

A single tear ran the length of her cheek. "Thank you, love."

Sirens blared as a police cruiser and then an ambulance sped by the building, their lights momentarily haunting the apartment with swirling specters of red and blue.

"I want you to have something," Wilma said, taking her arms from him just long enough to remove a pendant from around neck. She pressed it into his palm. "Take it."

A small green stone on a thin leather necklace, it was highly polished and bore a strange black symbol across the front. Consisting of a single straight line with a V shape attached to the top right side and an identical though inverted V attached to the right bottom side, it was unlike anything Deacon had ever seen.

"It's known as the Perthro Rune," she whispered. "I dreamed of it once. It was a very strange and nonsensical dream about horrible creatures coming up out of the ocean. In the dream I fled to the deep woods and it was there that I found this symbol carved into a large stone in a clearing. I'd never seen it before in my life, but days later I came across this necklace in a curious little shop on Boylston Street. I was shocked, but fascinated, convinced someone or something—perhaps the universe itself—was trying to tell me something. Of course I couldn't ignore it, so I researched its origins. Turns out it's a mysterious Norse rune believed to be the rune of fate and the unmanifest."

"Wilma, I can't take this, I—"

"It helps those doomed with psychological, emotional and physical addictions," she explained. "You see, in Norse mythology, doom was not used in the same way we use it today. It didn't necessarily mean death or destruction, but was closely defined as those aspects of ourselves we struggle to control that work to bring about our destinies. Some believe it even has the power to protect you from many things, including yourself."

SMOKE, IN CRIMSON

The sudden horrifying sound of violently flapping wings snapped Deacon's attention to the slider. Outside, Fay stood on the balcony in a long white nightgown, bloody hands pressed to the glass, a specter only his eyes could see, grinning at him as blood ran from her mouth and down over her chin in a steady stream. Behind her, in the night, the leathery wings of hideous demons fluttered as their jaws snapped, growling like the rabid things they were, drooling blood, bile and thick strings of diseased saliva.

Deacon looked from Fay's eyes to Wilma's. Darkness or light...

Those were the choices, *his* choices.

When he looked to the slider again, the horrors were gone.

"I suspected why it came to me, why I needed it, but I never truly knew why it was so important that I keep it," Wilma said, taking Deacon's hand and closing his fingers tight over the rune. "Now I do."

And so do you.

He fell back into her arms, his head on her chest, and they both held on tight.

A sudden, deafening, high-pitched squeal tore through his mind, ripping him from the darkness. Bolting upright from his previously slumped posture, Deacon frantically looked around. He was on a train breaking noisily as it slid slowly into a stop. With a hiss, the doors opened.

Dawn was breaking over the city. Had he ridden the trains all night?

Wilma, he thought. He looked around but he was alone in the car.

Disoriented and still not sober, Deacon couldn't be certain what was real and what had simply been his drunken, drug-fueled nightmares.

Until he opened his hand and found he'd been clutching the rune all along.

ALONE IN THE DEN, Deacon gathered his things, stuffing them back into his knapsack. The rain had picked up again. Sheets of it crashed through the darkness and against the windows with a steady drumming sound, breaking his concentration.

For a moment, sitting on the couch in the silence of the cottage, he allowed the fantasy to unfold before him. He and Lauren and Henry all living there together, a family, a *real* family, happy and loving each other and making a life—it all seemed so real, so possible. And yet he knew it could never be. Not for him.

Did you really think you'd be here forever, playing house with your sweet little readymade family?

If only.

SMOKE, IN CRIMSON

Deacon checked his watch. Just after midnight. Despite the late hour, he had no intention of staying the night. Not after the way things had ended with Lauren. He felt like an intruder now, and prolonging his stay and still being there come morning would only make things more awkward and unpleasant for her. He felt bad about Henry too, as he'd said he'd see him in the morning, but it was better this way. The sooner the kid figured out Deacon was not someone who should or could be a permanent fixture in his life the better.

Late hour and downpours be damned, he'd already decided to slip out quietly. It hurt to leave that way, but pain was something he'd long become accustomed to.

His things packed and his knapsack secured, Deacon checked his phone.

One voicemail from Lance Dillon flashed in his notifications. He'd forgotten all about it. With a sigh, he pulled it up and hit PLAY.

"Deacon, hello, it's Lance. I saw I had a missed call from you earlier so I'm calling back to see what's up. Should we miss each other again please leave a voicemail so I know the nature of your call and what's going on. I assume something must be happening or you wouldn't have called in the first place, yes? At any rate, get back to me as soon as you can, please. Whatever you have to tell me I'm eager to hear."

Don't be so sure, you smug sonofabitch.

A thick beam of light cut the surrounding shadows and glided slowly across the room, catching Deacon's attention. Whenever a car passed along the road on the other side of the cottage this happened, but this time the light didn't pass straight through.

This time it lingered.

Deacon put his phone aside, rose from the couch and made his way into the kitchen. The teacups from earlier were still on the table where Lauren had left them. The only light was from a small bulb on the stove, but it provided enough for him to safely negotiate the space. He listened a moment. All he could hear was the steady hum of the refrigerator and the driving rain.

The light remained, unmoving now and partially illuminating the wall behind him. Thankfully, one of the differences between Lauren's cottage and Fay's was a window on the wall opposite the kitchen which faced the road. The thick beam still shone directly through it, slicing through the otherwise dark room. Deacon stood just to the side of the window and leaned close enough to look out through the dark and rain-blurred pane without being seen.

The light was coming from a vehicle parked on the far side of the road.

Suddenly the headlights were extinguished, taking any visibility beyond the window along with them. Deacon returned to the den, pulled on his jacket, grabbed his phone

SMOKE, IN CRIMSON

and knapsack then quietly moved into the mudroom and slipped out the door onto the back porch.

The cold air hit him, and then then the deluge. Leaving his knapsack at the edge of the porch, he hurried around the side of the cottage opposite the beach and into a short driveway facing the road. Hiding behind Lauren's car, he crouched and stared through the rain until the vague silhouette of an old pickup truck separated from the darkness. Backed off the road and onto the beginnings of a patch of grass, it was purposely parked so that the front of the truck faced Lauren's cottage.

Still in a crouch, Deacon started toward it.

He only got a short distance before another light appeared, this one smaller and more contained. The driver of the truck had switched on the interior light, which allowed Deacon to clearly see Albert sitting behind the wheel fiddling with a flashlight and what appeared to be a white, previously coiled length of rope. He turned the flashlight on then off, as if to be sure it was functioning properly, then the interior light went out, returning him to darkness. With no glow from the dashboard, Deacon knew the truck was not running.

He also knew what Albert had planned.

Moving quickly, Deacon crossed the road, arcing to his right so he could remain undetected and come upon the vehicle from the rear rather than head-on.

When he reached the grass he waited, watched, his breathing heavy.

The rain had soaked him down, and he was cold but laser focused. He could feel things changing inside him, awakening. Things he despised but needed in order to do what had to be done.

Slowly, Deacon rose to his feet. Head bowed, his hands curled into fists. Those horrible things inside him were alive now, surging and crackling through his body like electrical current, growing stronger with each crashing beat of his heart.

As an animal-like guttural noise from deep inside him emerged, he began to run.

A few feet from the rear of the truck, Deacon leapt, completely clearing the bed with impossible ease and landing on the roof with feline-like agility. The vehicle shook from the impact, the roof denting and nearly caving in beneath his feet.

The driver's side door opened immediately. Albert's rotund frame tumbled out of the truck, whirling around and stumbling gracelessly, the flashlight in one hand and the rope in the other as he gawked up at the roof in an attempt to see exactly what had crashed onto it.

"I—I wasn't gonna do nothin'!" he yelled. "I was just—"

And then, through the darkness and rain, he saw what was waiting for him.

SMOKE, IN CRIMSON

Though he screamed, no one could hear it above the downpour. Though he ran, lumbering into the road with all of his might, Albert could not escape that which flew from the roof of his truck and descended upon him. Though he begged and pleaded and cried out, first in terror, and finally in agony, crying out for God, Jesus, and even his mother, he could not prevent it from ripping him to shreds like the feral creature it was.

Long after it was over, the rain kept falling, washing it all away like the bad dream it should have been.

CHAPTER **NINETEEN**

NONE OF IT SEEMED real. But then, had it ever?

An hour or so before dawn, the rain stopped. On a rural road a few miles from the beach, an old pickup truck traveling at a tremendous speed apparently spun out of control and struck a telephone pole. A fire quickly became an explosion as the gas tank erupted, engulfing the vehicle in flames. By the time fire and emergency vehicles arrived on scene it was an inferno, and whatever remained of the occupant was unrecognizable as even human, but one of the firefighters was relatively sure the truck belonged to a local man employed at a nearby gas station. Later, it would be theorized that the driver had been drinking and speeding, and likely lost control of the truck on the still slick roads.

Not so far away, on the beach, Deacon stood just beyond the reach of waves lapping shore. He stared at the ocean for what seemed a very long time, his mind a jumble of thoughts and strange visions. In those moments, with memories of gore and screams and torrential rains still playing out before him, he came very close to walking into the surf and letting it take him. In some ways Deacon wanted to die, but it was more about what the darkness did to him, the pain and chaos it wrought. He wanted it to stop, but knew one could not happen without the other.

Don't you know by now, baby? There is no death, not for us.

Deacon could only hope that was one more lie in a string of many, that maybe it was all a lie, a nightmare, *Fay's* nightmare, and he was just living in it like everyone else.

Even if you could, killing yourself won't stop this.

Visions of Fay wandering through the forest filled his head. In a long flowing gown, a witch in the dark woods searching for answers, searching for him, she moved as if gliding, her bare feet floating just above the forest floor, head thrown back, eyes rolled to white, mouth open and whispering ancient incantations of evil no human being was ever meant to possess.

Wake up. I want to wake up now. Fay, set me free.

We fear our dreams, but it's the nightmares of others that drive us to madness.

An odd jingling noise sounded in the distance.

Wake up and set me free, Fay. Let me go.

As the sound grew louder Deacon turned his attention from the ocean. Running across the sand in his direction was

SMOKE, IN CRIMSON

Larry, followed by Henry. Although the rain had managed to wash the blood and bodily fluids from Deacon's hands, face and neck, and he'd wiped down his jeans and boots with rags he'd found in Albert's truck, a fair amount of blood still stained the front of his shirt. He zipped his jacket closed and crouched to welcome Larry as he leapt toward him joyfully.

Deacon was met with a big lapping kiss and a wiggling mass of happiness. Holding the dog's head in his hands, he looked into Larry's eyes then kissed him gently on the nose. How could this amazing being only see the good in him? Or did he see both and choose to celebrate only one?

I wish I could see myself as this dog does.

"Hey," Deacon said to Henry as he approached.

"What are you doing?" the boy asked, out of breath and his cheeks bright red in the cold morning air. "Mom said you had to go."

"I'm sorry, Henry, but yeah, I do."

"Why?"

Deacon gave Larry another snuggle then rose to his feet. "I wish I could stay but—"

"Then why don't you?"

"I can't."

"Why?"

"It's just the way it is, pal." Deacon struggled to find the words. "I have to go, I—I don't have any choice. I've got things I need to take care of far away from here."

GREG F. GIFUNE

"Like what?"

Deacon sighed. "Adult things you wouldn't understand."

Henry considered this a moment. "Will you come back when you're done?"

"I don't—Henry, I don't know, I—"

"But maybe you will?" Henry looked like he might cry.

Don't do this, kid. Not over me. I'm not worth it.

"I don't know, but I want you to understand none of this has anything to do with you. If there was any way I could stay with you guys I would, it's just not possible for me right now. No matter how much I want to, I can't." Deacon reached into his pocket and handed Henry the rune. "But I want you to have something."

The boy stared at the green stone in his hand. "What is it?"

"Call it a good luck charm."

"Mom says there's no such thing, they're just for fun."

"She's probably right."

"Then how come you have it?"

"Someone special gave it to me a long time ago. Now I'd like you to have it."

"Why? It's just a shiny rock."

"That it is, but it'll probably do more good for you than it ever could me."

Henry seemed unconvinced.

318

SMOKE, IN CRIMSON

"You're a great kid, Henry. You and your mom take care of each other, okay? Be a good kid, and always try to do the right thing."

Henry nodded, his bottom lip trembling.

Not wanting to embarrass him or let him see his own emotions surfacing, Deacon looked away, back toward the road.

A dark figure stood atop the dunes behind them.

Unmoving, it stood facing them like a statue.

"Henry," Deacon said evenly. "I need you to take Larry and go home now."

"Why did you just leave like that? You didn't even say goodbye. You just *left*."

Deacon looked again. A second and third figure had joined the first along the dunes, as if having appeared magically while his attention was focused elsewhere. "I shouldn't have done that, and I'm sorry. But I need you to listen to me right now."

"Don't worry about it, we're leaving." Henry scowled at him and motioned to his dog. "C'mon, Larry, let's get out of here."

More dark figures lined the dunes now, watching... waiting...

Deacon crouched down so he was face-to-face with Henry. "You and Larry run home now, you hear me?" He gently squeezed the boy's shoulders. "Fast as you can."

Before he knew it, Henry was hugging him.

"It's gonna be all right," Deacon whispered in his ear, holding him tight. "You'll see. Take Larry and go home. Go on now, run. And don't look back, not even once."

Henry released him, nodded and wiped his eyes.

Goodbye, Henry. Goodbye, Larry.

As the boy and dog ran off, Deacon watched until they'd made it back to Lauren's cottage, keeping an eye on the figures to make sure they hadn't moved or attempted to pursue them.

Goodbye, Lauren, and I'm sorry. I would've loved for you three to be my family.

Deacon defiantly faced the figures that now lined the dunes.

We're your family, Deacon, the only family you'll ever know.

He headed for Fay's cottage.

Once he reached it, he unlocked the door then looked back. The beach and dunes were empty. The figures were no longer there.

But Deacon knew better.

They weren't gone.

THE MOMENT DEACON ENTERED the cottage he knew he wasn't alone.

SMOKE, IN CRIMSON

Lance stood in the kitchen in an ankle-length cashmere coat and a navy blue pinstripe suit, his hands in the pockets of his trousers as he surveyed the damage done to the wall. He then turned to the table and the items scattered across it, including an overflowing ashtray, several empty alcohol bottles, drugs, and the open mirror box.

"Well then," he said through a heavy sigh, his brow knit with dramatic insincerity. "Looks like you've been busy. I certainly hope you have something of value to tell me."

"I'm leaving town," Deacon said. "That ought to be of some value to you."

"I meant regarding my daughter."

"Fay's gone, Lance, and she's not coming back."

"And how, may I ask, have you arrived at that conclusion?"

Deacon set his knapsack on the floor. "How about we call it instinct?"

"In-other-words you've come up with nothing and there's been no contact."

"I believe she's alive if that helps."

"Then where is she?"

"Nowhere...everywhere...I don't know."

"Is that meant to be humorous?"

"Am I laughing?"

Lance cocked his head toward the hole in the wall. "Stevie had a lot of concerns about you staying here, but I

GREG F. GIFUNE

don't think even he believed you'd use this time to throw yourself a party or two and vandalize my property."

"You wanted me here, Lance. I told you there wasn't much I could do."

"I thought at least you'd try."

"I did."

Lance rolled his eyes. "Yes, given the condition of this place it seems so."

Deacon pointed toward the table. "See that thing? It's called a mirror box. It's a kind of spell box used by witches and practitioners of magic. It belonged to Fay."

"Fay's dabbled in that foolishness for years, what's your point?"

"It was hidden in the wall. She put it there for me to find."

Lance seemed genuinely surprised. "Why would she do such a thing?"

"Because she didn't want anyone else to find it first," Deacon said, removing her phone from his jacket pocket and holding it up. "Her phone was inside. It's wiped clean, except for a single short video."

"I see," he said. "Do I want to know what kind of video we're talking about?"

"It's a message."

"For you I take it?"

"That's right."

"May I see it?"

SMOKE, IN CRIMSON

"She said not to let the others see," Deacon explained. "What do you think she meant by that, Lance? Think she meant you too?"

He frowned. "Let's not forget that I *am* her father."

"You sure you want to play that card?"

Lance feigned ignorance. "Are you implying there's some reason I shouldn't?"

"Fuck it. Knock yourself out." Deacon tossed him the phone.

Before he could get his hands out of his pockets it bounced off Lance's chest and landed on the table. Face flushed, he snatched the phone from the table. It took him longer than seemed warranted, but he eventually located the video.

As it played, Deacon grabbed the only bottle on the table that wasn't empty, poured the rest of it into a glass and swallowed it down in a single gulp.

Sounds of the wind and ocean spilled from the speaker as Fay's voice echoed eerily through the kitchen.

"I know it's you, baby. It's all for you. It's happening. It's *happening*."

Lance remained where he was, scowling but transfixed.

"I don't know for sure how or when, but that doesn't matter now. None of that matters. It didn't have to be this way, baby. I know you don't understand yet. But you will. They're coming."

GREG F. GIFUNE

Splashing sounds from the ocean filled the room.

"It's a lie. All of it."

Fay's voice wavered, her breathing strained and heavy.

"It's okay to be afraid. You just don't know it yet. I'm on the other side of that veil, baby, and when you're here, that's when you'll understand. Nothing can undo what's been done, what *we've* done, but we can make it beautiful again, Deacon, so motherfucking *beautiful*. They're coming. But I'm ready."

"My God," Lance muttered.

"I'm going back," Fay's voice whispered as if in response. "But only so I can leave this for you. Don't let the others see. I'll find you, but if you have to come to me then come. You know what to do. Go back. Go back so you can go forward. Suffering is joy."

Even after the video ended, Lance continued staring at the phone. When he finally looked up, his eyes were moist. "What is she talking about?" he asked, placing the phone on the table. "Going back to go forward, suffering is joy, they're coming—what—what in God's name does all that mean?"

Rather than answer, Deacon let him twist in the wind a while.

"She's out of her mind," Lance said. "She's completely out of her mind."

"You're not wrong, but we both know it's more than that. Don't we, Lance."

324

SMOKE, IN CRIMSON

"Fay was always such a strange child." Lance began to pace near the stove, his head bowed. "She used to say she could hear things, music playing and voices, entire conversations going on. I can remember her saying, 'Can't you hear it too, Daddy?' Of course her mother and I simply assumed she was a child with a vivid imagination. She was always so sensitive. Even as a young girl, she wanted to help people, to comfort them. And then, when her mother took ill that all changed. *Fay* changed. We both did, I suppose. How could we not? But what I'd written off in her as whimsy and child's play turned decidedly...*darker*."

Turn, you sonofabitch. Turn on the end of that fucking rope around your neck.

"When my wife died things only got worse," Lance continued, still looking at the floor as he slowly paced back and forth. "Fay was young but too old for the whole *imaginary friend* thing. Yet she spoke of one often. An older man, she said, all dressed in black. It was beyond belief, really, and I of course never saw such a man for myself, but strange things did begin to happen. Fay would sometimes cry in her sleep. Usually it was just a quiet whimper, a sort of muted weeping. But there were times when it was loud enough to wake me. She'd say he was there with us, in the house, in the walls. She could hear him scratching she said, and claimed he was sometimes beneath the floors as well.

She swore she saw his shadow drift across the ceiling or past the windows."

A gust of wind shook the cottage.

"She said he was watching us. She'd say, '*He sees.*'"

Deacon squared his stance. "And what did he see, Lance?"

He finally looked up from the floor, eyes brimming with tears.

"What!" Deacon snapped. "What did he see?"

"I don't know what you're talking about."

"What did he see, Lance?"

"Where the hell is my daughter?"

"You haven't had a daughter in years, you fuck. Fay told me all about it. She told me all about *you*."

"My daughter is mentally ill! She's an alcoholic and a drug addict! You know that better than most, being those things yourself, so don't you *dare* come at me with some cockamamie sicko stories about—"

Deacon was on him so quickly Lance didn't realize what was happening until he'd been pinned against the far wall. "You did this to her, you piece of shit!"

"Get off of me this instant!"

Deacon slammed him against the wall until he stopped struggling. "You killed whatever light was in that little girl and drove her right into the dark, right into the arms of that fucking *thing* that tricked her into believing he was just a man, and her friend!"

SMOKE, IN CRIMSON

"There was no man, you ass!" As tears ran the length of Lance's face, his body went limp in Deacon's grasp. "It was all in her head, her sick twisted mind."

"Are you sure about that?" Deacon leaned in so close their faces nearly touched. "You can't fool me, Lance. Not me. You hear him too, don't you? You have for a long time now. Whispering to you, scratching at you from behind those walls, following you in the dark and coiling around you like a fucking snake every time it's quiet and you're all alone with nothing but your memories of what you did to that innocent little girl—your daughter, your fucking *child*. You've been running as long as Fay has. It's just in the opposite direction."

"Stop," Lance wept, his face twisted into a grimace as his body slumped.

Rather than let him slide to the floor, Deacon dragged him over to the table and dumped him into a chair. "You're gonna burn, asshole. Shit, you're burning right now."

"Who the hell are you to condemn me?" He wiped his eyes and fell forward, his arms on the table. "You're no goddamn hero."

"There are no heroes, Lance. Not in this story."

Lance looked up at him, his eyes pleading. "I never meant to hurt her."

Despite Deacon's rage, the man sitting before him was pathetic. He didn't feel sorry for him—he couldn't—but he understood that the rope around Lance's neck, the one that was slowly strangling the life from him, was of his own making. No one was going to have to push him off a cliff. He'd become a lemming running for the edge on his own long ago. Like Deacon, like Fay, like the others, there wasn't much left of him.

When darkness took you, it never left much behind.

"Why did you even bother to come here?" Lance asked quietly.

"You invited me, remember? I don't go where I'm not invited."

"I wanted your help, I—I still do, I *need* your help." He stared at Deacon desperately. "Help me. Help me bring Fay home. Can't you please help me?"

"Fay's not coming home, Lance," he said.

"Please, she—she's all I have."

Deacon grabbed his knapsack and tossed it over his shoulder. "Fuck you."

As Lance hung his head and wilted over the kitchen table, Deacon lit a cigarette then strode to the mudroom. He hesitated a moment, preparing himself for whatever was waiting for him out there.

And then, without looking back, he walked out the door.

CHAPTER **TWENTY**

THOUGH THE AREA WAS deathly quiet, in Deacon's absence a heavy fog had rolled in across the Atlantic, blanketing the beach in thick layers that moved eerily across the sand, up along the dunes and to the adjacent road beyond. His senses sharpened in the strange silence, and with a slow but deliberate pace, Deacon headed for the road, listening and watching for those things he knew were still stalking him but hidden now within the fog, concealed by its dense cover drifting and slowly roiling around him like dragon's breath.

I walked into this town on my own. I'm walking out the same way.

Indecipherable whispers circled then faded.

You can have each other, tear each other to pieces, I don't care anymore.

When Deacon felt concrete beneath his feet he knew he'd reached the road.

GREG F. GIFUNE

It's your world now, not mine. I'm gone, Fay, just one more bad dream.

With the beach to his right no longer visible through the fogbank, Deacon increased speed, his boots hitting pavement the only sound. He could feel something behind him, following him through the fog, getting closer as it gradually closed the gap between them.

Deacon stopped and turned.

Nothing...no one...

The dreams make us real, baby.

"Let me go," he said aloud.

A strange scraping sound answered, low to the ground but impossible to see in the fog until it rolled into sight and came to rest an inch or so from his feet.

Deacon didn't have to look. He knew it was a bottle.

Pick it up. Drink it, baby. Let the vodka quench your thirst.

"No," he said through gritted teeth.

Let it lead you to what you really want. What you really need.

Shaking his head no, but otherwise with as much economy of movement as possible, he allowed his knapsack to slide off his shoulder and onto the ground. The fog was becoming disorienting, and he could hear a faint voice calling to him somewhere in the distance. He knew this voice. It had been a long time since he'd heard it, but he knew it.

SMOKE, IN CRIMSON

Other voices accompanied it, relegated to the background, undertones of screams, growls and hisses.

"I'm waiting," the disembodied voice called.

"Look around you," Deacon said to the swirling void. "There are no enemies, not anymore. You've won, Dana. You won a long time ago."

As if in response, a screech echoed through the fog, bringing with it visions of dark figures exploding out at him, dragging him to the ground and wrapping him in their black cloaks. He struggled but there were too many smashing and clawing at him with their fists, and as he attempted to roll away, they kicked and stomped him, their war cries splintering him down to whatever remained of his tainted soul.

I'm in your head, Deacon, back where I belong.

He looked to the bottle at his feet.

And now you'll never get me out.

Deacon snatched the bottle, opened it and drank. "Fuck you," he gasped.

Mmmm, that's a good boy.

Angrily, he raised the bottle again, ignoring Dana's whispers until he swallowed the last drop. Stumbling, he threw the bottle into the fog. A moment later he heard it shatter.

Up ahead, the fog seemed to part just enough for Deacon to make out the old abandoned hotel at the very end of the beach. Dark figures scurried up the walls like insects, slithering into the blown-out openings that had once been windows and doors.

His head spun, and a sudden wave of darkness struck him, crushing him as it folded into itself, squeezing him tighter and plunging him deeper into nothingness.

Silence, unlike any he'd ever known.

THE SOUND OF WATER slowly dripping came to him first. As he drifted through the darkness and closer to the light, Deacon felt a cold hard surface beneath him. But he wasn't on the street anymore. This was somewhere else, a cement floor, damp and cold.

His body ached, and his head was hazy, his vision slightly blurred. Above him was a bare ceiling, arched and high, all exposed girders and open spaces where a roof had once been, the grey sky beyond it empty and still.

Deacon rolled onto his side then managed to sit up. The area was long forgotten and empty except for some debris and trash. Wind blew through the openings, bringing with it the smell of the nearby ocean. THE SEA VIEW, they'd taken him to the ruins of the old hotel, to the front of the building and what had once been the lobby. Groggily, he looked around.

A woman stood in a nearby doorway, her back to him. Dressed in a long gown of black lace, dated and tattered, dusty and draped with cobwebs, it looked and smelled like something long in the grave. Contrasting with her short blonde hair, it blew in the wind, dancing and entangling her as if alive.

"Fay…"

When she spoke to him it was in a robotic monotone, a manner in which he'd never heard Fay speak before. "When are you going to realize your precious little stories of redemption—your one night stands you couldn't bring yourself to bleed, the lost little girls you wanted so desperately to save, your pitiful attempted rehabs with that charlatan filth Felix, an exterminator of your own kind—are never going to save you? Not from this. Not from me. There's only slavery now. Embrace what you are, baby. No matter how many times you try or how hard you promise yourself you'll do better, you'll fail. It's always just a matter of time. You can't outrun the things that live in your blood."

Deacon tried to stand but was too weak. "Am I dreaming?"

"What difference does it make?"

On the floor next to him was the bottle of vodka, empty and surrounded by numerous cigarette butts stamped out and smoked down to the filters. All he remembered was the fog and the things within in. He felt nauseous and sick to his stomach, and his blurred vision left him off-balance and lightheaded.

"What's wrong with me?"

"You're drunk, baby. You're always drunk or stoned. It's just a matter of what you're taking." Fay slowly turned and faced him. Her eyes were completely black, shiny like polished onyx. "Booze, weed, pills, acid, mushrooms, coke..."

Deacon tried to stand again but fell over.

"Fear…lust…rage…violence…" A smile curled her lips. *"Blood…"*

Struggling to his hands and knees, he reached for her, but she was too far away and the room had begun to tilt and spin.

Fay opened her arms as if to receive him, but instead fell back and away through the doorway and into the mist.

For Christ's sake, Deacon, you're the god damn bait.

Fog rolled in, slowly filling much of the large open space.

Wake up, Fay. Wake up.

Deacon snapped out of it, as if he'd suddenly come awake himself.

Something moved to his left, from deeper within the building. Deacon staggered to his side, his vision slowly clearing. A dark figure rushed at him through the fog, its arms extended, clawed hands reaching for him.

A leg sweep knocked its feet out from under it. As it crashed to the cement floor Deacon followed, straddling it. The sickly pale face and red eyes pierced the fog, jaws snapping and foaming like a rabid animal. Cocking back his fist, Deacon struck the creature again and again, until things in its face began to snap and shatter and give way.

SMOKE, IN CRIMSON

When its skull became a frothy slop, Deacon rolled off and staggered to his feet, his face and neck bathed in its blood, his fist equally bloody, caked with bone and dripping fluid.

In the interim, more creatures had circled him. They could've attacked, but hadn't, and just as Deacon was certain they would, they returned to the fog instead.

They'd been called off.

It was her eyes Deacon saw first. Adorned heavily with silver shadow and liner, her black pinpoint pupils were surrounded by an orange iris resembling a sea of fire, the sclera bloodshot. Only half her head was shaved now, the skin there littered with tattoos of skulls and demons, the other sporting razor-straight hair dyed blood-red that hung nearly to her shoulder. She wore a horrific and profane crown fashioned from polished bone, the appendages clamped down across her forehead and temples a series of severed human fingers strung together and separated by the long teeth of what appeared to be some sort of animal.

Dana's not what you knew, Felix had told him. *Not anymore.*

The inverted cross earrings had been replaced by daggers, and two smaller versions were now instead tattooed at the outside corner of each eye. She sported considerably more ink and piercings than years before, including a pentagram on her throat and numerous nose and lip piercings. Her ears were adorned with silver grids of lightweight chains that dangled from her lobes like glistening spider webs.

She's way worse.

Dana's body was changed as well, stronger, lither, more streamlined than before. Gone was the Salvation Army wardrobe, replaced with a skintight one-piece outfit of black leather, the front open to nearly her midriff and showing off an enormous tattoo of an ankh between her breasts. On her feet she wore knee-high black boots with intricate lacings and buckles, the heels large and square.

She's…something else now.

"Who were you expecting, Lucy Westerna?"

Even her voice was not as he remembered it, deeper, hoarser.

"Still got that devastating wit, I see."

Dana watched him with those horrible eyes of fire. "Tell me," she said, slowly striding back and forth before him. "What else do you see, Deacon?"

"I see you've developed quite a flair for the theatrical in your old age," he said. "You're a long way from used army jackets and Goodwill sneakers, huh?"

The fog moved between them, drifting.

"The life…the dreams…they change you. I'm *so* much more powerful now."

"You're as vulnerable as ever. Thankfully we're only indestructible in folklore."

"Only the weak loathe themselves. I knew you'd be no different."

SMOKE, IN CRIMSON

"What do you care? It's Fay you want, not me."

She brought a hand to her face and let two fingers rest against her black lips. Dana always gnawed her fingernails down to the quick. Now they were long and tapered to sharp points and painted to match her lips. "What I want…is everything."

"It's a bad dream—you, me, Fay—all of it. But soon, for you, it'll be over."

"You'd like that, wouldn't you?" Dana smiled, revealing blood-stained teeth. "You've learned nothing over these years. The rest of us have continued evolving."

"Is that what you call this?"

"You're still the weak and frightened rodent you always were." Her upper lip curled into a snarl. "A liar and a fraud, you're addicted to the rush, the orgasm. You can't live without it, but you want none of the consequence, none of the responsibility. What's that old saying? The more things change the more they stay the same?"

"Why am I so important?"

"You're not."

"Then why bother with me?"

"It's an opportunity to end you like I should've done back in the day."

Blood and gore trickled between his fingers. "You didn't have the fucking juice."

Dana laughed quietly. There was something profane

about the sound of it. "You don't deserve to be one of us, little worm, you never did. Your torn-between-two-worlds morality play routine was always so god damn tiresome. Following Fay around like some lost needy kitten and pretending you were better than the rest of us. I actually felt sorry for you…until it all fell apart."

"*You* went to the desert," he reminded her. "You're the one that left."

"You were already out."

"It's not my fault Fay chose me."

"You always held a special place in her heart," Dana said. "But Fay's never chosen anyone other than Fay. It's not in her nature. You *still* don't see that?"

"Then why are you trying to use me to lure her out into the open?"

"Because it's time to put an end to you both," she said, spitting the words at him.

"Yeah, I heard she told you to go fuck yourself not once but twice on the whole let's be a team again thing." This time Deacon smiled. "Love hurts, doesn't it?"

"Where is she?" Dana growled, her fire eyes glowing through the rolling fog.

"Closer than we realize."

"Oh, I know she's close, I can feel her." Another smile slithered across her face as she slowly licked her black lips. "I can smell her pretty pink cunt."

SMOKE, IN CRIMSON

Deacon wiped his hands on his jeans then dug his cigarettes from his jacket pocket. "You were always the most powerful of the three of us, even back then." He lit his cigarette then returned the pack and lighter to his pocket. "You just didn't know it yet. You loved what you were, got off on it. You never had second thoughts or remorse, regret, none of that. You were a god damn shark, living to hunt and eat, a predator with no conscience, a soulless machine. But you know what else you were? A moron that mistakes ruthlessness and brutality for smarts. You were always the dumbest of us, Dana, and despite all your *evolution*, crazy looks and B-movie bullshit you're working these days to scare the marks, you're still just as fucking stupid as you ever were."

"You always thought you were the smartest, well now you'll learn that—"

"Fay's the smartest," he interrupted. "She's outsmarted us this time too, letting it all play out, and when it ends— exactly as she knows it will—then there she'll be. Fay's not missing, and she sure as hell isn't on the run. She's watching over all this in her dreams. Problem for you is, she and I, we dream in chess. You're playing checkers."

Dana moved closer, partially concealed in the fog now. "I could enslave you, make you eat my shit for eternity, and there's nothing you could do to stop me, *you* don't have the fucking juice. Or, I could have them slaughter you whenever I say." She motioned to the walls, and the things crawling along them. "But I've waited so long to rip you apart, I'm not about to deprive myself of that joy. *That's* why I lured you here."

"You didn't lure me here, Dana."

"You walked right into my trap."

"No," Deacon said, taking a final drag before flicking his cigarette into the fog. "You walked right into mine."

Dana's eyes of fire narrowed.

A deafening boom erupted, and the thing before him was vaulted backward into the fog in an explosion of blood and bone and bodily fluids.

The things on the walls scattered.

From behind Deacon, Felix emerged, a shotgun in hand and still smoking. His long black leather coat flapping as he spun, steely eyes searching the fog, he pumped the shotgun and fired again and again, blowing the crawlers off the walls and into pieces. Screeches of agony echoed along the high ceilings as chunks of flesh and bone rained down from above.

Deacon moved forward, deeper into the fog. On the floor, Dana lay still in a growing pool of blood, her intestines strewn like a nest of bloody snakes beside the ravaged cavity that had been her midsection. She coughed, spewing black blood into the air which fell back onto her, spattering across her face and neck.

As their eyes met, Deacon saw sorrow along with the shock, a quick glimpse of who Dana had been before the disease. But as he held her gaze, it was their history that played out before him. Her touch, her smell, her taste, her *evil*—he remembered it all.

Without looking at her, Felix racked the shotgun, lowered the barrel and fired, exploding Dana's face and skull. "For all the horror and operatic bullshit," he said with inconceivable calm. "End of the day, your kind's no harder to kill than anything else."

"They're not my kind."

The shotgun was beneath Deacon's chin so fast he had no chance to block it.

"Sure about that?" Felix asked.

Deacon closed his eyes. "Do it," he whispered, trembling. "Please, just do it."

"The day might come when I have to." Felix lowered the shotgun. "But that day is not today."

A moment later, Deacon opened his eyes. Felix was gone.

Deacon crossed the room and stepped out onto the sand. The fog was still heavy but beginning to dissipate. In the distance, on the far dunes, Fay stood in her black gown, staring out at the ocean, the wind in her hair.

Behind him, inside the old hotel, dead things caught fire and began to burn.

As the ashes escaped with the wind, numerous humanoid forms began to emerge from the ocean, breaking the waves.

GREG F. GIFUNE

It was a very strange and nonsensical dream about horrible creatures coming up out of the ocean...

Fay opened her arms in welcome, as if willing them into existence, and threw her head back, lips moving in silent prayer, casting her spells even now.

A dozen or more hideous dark beings shuffled through the surf toward shore.

No end. No beginning.

Back into darkness, naked and alone as a newborn, all sound had ceased. Deacon felt the weight of the dark pass through him, into his chest and head, tearing again at his soul. Fay's black magic alive in him once more, he floated off into nothingness.

The darkness washed him. But not clean. Never clean.

No, baby. It only blinds us to the light.

Deacon's screams carried across the dunes to the water, as they would forever now, conjurers and slaves both, tethered to a netherworld of wickedness and unholy dreams.

CHAPTER **TWENTY-ONE**

A LONE MAN WITH a knapsack over his shoulder walked along a lonely rural road heading out of town. Quite a distance behind him, a police cruiser followed at a slow creep, as it had for several minutes. But as the walker neared the town line, the police car sped up, passed the man then pulled over to the side of the road, blue lights flashing.

Stevie stepped out of the cruiser with what appeared to be significant effort. He mumbled something into the radio on his shoulder then sauntered over to Deacon, who had come to a stop once the car passed him.

"Talked to Mr. Dillon," Stevie said with a frown. "He told me you were leaving and had nothing more for him."

"That's right."

"Gonna cut and run just like that?"

"Just like that, Stevie."

Hands on his hips, the cop stayed quiet a moment. "Can't say I'm surprised," he finally offered. "Wish I could, but I can't. Mr. Dillon's mighty upset, more than I've ever seen the man."

"I imagine so."

"And you don't know anything more?"

"No."

"So, where you headed?"

"I'll know when I get there."

"All right," Stevie said, nervously wiping at his nose. "I've got your number. Soon as I get to the bottom of what happened to Gina's grave I'll be sure to let you know. And as I said, I give you my word those responsible will be punished."

"Okay," Deacon muttered. He could think of nothing else to say.

"Did you work out the particulars with Pete about getting that stone replaced?"

"Is that an official police question?"

Stevie shrugged. "Just figured if it was a problem I could help, that's all. Save you another trip to town and get it taken care of so you wouldn't have to worry about it."

"I appreciate that," Deacon said. "I have no doubt you'll do the right thing, Stevie. You always do, and with no ulterior motives whatsoever."

Stevie stared at him for what seemed a very long time. "Hell of an accident in town last night," he said grimly.

SMOKE, IN CRIMSON

"Wasn't much left of the driver or his truck. Figure he must've been drinking, smashed right into a telephone pole. Gas tank blew. Truck and the driver burned up real bad. Turns out it was the same fella you warned me about that was harassing Lauren and her boy."

"That's a shame," Deacon said.

"Albert lived alone, had no family, no real friends. He wasn't what I'd call the most popular guy in town. Sadly, truth is, nobody's gonna miss him."

Nobody's gonna miss any of us.

"Then maybe everybody's better off."

"Maybe so," Stevie said with another nod.

It's all a mindfuck, baby.

"If there's nothing else…"

Stevie continued standing in front of him, blocking his way. "Don't ever come back here," he said quietly, but firmly. "Not ever. Not *ever*, Deacon. There's nothing here for you anymore."

"There never was, Stevie."

Wind blew through the trees lining either side of the road.

The last thing Deacon remembered was watching the branches rock and sway before just as quickly becoming still, and the stark silence of the long, desolate, haunted road before him.

Wake up, Fay…

GREG F. GIFUNE

HOLLYWOOD WAS NOTHING LIKE his dreams. Their bungalow sat at the outskirts of a long abandoned industrial area near the highway, on a small patch of scorched earth and dead grass surrounded by a rusty chain-link fence. A boxy number with a flat roof and arched doorways, from a distance it looked as forgotten and unoccupied as the rest of the neighborhood. They'd settled there a while ago, but Deacon couldn't remember precisely how long it had been. Not that it mattered. This place wouldn't last any longer than the string of others before it and those awaiting them after it.

The sun was just beginning to rise. Against an orange, fiery sky, a couple palm trees near the road danced as the Santa Anna winds blew.

"What are you doing?"

Her voice brought him around, but rather than answer the obvious, Deacon raised his glass, took a sip then said, "I didn't realize you were awake."

Fay moved from the dark hallway into the room, took the drink from his hand and had a sip. The bungalow, unkempt and messy, was quiet and still mostly dark. "For now," she said, returning the glass of vodka to him. "I was having a horrible nightmare."

His eyes wandered over her. Her blonde hair was mussed from bed. She wore no makeup, and was dressed in

SMOKE, IN CRIMSON

a stained t-shirt, nothing more. "Is there some other kind?" Deacon asked.

"We were on a beach like the one back home at the cottage, remember? But it wasn't that beach. It was somewhere else. *We* were somewhere else. We didn't know where, though, and we couldn't remember our names. We were lost." Fay grimaced. "We were dead."

Deacon remained slumped in the old recliner where she'd found him, nude. "Fitting," he said, sipping his drink.

"I can hear you thinking," Fay said, grabbed a pack of cigarettes and a lighter from the cheap coffee table between them. "Why are you always such an unappealing zombie afterward?"

"What a sadly appropriate term," he said. "Imagine, me as a living corpse, decaying from the inside out."

Fay smiled as she lit the cigarette.

"I'm glad I'm so amusing."

Her smile died as she exhaled her first drag at him.

"Sorry," Deacon said. "I'm just tired."

"That's odd. I did all the work."

He referenced memories, sighed. "Here's to you," he said, raising his glass again.

"Do you plan to sit there and get drunk all day?"

"You're more than welcome to join me."

Fay moved closer, stood before the recliner and raised a foot. It came to rest in his crotch. "There's always him." She cocked her head in the direction of the bedroom.

347

"Haven't you had enough?"

She worked her foot slowly back and forth. "He'd take me dancing if I asked."

Finding himself dangling once more in that strange chasm between absolute intoxication and a more genuinely altered state of consciousness, Deacon finished his drink then set the glass down on the table. As he leaned forward to do so, Fay pressed her foot down harder against his now erect cock. "So ask."

"I'd rather stay here. I'd rather stay high."

"Why do we do it?" he asked quietly.

Fay rolled her eyes. "Not this shit again."

"Answer me."

"It's an addiction."

"We're junkies."

She slowly licked her lips, pushing harder. "Uh-huh."

Leaning back, Deacon opened his legs wider, pushing back against her foot. "What the fuck have you done to me?"

"Baby," Fay said, grinning like a demon. "What the fuck have *you* done to *me*?"

Shuddering, Deacon threw his head back and came across her bare foot.

"Shhh," Fay said playfully. "You'll wake him."

As she moved away, he squinted, locating her through the montage of pictures clogging his mind's eye. Through the near-dark, he found her at the other end of the bungalow, leaned against the bedroom door wearing nothing now but that same demonic smile. Clutched in her hands was the ankh she normally wore around her neck, the razor point sparkling through the shadows.

Deacon's eyes closed. Nearly sated, he wanted to sleep, but all he could see in the darkness of his dreams was Fay plunging the ankh into the unsuspecting stranger, her mouth open to accommodate the spray of arterial blood spattering their nude bodies.

He licked his dry lips, as somewhere deep inside him, where some semblance of whom and what he'd once been, watched helplessly.

"I'll be right in."

In the quiet that followed. Deacon swore he heard Fay say she loved him. But it was other things he thought of.

Snowflakes falling through the glow of streetlights…the smell of the ocean on a cold winter night…a gleeful dog's wet nose against his face…a family—a wife and a son and a home he wanted so desperately—doomed by his weakness and burning away before he could ever truly know such a life. The sensation of a sacred polished stone in the palm of his hand…the sound of Gina's laughter before it all went bad…the warmth of the sun on his naked flesh…and love. The love he'd had for his sister. The love he felt when he first saw Fay, and his desire to save her, to rescue her, unaware that she'd neither been a damsel in distress, nor he a knight in shining armor.

No end...no beginning...

Alone in the darkness of the bungalow, with the lunacy of illusion fading, Deacon watched it all fall through his mind, a waterfall of blood.

He looked to the bedroom doorway. Fay was gone.

Smoke coiled and turned in the darkness, her diseased dreams the tides in an ocean of crimson, rising and receding while all she left behind beckoned him like a siren's song from which there was no escape.

Deacon pushed himself up and out of the recliner. Ignoring his empty glass, he grabbed the bottle from the coffee table instead and took a long drink of vodka.

The life...the dreams...they change you.

For the first time in a long while, he thought about the beach, the dunes and the little town on the other side of the country he'd never again know.

Beneath the bungalow, horrific things shifted and scuttled about, scratching at the floor and along the concrete walls of the crawlspace below.

There's no escape, baby, not from Hell.

He made himself more promises, told himself more lies, and believed every one of them. From the bedroom, a muffled cry bled through the darkness, mingling with Fay's sudden laughter.